Lyrics and Lust

A Novel by Khari Toure'

ISBN: 979-8-9856414-0-0

This novel is a work of fiction. The names, characters, and incidents portrayed in it are the work of the author's imagination. Any resemblance to actual people, living or dead, events or localities is entirely coincidental.

Published by Toure Publishing

1st edition 2025

For my grandmother,

Mary Lee Lacy.

Trigger Warning

This book contains mature themes, including sexual content, violence, and the harsh realities of human trafficking.

While writing this book, I wanted to shed light on the thousands of missing and trafficked Black women across America—many of whom are never found. By sharing this story, I aim to raise awareness about a crisis that is often overlooked.

Contents

Death and life are in the power of the tongue.

Proverbs 18:21

Prologue

December 6th, 2000

10:20 Eastern Standard Time

Midtown Atlanta

Sixteen-year-old Brianna Johnson strolled down Midtown Atlanta, her small hips swaying in tight blue jeans and a white crop top. She scanned the street, hoping to find another trick for a quick car date.

Two hundred dollars sat in her bra - one hundred short of what she owed. Her pimp warned her that if she came back with less than three hundred dollars, he would beat her. She didn't want to get beat again.

A blue Hyundai pulled up to the curb. Brianna stopped and looked inside. A man sat behind the wheel, wearing an Army uniform. He had short, cropped hair, and his skin had a golden hue that reminded her of Justin Timberlake. He smiled, revealing dimples and perfect white teeth.

"Can I have a date with you?" he asked.

Brianna hesitated. A few months ago, an undercover cop had arrested her. She wasn't going back to juvenile hall.

"Naw, you look like the police!" she said, her Southern twang stronger than usual. The man chuckled and shook his head. He reached into his pocket and pulled out a stack of twenty-dollar bills.

"I'm on leave from the Army. I got plenty of money," he winked, glancing around to make sure no one was watching them. "Now get in. I'll face a court-martial if I get caught soliciting." Brianna hesitated for only a moment before getting into the passenger seat.

The man hit the gas, speeding onto the highway. Lil' Kim's *How Many Licks?* Blasted from the speakers. He turned up the volume and shot Brianna a glance.

"I got a room in College Park," he said. "I'll bring you back after our date."

Brianna nodded, losing herself in the beat of the song.

"What's your name?" he asked.

"Peaches," she replied.

He raised an eyebrow and smirked. "A real Georgia peach, huh? My name's Cutter." He nodded along to the music.

Cutter? What kind of name is that? Briana wondered.

Brianna stared out the window as her thoughts drifted back to her mother and the reason she had run away from home. She recalled her mother's reaction when Brianna revealed that her stepfather had tried to rape her. Tears welled in Brianna's eyes as she remembered how her mother defended him, accusing Brianna of making it all up.

That day, Brianna knew she couldn't stay in that house. So, she packed her bags and ran.

Homeless and alone, she met an older man who promised to care for her. But he turned out to be a violent and controlling pimp, running an underage sex trafficking ring in Atlanta. With no one to help her, Brianna was forced to sell her body to survive.

Brianna was so absorbed in her thoughts that she lost track of time. Looking out the window, she noticed the man had driven off the interstate. The car was now on a deserted street, far from College Park. Panic set in as her instincts told her that something wasn't right.

"This ain't College Park," she said, glancing around. "Where are you takin' me?"

Cutter's lips curled into a sinister smirk. He turned to her, his eyes cold and empty.

"Oh, I got a special place for you," he said in a low, chilling voice.

A shiver ran down Brianna's spine.

"Let me out this damn car!" she snapped, reaching for the door handle.

"Calm down, Peaches. We're almost there."

Brianna's heart pounded. She'd seen a news report about missing girls in Atlanta. No bodies had been found, but there were rumors that a serial killer was on the loose, kidnapping and killing young girls.

Is this the serial killer? Where is he taking me?

"Take me back!" Brianna screamed, her Southern accent thick with desperation.

"Take me back…Take me back," Cutter laughed, changing his voice to imitate her Southern accent. He slammed his foot on the gas. The car sped up.

Brianna reached into her purse for her pocketknife. Before she could grab it, something sharp pressed against her side. Her eyes widened in terror as she stared at the large knife pressing into her stomach.

"Don't do anything stupid," Cutter said with an evil grin. "Don't make me slice you like a peach! Ok, Peaches?"

Brianna's body froze in fear. *I'm being kidnapped.* "What do you want from me?" she whimpered.

"I want you to shut up!" He commanded.

"Please … let me go," she sobbed, her bold attitude replaced by a fear-filled voice.

Cutter didn't respond. He kept driving into the darkness until they reached an abandoned house tucked behind a thick wall of trees. He pulled around back, parking next to a storage shed.

Brianna barely had time to scream before he yanked her out of the car. He unlocked a brass padlock and shoved her inside. A single light bulb flickered above, casting shadows along the walls. Chainsaws, shovels, drills, and sledgehammers lined the shelves. The stench of bleach filled the air.

The light was just bright enough for Brianna to see her captor. He was slender, with steel-blue eyes and tightly cropped brown hair. He quickly locked the shed and placed the keys on a workbench.

"You remind me of her," he hissed through gritted teeth.

"Who?" Brianna asked, trying to keep her voice steady.

"Dionne."

She swallowed. "Who is Dionne?"

Cutter's eyes gleamed with an evil intensity. "Dionne was the last girl I picked up."

Brianna began to hyperventilate.

I should've never gotten in his car.

Through her tears, she saw the silver military dog tags around his neck. She focused on the name.

Vincent! His first name was Vincent!

Vincent pulled a black ball gag from his pocket and strapped it tightly around her mouth, muffling her cries. Brianna's eyes darted to the knife resting on the workbench.

I'm going to die if I don't fight back!

Brianna's survival instincts kicked in. She lunged at Vincent, kicking him between his legs. He roared in pain and stumbled. She grabbed the knife and plunged it into his shoulder, causing him to scream and collapse.

Brianna snatched the keys from the workbench and bolted towards the door, her hands shaking as she fumbled to unlock it.

She bent down to pick them up – then froze.

Brianna saw Vincent looming over her. His face twisted in rage.

"You shouldn't have done that, Peaches…"

With one swift motion, he lunged toward her. Her screams were never heard.

1

Praise Poem

December 10th, 2000
6:50 a.m.
Oakland, California

Carol Simmons sang along to her favorite gospel song, *Order My Steps*, as it played from a small CD player in the basement of Holy Tabernacle Church. At sixty years old, her body was tired, but she was determined to scrub the moldy walls caused by leaky water pipes.

Order my steps in your word, dear Lord, she sang, scrubbing with a hard-bristled brush. She hadn't slept well the night before. Chest pains kept her tossing and turning. Despite the rough night, she arrived early to clean the basement. It was in this basement, damp with leaky pipes, that Carol taught Sunday school.

Holy Tabernacle sat in the heart of the *Murder Dubs*, a place where gunfire was more common than gospel hymns and where kids learned to run before they learned to read. However, teaching Sunday school was worth the risk if she could keep just one child away from the dangers of East Oakland's streets.

After scrubbing the last patch of mold, she turned off the CD player, wiped the sweat from her forehead, and climbed the stairs to the sanctuary. As she sat on a back pew to catch her breath, she heard someone knock on the church door.

Carol's face lit up when she opened the door and saw her grandson, Kareem, standing outside. He was dressed in a Navy Blue suit and holding a Bible and a notepad.

"Good morning, Granny," Kareem said with a warm smile.

She hugged him tight. "Good morning, grandson."

At thirteen, Kareem was tall, with broad shoulders that seemed to grow by the day. His thick, wavy hair and piercing brown eyes reminded Carol of his father at that age. As the door shut behind them, Kareem asked, "Why did you leave the house so early?"

Carol hesitated. She didn't want to tell him that her chest pains had made sleeping difficult. "I came in early to clean the church," she said while walking towards the pews. "Did you finish writing your poem for Youth Sunday?" she asked, trying to change the subject.

Kareem grinned. "I finished it last night. It's called *Spiritual Warfare*. I wrote it after your Sunday school lesson last weekend. Remember when you said we aren't fighting against flesh and blood but against spiritual wickedness in high places?"

Carol's eyes gleamed. "Ephesians 6:12. You have an amazing memory, grandson."

Kareem beamed. "It runs in the family."

The children arrived at church, and Carol started Sunday School with the story of Daniel and the Lion's Den. The class listened while she made ferocious sounds, imitating lions and using her hands as paws. The kids giggled, and Kareem lowered his head in embarrassment.

After finishing the story, Carol asked, "What gave Daniel the courage to face the lions?"

Leah, the pastor's nine-year-old daughter, raised her hand. "Daniel was brave and not afraid of lions."

Carol smiled. "Good answer."

Six-year-old Jason spoke next. "The lions thought Daniel was one of them, so they didn't eat him!"

The class laughed at his response, but Carol quickly reminded them that Daniel's story was no laughing matter.

Kareem raised his hand. "Without a test, we have no testimony! Daniel's faith was tested, but his trust in God kept him safe."

Carol clapped. "That's exactly right," she said, her voice serious. "There is evil in this world," she warned. "Evil is always lurking, prowling like a lion looking for its prey. But if you have unwavering faith that God will protect you, there is no reason to fear the wickedness of this world."

A church deacon interrupted to announce Youth Sunday. Carol led the children upstairs to change into their choir robes.

Every fourth Sunday, the church held a youth service. The new pastor, Pastor Banks, believed it would attract more single mothers - and it worked. Within months, the congregation grew from a few hundred to over a thousand members.

As the children dressed, Carol watched Kareem. He looked just like his father. It had been over a decade since Kareem's parents were murdered just blocks from the church. A burglar shot and killed them months after Kareem was born. The killer spared Kareem, leaving him crying in his crib. Despite numerous investigations, their murders remained unsolved.

After the tragic death of her son, Carol gained custody of Kareem. She joined the church and gave her life to Christ. Although she couldn't save her son from Oakland's crime-ridden streets, she was determined to protect her grandson, Kareem.

"Ready to share your poem?" Carol asked Kareem. She organized Sunday school lessons as she spoke. "Everyone loves hearing your work on Youth Sundays."

"I'm ready," he said, pacing. "But I'm still nervous. I need some air."

Kareem walked outside towards the church parking lot. He spotted the shiny black Bentley. It sat in the pastor's reserved spot, being guarded by a deacon. Kareem frowned. *Why did church members struggle to pay bills while Pastor Banks drove such a fancy car?* The pastor's daughter, Leah, never wore the same dress twice.

Pastor Aaron Banks was a thirty-six-year-old single father who had been installed as the church's new pastor a few months ago. His deep voice and strong presence filled the church each Sunday morning. Many women in the congregation found themselves drawn to the handsome new leader. Under his guidance, the church experienced rapid growth. Soon, it became the largest church in Oakland.

Kareem's mind then drifted back to an argument he had with his grandmother. She'd been upset when he called Pastor Banks a fraud. "He only cares about money!" Kareem had insisted. *Why couldn't she see it?*

As church members filled the pews, Kareem went inside and sat with the congregation. Leah Banks, the pastor's daughter, sat beside his grandmother. He sat beside her and watched the children's choir march to the pulpit in green and gold robes, singing *This Little Light of Mine*.

After the children's performance, it was time for Kareem's spoken word. Ministers and church members alike were impressed by his poetry. Some even said he would become a great preacher one day.

Kareem walked to the front of the church and faced the congregation. His grandmother beamed with pride.

"The poem I wrote is called *Spiritual Warfare*," he announced, his voice deep and confident beyond his years. For three minutes, Kareem read his poem. When he finished, the congregation stood up, clapping and shouting praises.

Hallelujah! someone shouted.

That young man has an anointing! Another voice rang through the church.

Pastor Banks stepped up to the pulpit, smiling proudly. His Yves Saint Laurent suit shimmered under the lights. When he raised his Bible, the congregation gasped, revealing a diamond-encrusted Rolex watch, several rings, and a bracelet. Women in the church whispered about how good he looked in his suit.

"It's a blessing to see so many young children here, praising the Lord," Pastor Banks declared, his deep voice echoing through the church. "'Train up a child in the way he should go, and when he is old, he will not depart from it.'"

"Amen!" the congregation responded in unison.

"Now, brothers and sisters," Pastor Banks continued, raising his arms, "God has placed it on my heart to heal someone today! Some of you are sick and suffering. Come to the pulpit now to be healed!"

Carol Simmons squeezed Kareem's hand, then rose from her seat.

"It doesn't matter what the doctors say," Pastor Banks preached. "Faith and prayer are the only prescriptions you need!"

"Hallelujah!" someone shouted as Carol stepped forward.

Kareem watched as the pastor opened a jar of oil and drizzled it over his grandmother's head.

"Lord, we ask you to heal Sister Simmons!" he prayed loudly. "In the name of Jeeeeesus… be healed!"

Pastor Banks pressed his hand to Carol's forehead. She jumped, waving her arms, and began shouting praises. Tears streamed down her face as she raised her hands to the sky in worship. The church broke into a powerful rendition of *Can't Nobody Do Me Like Jesus.*

Kareem watched as his grandmother returned to her seat, while the congregation clapped and swayed to the music.

Sister Austin, a six-foot-tall woman, suddenly became overcome with the Holy Spirit. She ran down the aisle toward Kareem's pew. He quickly moved aside as ushers rushed to surround her. In her excitement, she knocked off an usher's wig. Kareem chuckled under his breath. The last time Sister Austin caught the Holy Ghost, she knocked out a deacon's front tooth.

Pastor Banks began his sermon on the dangers of sin. The congregation responded with shouts of "Amen!" As the sermon ended, Kareem knew what was coming next: Offering time.

"Who wants to be blessed by God today?" Pastor Banks asked with a broad smile, his gaze piercing the congregation. Every hand in the congregation shot up.

"If you want God's blessings, you must give to Him first!" he preached. "Dig deep into your pockets so we can continue our ministry. It's a financial burden to run the church, print tracts, and care for the homeless."

Kareem watched as his grandmother placed a hundred-dollar bill into a tithing envelope. He shook his head. She could barely afford her bills, yet she continued to give money to the church. He knew better than to voice his opinion on the matter, though. His grandmother was a devout believer. After the service, they made their way to the grocery store.

2

Granny's Soul Food

Carol Simmons thanked the cashier and checked her receipt. She couldn't believe she had spent over fifty dollars on groceries for Sunday's dinner. Money was tight, but she wanted to make a special meal for Kareem to celebrate his good grades.

She smiled as Kareem grabbed all the grocery bags and carried them to the bus stop without complaint.

"Grandson, I can carry one of those," Carol said, reaching for a bag. Kareem grinned and pulled away. "Nope! You're already carrying that fifty-pound Bible." He chuckled, glancing at the oversized leather-bound book she always brought to church.

"My Bible doesn't weigh fifty pounds," she replied, pulling the Bible closer to her. "It's just large print!" She laughed, poking his arm.

By the time they got home, Carol was exhausted. Kareem noticed and suggested she take a break.

"You've been up since early this morning," he said. "Why don't you rest, Granny?"

"Everything is fine," she insisted. "Go play your video games. I'm cooking fried chicken, collard greens, and cornbread for dinner."

Mmm, Kareem hummed, licking his lips. He loved soul food. When he went to his room, Kareem spotted a gift-wrapped package on top of his PlayStation. He carefully removed the paper and opened the box to reveal *Madden 2000* - the video game he had wanted for months. His grandmother had removed the price tag, but Kareem knew it cost more than forty dollars - money she couldn't afford.

Kareem walked into the kitchen and hugged her. "Thank you, Granny, but we can't afford this. I can borrow games from my friends."

"You deserve this, Kareem," she said, playfully swatting at him with a box of cornbread mix. "Now get out of my kitchen."

As soon as he left, Carol leaned against the counter. She needed energy. She went to her room, turned on her Sony boombox, and played Kirk Franklin's *Stomp Remix*. The gospel beat filled the house, and soon, she was dancing. Kareem stood in her doorway, laughing.

"I don't care what some Christians think," she said, moving to the rhythm. "This song makes me want to dance and praise God," she said joyfully. Kareem walked into the room, raised his hands, and joined her, stomping to the music. When the song ended, they laughed together.

"Can I have the poem you read in church today?" Carol asked, sitting on the edge of her bed. "It touched my soul." Kareem pulled a folded paper from his pocket and handed it to her before returning to his game.

Not long after, the aroma of soul food filled the house. Kareem snuck into the kitchen and reached for a piece of fried chicken, but his hand was slapped away before he could take it.

Smack! "Boy…you know better than that! Wash your hands before dinner, and I'll make you a plate."

After washing his hands and saying grace, Kareem began to eat. His granny had cooked fried chicken, collard greens, yams, cornbread, and peach cobbler for dessert.

As he ate, Carol reached for his hand and smiled. "Your poems are making a difference in church," she said. "You have a gift. Use it wisely. Proverbs 18:21 states, *'Death and life are in the power of the tongue.* Words can heal or hurt. Be mindful of what you write."

Kareem fidgeted with his fork. "Do you think my parents would be proud of me?"

Carol took a deep breath, holding back tears. She wasn't surprised by his question. Lately, he had been asking more about the parents he never knew.

"They would be so proud," she said softly. "You've grown into a smart, strong, and amazing young man." She let the words sink in before asking, "Have you given any thought to what you want to do after college?"

Kareem nodded. "I want to go into real estate. Realtors make a lot of money." He'd watched a TV show about real estate and was amazed by the wealth. "I'm going to sell expensive houses and buy you a mansion!"

Carol chuckled. "That's sweet, but I don't need a mansion. Your hugs are priceless! And when you become wealthy, always help those who are less fortunate. Remember, the best *things* in life aren't *things*."

After dinner, Kareem started washing the dishes. Carol turned her chair toward him.

"I've noticed Leah Banks has been around you a lot," she said. "She has a crush on you."

Kareem sighed. "She's just a friend. All she talks about is fashion and clothes. It would never work out."

Carol chuckled. "When you start dating, always treat a woman with respect. Be a gentleman."

"I will," Kareem said. "But I'm not rubbing any girl's stinky feet!"

Carol burst into laughter. Kareem smiled, but his expression changed when he saw her clutch her chest.

His hands froze in the sink. "Granny, are you okay?" he asked, worried.

She took a deep breath. "I think I just need to rest," she said. "I'm going to read my Bible in bed for a while. Finish washing the dishes. We can't afford to have the exterminator come out again."

"All right," Kareem replied as he watched his grandmother rise from the dinner table and stumble towards her bedroom.

A devoted Christian, she turned to her Bible for comfort. She couldn't afford the healthcare she needed because her Social Security and retirement checks barely covered the bills. She opened the Book of Psalms and began to read. Minutes later, she felt lightheaded. A sharp pain spread through her chest, and her jaw went numb.

Kareem peeked into her room and panicked. She was lying in bed, clutching her chest.

"Granny, I'm calling an ambulance!" He sprinted to the living room and dialed 911.

"911, what's your emergency?"

"Please send an ambulance! My grandmother is having a heart attack!" Kareem's voice shook. "Please hurry!"

The dispatcher asked questions, but Kareem felt overwhelmed.

"She's in bed! I don't know if she's breathing! Just hurry!"

He dropped the phone and ran back to her room. Her skin had gone pale. Tears ran down her face as she stared at him helplessly.

"It's going to be okay, Granny," he said, trying to stay calm. "Help is on the way."

Carol looked at him. "I love you," she whispered so softly he barely heard her. Suddenly, Carol Simmons closed her eyes.

"Granny! Granny, wake up!" Kareem shouted, shaking her. "The ambulance is coming!"

He tried CPR, just as he had learned in school, but she didn't respond. Minutes later, paramedics burst into the room.

"Help her!" Kareem yelled. "Please don't let her die!"

The paramedics worked desperately, but it was too late. Carol Simmons was gone.

Kareem stood frozen, staring at her lifeless body. His vision blurred with tears as his world shattered around him.

3

Motherless Child

Kareem stared through the rain-streaked windshield, watching the raindrops slam against the windshield of his social worker's car. Raindrops pounded against the car like tiny fists, drowning out everything except the low murmur of the engine. He used to believe that rain meant angels were crying. But on the day of his grandmother's funeral, Kareem no longer believed in angels or the goodness of God.

When Kareem entered the church, his eyes locked onto the black casket at the front. His feet felt heavy as he walked up the aisle. He could feel the silent stares of mourners as he passed. Reaching the front pew, he sat next to Leah Banks. She wore a black dress, matching shoes, and a jacket. Her tear-filled eyes met his.

"I'm sorry, Kareem," she whispered. He took a deep breath but said nothing. His grandmother—his only family—was gone. He'd never felt so alone.

Pastor Banks delivered a brief yet emotional eulogy. Many people cried. After the service, Kareem and his social worker joined the funeral procession to the cemetery. The rain continued, making the burial brief. Pastor Banks read a verse from Proverbs before the casket was lowered into the ground.

Kareem approached Pastor Banks, his voice shaky. "Why didn't God heal my grandmother?"

Pastor Banks cleared his throat. "Sometimes, God works in mysterious ways, Kareem. Your grandmother is at peace now. She's free from pain."

Kareem looked down, his hands gripping his grandmother's Bible. Anger, sadness, and confusion swirled inside him. The church members offered their condolences, but no one offered him a place to stay. His grandmother had always told him to trust in God, but now he felt abandoned.

His grip tightened on the Bible. *God, why? Why did you take my grandmother away from me?* Kareem asked. *Why did you take my parents?* He searched for answers, but none came. The emptiness in his heart only grew.

Pastor Banks handed Kareem a business card with the church's logo. "If you ever want to visit, call me. I'll arrange for the church van to pick you up."

Then, Pastor Banks turned to the social worker, his eyes lingering on her figure. Smiling, he slid another card into her hand. "Feel free to call me anytime. I care about Kareem's well-being."

Kareem overheard him flirting but felt too numb to react. He'd seen plenty of women seduced by the pastor's charisma and charm. He glanced down at the Bible in his hands. The same one his grandmother had cherished. The same one she had read every night. But now, it felt like an empty book. *Where was God now?*

"Kareem, are you ready to go?" his social worker asked.

"Yes," he said, his voice trembling. Tears filled his eyes as he dropped the Bible onto the cold, hard earth of his grandmother's grave and walked away. He felt God had abandoned him, so he abandoned his faith in God.

Leah saw Kareem drop the Bible. "Daddy, Kareem dropped his bible!" she exclaimed.

"It's ok, Leah," Pastor Banks replied, smiling at the departing social worker.

"Why did he drop it?" Leah asked. "Maybe it slipped from his hands after getting wet from the rain," he suggested. Leah glanced at her shoes, noticing the rain had ruined her new boots.

"Daddy, can we go shopping? I need new boots."

"Of course, daughter. Let's go shopping," he said, walking to his brand-new Bentley.

During the drive back to his foster home, the social worker tried to cheer Kareem up.

"You've been through so much, and I'm proud of how you've handled it," she said. "Fortunately, your grandmother had a good life insurance policy, so you'll have enough money to attend college."

Even in her death, she's taking care of me, Kareem thought to himself. Part of him wanted to go back to the cemetery, sit next to her grave, and never leave. *I'll always love you, Granny,* he told himself, his tears dripping on her obituary.

4

Studio Session

Oakland, California

14 years later

Keith Hicks sat in his recording studio nodding to the beat he'd just created. A maestro behind the mixing board, he'd spent the past hour blending beats and melodies into beautiful music. With a deep bassline and an 808 drum kit, he produced a slow, sensual beat with a 90s R&B vibe. *Kareem is going to love this track!* Keith thought.

Keith *Hitmaker* Hicks was one of the most creative producers in the country. Over the past decade, he'd produced some of the biggest gospel and hip-hop hits. His talent for blending diverse genres, including gospel, funk, hip-hop, jazz, R&B, and pop, sets him apart. Every track he created sounded original and timeless.

Keith's love for music began at a young age. It started with a cheap Casio keyboard his mother bought him for Christmas when he was six. By twelve, he'd learned to play multiple instruments and became the musical director at his church. Now, he owned *Inspirational Sounds*, his recording studio, where he created beats as one of the music industry's top producers.

With his tall, muscular build, Keith resembled a football player more than a music producer. At six feet four inches and 260 pounds, he had a powerful presence. But despite his size, Keith was a gentle giant, always cracking jokes and making people laugh. He was also a devout Christian, spending most of his time in church or the studio. When he wasn't making music, he was with his girlfriend, Tasha Jennings.

"Ayyyyy, I like that beat," Tasha said as she entered the recording studio. Keith swiveled in his chair and smiled as he took in the sight of her.

Tasha Jennings was a gorgeous Southern girl from Alabama with curly hair, smooth brown skin, and a radiant smile. Although she was only five feet tall, her confidence made up for her small stature. Their church friends often called them *Beauty and the Brawn* because of their size difference.

"Hey, love," Keith said, pulling her into a hug before kissing her. As he sat back down, Tasha rested her hands on his shoulders, kneading the tension from his muscles. Her perfume lingered in the air as she leaned in. "Is that beat for Kareem?"

Keith grinned and nodded. "Yeah, babe! This is the final track for his new album, *Lyrics and Lust*." He turned back to the computer, importing the tracks into Pro Tools.

Keith and Kareem had been best friends since college. They first met at a student rally at Cal Berkeley, where Kareem performed a spoken-word poem protesting rising tuition costs and the lack of diversity on campus. Keith liked Kareem's passion. They started working on spoken-word projects and became best friends.

Keith chuckled, remembering how Kareem had helped him get together with Tasha. During his junior year, Keith was too nervous to approach her, so he asked Kareem to write a love poem. After Keith recited the poem to Tasha, they became a couple.

Keith had two more songs to mix and master for Kareem's spoken-word album, *Lyrics and Lust*. The first single, *Sweet Tooth*, was already a hit, racking up over a million streams on Spotify. Meanwhile, Tasha's best friend, Maya Rivers, had booked a session that morning. She had an incredible voice and was ready to start recording her gospel album.

The studio buzzer rang. Keith checked the security camera and saw Kareem. He hit the unlock button.

"Hey! What's good?" Kareem greeted Keith, giving him dap. "What are you two lovebirds up to?"

"I was just playing one of your beats for Tasha," Keith said with a grin. "This album is going to be fire. We're bringing grown and sexy music back!"

"I just saw the numbers for *Sweet Tooth*—it's blowing up on Spotify and Apple Music!" Kareem said, his eyes gleaming with excitement. "Let's finish this album today."

"Don't forget Maya's session," Tasha reminded. Keith leaned back from the mixing board and smiled. "I know, baby! I finished the music for her song, *Hug You in Heaven*, last night."

"Maya, huh?" Kareem smirked. "She's from your church? What does she look like? Hopefully, not like that singer you brought in a few weeks ago."

"Who? Sister Walker?" Tasha laughed.

"Yes! Sister Walker! The one with the mustache and body shaped like a wisdom tooth," Kareem teased.

"Stop it!" Keith chuckled, shaking his head. "Sister Walker may not be the most attractive woman, but she can sing!"

"You better stop talking about God's people!" Tasha warned Kareem, shaking her fist playfully.

Kareem smirked. "Can your friend sing like Jill Scott, Ledisi, or Jennifer Hudson?"

"Boy, she can saaaaang," Tasha said, emphasizing the last word. "I've been telling her for years to get in the studio. Now that she's back from college, she's finally ready to record her gospel EP."

Before anyone could respond, Tasha's phone dinged.

"That's Maya," she said, glancing at the screen. "She's outside."

Kareem opened the door and froze. His jaw nearly hit the floor.

Maya Rivers stood five feet six inches tall, her complexion the color of mocha, her smooth brown skin glowing. Her deep dimples made her alluring smile even more beautiful. She wore a crisp white blouse and fitted jeans that hugged her curvy hips just right.

"Hello, I'm Kareem," he said, extending his hand. His gaze lingered a little longer than necessary.

"Nice to meet you, Kareem. I'm Maya," she replied, shaking his hand. The moment their eyes met, his heart raced. Love at first sight was real.

"This is a nice studio, Keith," Maya said, admiring the platinum plaques on the wall.

"Thanks, Maya! I'm excited about collaborating with you," Keith replied. Tasha smirked and nudged Kareem. "Not Sister Walker, is she??"

"What about Sister Walker?" Maya asked, her gaze fixed on Kareem.

"Oh, it's nothing," he replied, trying to avoid the fact that he'd talked bad about Sister Walker earlier. Maya sized Kareem up from head to toe before stepping back and folding her arms across her chest.

"So, you're the poet Keith and Tasha have been hyping up all these years?"

"That's me," Kareem said, flashing a flirtatious smile. "I heard you could sing."

"I've been singing in church since I was a kid," Maya said, setting her purse on the coffee table. "Now that I've graduated from Howard University, I'm ready to record my gospel album."

"So, you only sing gospel?" Kareem asked, curious.

"Yes," Maya replied firmly. "No secular music."

"Did you hear that, Kareem?" Tasha teased. "No secular music. That means she won't be singing on your album—since your music is as *secular* or, should I say, *sexular* as it gets." She winked at Maya.

"Are all your poems about sex?" Maya asked.

"Not all," Kareem said defensively. "I write about a lot of things—politics, love, culture. But erotica is my specialty. My new album, *Lyrics and Lust,* drops soon."

"Lyrics and Lust?" Maya repeated, sounding uninterested.

"Yeah," Kareem said confidently. "I'm about to lay down vocals for my new single, *Go Deep,* today."

Maya glanced at her phone, suddenly disinterested. Keith looked up from his computer and motioned for Kareem to enter the vocal booth. Kareem stepped into the booth and adjusted the microphone.

"Maya, give us twenty minutes, and then we'll start your session," Keith said. Maya nodded and sat on the couch with Tasha. As the beat poured through the headphones, Kareem closed his eyes and started performing his erotic poem, *Go Deep,* over the sensual rhythm Keith had created:

I'm going deep
I want to explore the contour of your ocean floor
I want you to feel my manhood slide
Deep inside
Your womanly waters
I'll hold my breath
While my tongue dives deep
And explores
Your underwater caverns
Where no man's tongue has ever gone before

When he exited the booth, Kareem saw Maya with her eyes closed, AirPods in her ears. He frowned.

"You didn't like the poem?" he asked.

Maya put her AirPods away before responding. "I don't mean to sound preachy, but I don't listen to erotic music. But, if that's your thing, then, do you!"

"I hope you're not one of those holier-than-thou Christians," Kareem said, raising an eyebrow. "You do know the Song of Solomon talks about erotic love, right?"

Maya's brows lifted in surprise. "So, you're a Bible scholar now?"

Kareem smirked. "I was raised in the church."

Maya fell silent. That bit of information intrigued her. There could be more to him than just good looks.

"Sex sells," Kareem added. "My song *Sweet Tooth* already has over a million streams."

Maya crossed her arms, unimpressed. "Sex does sell. Too bad *celibacy* doesn't sell as well."

Sensing the tension, Keith jumped in to lighten the mood. "Maya, please don't tell anyone at church I produced this album," Keith joked, closing Kareem's session. "I don't need your dad or the ministers giving me the side-eye on Sunday!" Everyone burst into laughter.

Keith, Tasha, and Maya were all members of *Agape Assembly*, a holiness church in Oakland. Maya's father was the pastor.

Maya turned back to Kareem. "Are all the songs on your album erotic?"

"Yeah, it's full of baby-making music," Kareem admitted with a grin. "But I'm thinking about adding a few love songs."

"That would be nice," Maya said. "We need more love songs."

Kareem nodded. "I'm working on a love poem called Intimate."

Tasha snickered. "Kareem, stop! You don't want to be *intimate* with a woman. You want her to come over so you can get *into it!*"

Laughter erupted again.

Maya took a deep breath as she stepped into the vocal booth. Despite years of singing, this was her first time in a professional studio. Kareem noticed her nerves and gave her an encouraging nod before lowering the mic to her height.

"Alright, Maya, the track is ready," Keith said, pressing the talkback button. Maya nodded as the instrumental began to play. The song had a smooth gospel feel with a mid-tempo beat and melodic chords. She closed her eyes and started singing *Hug You in Heaven,* an emotional ballad she wrote for her late mother:

Mama, I wish you were still here

I would give up all my material possessions

If God would open the curtains of heaven

And allow me to hug you for a few seconds

And tell you how much I love you

And miss you

Maya's voice soared, full of raw emotion. Kareem felt something stir deep inside him. The lyrics and melody reminded him of his grandmother. "That was beautiful," he complimented when she stepped out of the booth. "Thank you," Maya whispered. "I wrote this song for my mom after she passed away from ovarian cancer a few years ago." Kareem's expression softened. "I'm sorry for your loss."

Tasha suddenly broke the moment. "So, what's the plan after the studio?" Keith suggested bowling. Kareem turned to Maya with a playful grin. "You any good at bowling?"

Maya smirked. "Are you ready to lose?" Kareem laughed. "We'll see about that."

After three intense games filled with laughter, Kareem asked Maya to go on a date. His face lit up when she said yes.

5

Kabul, Afghanistan

Vincent gripped his prized Bowie knife, studying its razor-sharp edge. He ran his thumb across it - too dull. He reached for the whetstone and began sharpening it, keeping a precise angle. His father's words echoed in his mind: *the sharper the knife, the more efficient the kill.*

Vincent stored his knife collection inside his private armory, hidden within the walls of a high-security compound in Afghanistan. His luxurious bunker was a stark contrast to the poverty beyond the gates. After sharpening the blade, he slid the blade beneath his turban, and left the compound, disappearing into the darkness.

Vincent Thomas was a notorious and feared mercenary. He'd fought in Iraq, Yemen, Ukraine, Syria, and Somalia. Now, in his mid-forties, he worked as a private military contractor, earning millions. But it wasn't money that drove him to become a mercenary - it was his insatiable thirst for blood and the thrill of killing.

Vincent's thirst for violence began at a young age. When he was seven, he saw a news story about John Wayne Gacy, a serial killer who murdered dozens of people and hid their bodies beneath the crawl space of his home. Vincent was fascinated. Soon after, he killed a neighbor's cat that had been hunting mice in the crawl space beneath his house. Rather than feel remorse, Vincent felt excitement. He soon began torturing and killing other small animals. It was only a matter of time before he started killing people.

At twelve, his life fell apart. His father divorced his mother and married a woman he met overseas. His mother spiraled into alcoholism, cursing her ex-husband and his new wife, Tracy. When the court granted his father custody, Vincent's hatred for Tracy increased.

Tracy. The woman who replaced his mother. The woman who stole his father. Vincent didn't just hate her. He resented her. And one night, when the weight of that hatred became too much to bear, he acted on it. A twisted smirk spread across Vincent's face as he remembered the night he took his revenge on Tracy.

It happened on a Saturday night. Teenage Vincent was staying at a friend's house up the street. He waited for everyone to fall asleep before sneaking out of the window and returning home to spy on his stepmother, who he suspected was cheating on his father while he was stationed overseas. As Vincent approached his home, he spotted a silver Ford Mustang parked in the driveway. He quickly memorized the vehicle's license plate and quietly crept into his house through the crawl space.

Once inside, he heard muffled moans coming from Tracy's bedroom upstairs. Vincent crept up the stairs and peered into his stepmother's bedroom door, where he saw her having sex with an unknown man. He peeked through the door and saw Tracy handcuffed, blindfolded, and gagged, tangled in sheets with another man. A shiver of excitement ran down his spine.

Vincent tiptoed into his room and retrieved his torture kit - one that contained razors, duct tape, rubber gloves, handcuffs, and a Bowie Knife. He waited.

When the stranger left, and Tracy fell asleep, Vincent moved. He slid on rubber gloves, grabbed his torture kit, and crept into her room. In one swift motion, he shoved her face into the pillow, muffling her scream as he snapped the handcuffs onto her wrists.

When he flipped on the light, her eyes widened in horror. She was bound, gagged, and helpless. Vincent smiled. He drew his Bowie knife. With one clean stroke, he stabbed her to death. The ball gag muffled her screams.

When it was over, he staged the scene. He cut her hands to make it look like she had fought back. The setup had to be perfect. He had spent hours in the public library studying forensic science. Once he finished, he slipped out through the crawl space and dumped his torture kit in a creek. Then, he crawled back through his friend's window as if he'd never left.

The next day, Vincent returned home with his friend. When they entered Tracy's room, Vincent pretended to be horrified. His friend fainted at the sight of the blood-soaked bed.

The police arrived and found no signs of forced entry. Vincent provided them with a lead - the Mustang's license plate. They arrested the man and charged him with murder. A forensic pathologist called it a crime of passion.

Vincent was never suspected because his weekend at a friend's house served as an alibi. Vincent had successfully committed his first kill - the first of many.

When his father returned for the funeral, he sent Vincent to military boarding school. While there, Vincent excelled, focusing his studies on warfare and weapons. He wore the school's Latin motto, *Aut vincere aut mori,* meaning *Either conquer or die* across his chest. His classmates nicknamed him *Cutter* because he was fascinated with Bowie knives, bayonets, and hatchets. He graduated at the top of his class. Then, he joined *Murky Waters,* an elite mercenary unit. And the killing continued.

Murky Waters was a notorious organization known for their ruthless methods and connections to high-profile political figures. They only hired the best: Navy Seals, Marines, and special ops leaders. As one of their assassins, Vincent killed without fear of prosecution. American troops followed the Uniform Code of Military Justice. Mercenaries like him followed no code.

Vincent spent nearly a decade in black ops—assassinations, spying, kidnappings, torture. Now, in Afghanistan, he earned hefty paychecks killing Taliban militants. He was well-liked by his comrades and respected for his military knowledge. However, on the inside, in the hidden recesses of his heart, a ravenous monster lurked. Tonight, he would kill again.

***

Kabul, Afghanistan, was a city scarred by war. Once called a city of gardens, Kabul was now a heartless place filled with death and destruction. Its rampant poverty and desperate people made it a serial killer's paradise.

Murky Waters rarely allowed anyone to venture outside their military headquarters alone due to the extreme danger that lurked in the city. Vincent, however, was hungry for a kill, so he dressed like a local to hide his identity. His full beard helped him look like an Afghan. He had a hunting knife, two grenades, and a 9mm Glock hidden in a holster in case he ran into trouble.

In Kabul, corruption thrived. Vincent learned the language and met crooked soldiers selling girls for cash. Women here were easy targets. He paid one soldier to bring a girl from the slums to his hotel. Vincent paid a soldier to bring a girl from a poor neighborhood to his hotel room.

When Vincent opened the door, the soldier stood with a young Afghan girl in a traditional blue burqa that covered her completely. Her face showed fear.

In one swift motion, Vincent ripped off her burqa with his hunting knife and shoved a large ball gag deep into her mouth to muffle her screams.

"What are you doing?!" The soldier yelled in broken English as he pulled out his revolver. In a swift movement, Vincent plunged his Bowie knife deep into the soldier's ribs, preventing him from screaming and killing him instantly.

Vincent turned to the terrified girl. Tears streamed down her face. The ball gag in her mouth muffled her desperate screams as salty tears and drool cascaded down her chin. A wave of excitement washed over Vincent as he prepared to take her life.

6

A Great Date

Maya Rivers was living her best life. At the age of twenty-five, she was single by choice. Being single and celibate allowed her to focus on building her nonprofit, *A Safe Space*, for at-risk girls in Oakland. It also allowed her to avoid the drama and distractions of modern-day dating. But then came Kareem, and everything changed.

Kareem caught her eye the moment she entered the recording studio. He was extremely handsome - tall and muscular, with piercing brown eyes, a deep baritone voice, and a beard. Kareem was the type who made a woman look twice.

At first, she was hesitant about dating a man who wasn't a Christian. Plus, Kareem seemed like a player. But at the bowling alley, her opinion began to change. He opened every door for her and insisted on paying for her food. He was courteous and respectful. There was more to Kareem than his good looks. She wanted to get to know the man behind the erotic poetry. So, she agreed to go on a date.

Maya sprayed her favorite Chanel No. 5 perfume between her breasts and behind her earlobes before applying Mac lip gloss to her full lips. Then, she stood in front of the full-length mirror, admiring how the form-fitting black jeans and grey blouse she had purchased complimented her God-given curves.

Maya wasn't conceited, but she knew men were attracted to her. In high school, she was teased for the size of her hips and thighs. Now, women were spending thousands of dollars on BBLs to obtain a body like hers. The more Maya gazed into the mirror, the more she noticed the same almond-shaped eyes and high cheekbones that mirrored her mother's features.

Maya's mind drifted back to the painful memories of her mother as she lay on the hospital bed dying from cancer. Maya had flown home from college and told her mother that she'd caught her boyfriend cheating with her college roommate.

Her mother's voice, though weak, was steady as she stroked Maya's hair and told her not to cry over a man who didn't love her. "One day, you will meet a man who will love you rather than lust after you. Until then, do as the bible says and *guard your heart, for everything you do flows from it,*" her mother urged before passing away weeks later.

"How's my daughter doing?" Her father's deep, rich voice called out. She turned around and saw her father standing in her doorway. Pastor Rivers was tall, with smooth brown skin, a shaved head, and a distinguished grey beard.

"How did the conference go, Dad?" Maya asked.

"It was good. Just a bunch of old pastors trying to come up with ideas to empower the community," he replied. "Is that Chanel No. 5 I smell? That was your mother's favorite perfume," he said, smiling. "Going on a date?" he asked, raising an eyebrow.

Maya fidgeted. "Just… a friend. Maybe I'll bring him to church."

Her dad chuckled. "I'd love to meet him. You haven't introduced anyone in years."

"That's because you scare them all away," she said, poking him playfully in the chest. Glancing at the clock, she grabbed her purse and rushed out the door to meet Kareem.

Maya smiled when she saw Kareem leaning against his glossy black Mercedes. Dressed in a tailored navy blue blazer that accentuated his muscular physique and a fitted white V-neck, he exuded confidence and power.

Kareem flashed a seductive grin as he walked towards her. He wrapped his muscular arms around her, making her feel safe and protected. Maya smiled as she inhaled the scent of his sandalwood and citrus-scented cologne. *He smells so good.*

"It's so good to see you," he said, his voice deep and smooth. He handed Maya a large gold box tied with a white ribbon. She opened it to find a dozen long-stemmed red roses. She breathed in their aroma and thanked him. *Such a gentleman,* she thought.

"Where are we going?" Maya asked while Kareem opened the car door and helped her slide in. "I've made reservations at Lake Chalet," he replied.

"How was your day at work?" Maya asked as they drove towards Lake Merritt. "It was great," he said, smiling. "I sold a nice home in Tiburon today."

"Congratulations," Maya said. "Do you like being a realtor?" she asked. A grin spread across Kareem's face. "I love it," he said. "The money is great, and I can make my schedule. I can also enjoy other activities, such as reading, traveling, writing, recording poetry, and working out.

Maya's eyes lit up. "I took some interior design courses at Howard University," she said. "Interior design has always been one of my passions."

"Maybe I can hire you to decorate this home I'm renovating," Kareem suggested. Maya smiled softly. "I'd be happy to help," she replied.

Kareem asked her how her day had gone. Maya let out a heavy sigh. "It was ok," she huffed. "I'm a social worker. Helping disadvantaged kids is another one of my passions," she said, gazing out the car window. "I see so many young girls being sex-trafficked out here in Oakland - it breaks my heart. I'm working on opening a home called *A Safe Space* to help get these at-risk girls off the streets."

"That's needed," he said, shaking his head sadly.

"These streets are infested with pimps, predators, and pedophiles, all preying on innocent young Black girls," Maya said while shaking her head in frustration. "Our ancestors didn't fight to free themselves from centuries of slavery just to have their descendants enslaved and trafficked on the street. Did you know over 90,000 Black women are currently missing in America?"

Kareem's mouth dropped open in disbelief. "Are you serious? 90,000 Black women are missing in America?"

Maya nodded, adding that Black women, making up less than 8% of the population, account for 40% of sex trafficking victims. In Oakland alone, over 500 of the 1,500 missing people are Black women. She explained that criminals targeted Black girls because they were less likely to be searched.

Kareem's face furrowed with concern. *90,000 missing Black women in this country?* Kareem thought, his mind spinning as he processed the information. *Is the F.B.I. or law enforcement even looking for them?* After a pause, Maya said, "Sorry, I don't want to ruin our date with a sad topic." Kareem reassured her, "No, I'm glad you did. I admire your passion for helping our people. Let me know if I can help." He saw the corners of Maya's mouth curl into a gentle smile.

Kareem parked his car at Lake Chalet, a waterfront restaurant in Oakland, and handed his keys to the valet. They chose to dine on the outdoor deck, taking in the sunny day and the lake view. As they settled in, Kareem complimented Maya's singing abilities.

"I love your voice," Kareem admitted. "I can see you becoming one of the gospel greats like Shirley Caesar, Karen Clark-Sheard, CeCe Winans, Yolanda Adams, Le'Andria Johnson, and Tamela Mann," Kareem said, running off the names of some famous gospel singers.

Maya gasped and clapped her hands. "My mama used to play Shirley Caesar and CeCe Winans all the time! Le'Andria Johnson and Karen Clark-Sheard are two of my favorites!"

A waitress approached their table, ready to take their order. Maya picked the Dungeness crab cakes and guava strawberry lemonade, while Kareem ordered crispy fried chicken wings and lemonade. After the waitress left, Maya looked at Kareem with curiosity. "You know a lot about gospel music," she said. You said that you grew up in the church."

Kareem shared with Maya that his parents had died when he was a baby, and his grandmother had raised him in the church until she passed away. He also discussed his challenging time in a foster home before attending college and becoming a successful realtor. Something about Maya made him feel comfortable sharing his family history with her.

Maya's voice was soft but sincere as she said, "You've had a rough life.

"I've had a difficult life," Kareem admitted, "but my struggles have made me stronger. Everything I've experienced has helped me become the man I am today."

Maya felt sympathetic for Kareem. Growing up, she never had to worry about financial struggles or her family's fate. Her father was a successful businessman and a pastor of his church. Her mother served as an Oakland councilwoman before retiring and passing away from cancer. She couldn't imagine the pain of losing her entire family.

"Where did you go to church?" she asked Kareem. *Holy Tabernacle,* he replied, and Maya's eyes widened.

"That's Bishop Banks church!" she exclaimed. "It's now a megachurch, with over 10,000 members. I'm singing at their Gospel concert in a few months."

"Yeah, he was the pastor when I went there," he said quietly, his expression darkening.

"Why don't you go to church anymore? Tasha and Keith told me they've been inviting you for years."

Kareem sighed. "I don't trust organized religion. Too many churches prioritize power and money over faith. Some of the biggest hypocrites are in the church. Too many pimps in the pulpit."

Maya surprised him by nodding. "I agree. There are many false prophets in the world. But my church isn't like that." She smiled warmly and placed her hand on his. "Don't let one bad church experience keep you from God's love. You might have left the church, but God never left you."

Kareem smiled, locking eyes with her. She was different from anyone he had dated. Maya was kind, caring, and genuine.

The waitress arrived with their appetizers and took their entrée orders. Maya chose the Seafood Linguini, and Kareem ordered Grilled Fish Tacos with guacamole. He took a sip of lemonade and studied her.

"You mentioned celibacy at the studio," he said. "Are you celibate?"

Maya set down her guava-strawberry lemonade and nodded. "Yes. It's been three years. I haven't had sex since college. Maya sighed. "My ex cheated on me with my college roommate. Most men lose interest when I tell them I'm waiting until marriage."

Kareem shook his head. "That's old school. These days, most men won't wait when there are so many available women."

"Well, I'm not going to settle for anybody just to say I have somebody," Maya responded. "I believe in dating with a purpose. I want a relationship that leads to marriage."

Kareem raised an eyebrow. "Dating with a purpose? What does that mean?"

Maya smiled. "Dating without a purpose is like driving without a destination—you get lost. I know where I'm going. My destination is marriage. I want my children to experience the same joy, security, and family structure I had growing up in a two-parent home."

Kareem nodded. "I respect that. You should write a book about it." Maya laughed. "Funny you say that. I started writing one in college after my breakup. Thanks for the confirmation."

"Real love is rare nowadays, but that's what I want. I'm fine with being single until my future husband finds me. Someone I can grow old and grey with," Maya said while looking into Kareem's eyes.

Kareem grinned. "I think I see a little grey in your hair already." Maya gasped, laughing. "Oh, you got jokes, huh?"

He smiled, his voice turning serious. "You're worth waiting for. I know a diamond when I see one."

"Thank you, Kareem," Maya said, blushing. Her dimples deepened as she smiled. His charm was growing on her by the minute.

The waiter arrived with their entrees. Kareem closed his eyes as Maya prayed before they ate.

"I'm curious. What inspired you to start writing erotic poetry?" Maya asked. Kareem paused before answering. "I've written poetry since I was a child, but a year ago, I entered an erotic poetry slam. I won. What surprised me was the intense reaction from the women in the audience. That's when I realized erotica was something special."

Maya looked at him thoughtfully. "What attracted you to me?"

Kareem didn't hesitate. "Your curves caught my eye, but your smile captured my heart."

Maya couldn't hide the smile forming at the corners of her lips. He had game. Kareem was a poet. He was polished. He seemed to know the right words to say. Part of her wondered if he was always this smooth or if he was being sincere.

They continued talking and laughing, sharing stories about their lives. They discussed politics, religion, and relationships. Their conversation flowed so naturally that it felt like they had known each other for years. After leaving the restaurant, Kareem pointed to a sleek black gondola gliding across the shimmering lake. "Have you ever been on one of those?" Maya said no.

A smile spread across Kareem's face. "Tonight's your lucky night. I made a reservation for a sunset gondola ride."

They boarded the boat, and the gondolier began to sing as he steered them across Lake Merritt. Kareem opened a bottle of wine while Maya unwrapped a selection of cheeses and strawberries. As they took in the peaceful surroundings, Maya let out a sigh. "What a beautiful view."

Kareem wrapped his arm around her waist. "Your face is the most beautiful view of all."

Maya blushed. "You always know just what to say."

Kareem grinned. "That's because I'm romantic." He pulled her into a hug. She laughed. "No, you're not."

"Yes, I am. I wrote you a love poem."

Maya's eyes lit up. "You wrote me a poem? I want to hear it!"

Kareem smirked. "You have to ask me to spit it first."

Maya frowned. "Why do I have to say 'spit'? That sounds so disgusting."

Kareem tilted his head back and stayed silent, waiting. Maya sighed. "Fine. Spit it."

Kareem looked directly into her eyes and began to freestyle the lyrics to a love poem while holding her hand. In the poem, he included her ideas of dating with a purpose and growing old together. Her eyes welled up as she listened to the lyrics. When he finished, she exhaled.

"That was one of the most beautiful poems I've ever heard." Her voice was soft, full of emotion. She turned away slightly, hoping to hide her reaction.

"Look at them," she said, pointing to an elderly couple sitting on a park bench. From their gondola, they watched as the elderly man tenderly kissed his wife's hand before massaging her back in slow, circular motions over the blue fabric of her matching Adidas sweatsuit.

"Aww... they're twinning! That's so cute," Maya gushed. "I love seeing old folks in love." She turned back to Kareem. "The words in your poem—that's the kind of love I want."

After their gondola ride, Kareem helped Maya out of the boat and tipped the gondolier. For a moment, they stood in silence, taking in the beauty of the setting sun. This was the most romantic date Maya had ever been on. She smiled to herself, then turned to Kareem.

"Kareem, can I tell you something?"

"Of course," he said.

"Your grandmother did an amazing job raising you."

The mention of his grandmother and the kindest compliment a woman had ever given him left Kareem speechless. He smiled as he stared into Maya's eyes and whispered, "Thank you."

Kareem pulled Maya into a tight embrace. He'd dated many beautiful, but he always kept his emotions in check, never letting himself get too attached. But with Maya, it was different. As he held her close, he felt the warmth of her body and the softness of her skin. There was something special about her. Something that made him want to stay by her side forever.

7

Passion Party

"I'm the baddest bitch!" Leah Banks said to herself, admiring her reflection in the full-length mirror.

She smoothed a manicured hand over the sleek black fabric of her Oscar de la Renta dress. Her Louboutin heels clicked against the floor as she moved closer to the mirror, absorbing the image of a woman who had everything - style, money, and curves that turned heads. Leah felt like a million bucks.

A satisfied smile spread across her face. She'd recently gotten breast implants, going from an A cup to a D cup. She loved the attention she got from men whenever she wore low-cut tops or V-neck sweaters that flaunted her new curves.

As the daughter of a powerful preacher, Leah enjoyed the finer things in life—designer fashion, five-star restaurants, and luxury cars. Her father, Bishop Banks, was one of the wealthiest preachers in the country, and she reaped the benefits.

Leah glanced at her diamond Cartier watch—9 p.m. already. *Damn, I don't want to miss the male strippers,* she thought, grabbing her Chanel handbag and heading to a passion party hosted by a friend.

When Leah arrived, her friend greeted her at the door. She sampled some party treats—a penis-shaped cake, adult cookies, and chocolate-covered strawberries. She ordered a *Sex on the Beach* cocktail and leaned toward the hostess.

"I hope you got some fine-ass male strippers coming through tonight, girl?" Leah teased.

The hostess smirked. "Leah, you're wild. There are no strippers tonight. I planned a more conservative evening—this is an older crowd."

"No strippers?" Leah pouted. "Oh well, at least I can buy a new sex toy." Shopping was Leah's second favorite pastime after sex, and when she had bad sex, she'd always cheer herself up by going shopping.

Leah's closest friends were a tight-knit sisterhood that understood the importance of discretion. They kept their passion parties private. Because Leah was Bishop Banks's daughter, she had to keep her sexual activities secret.

The hostess held up a sleek, new vibrator. "Ladies, this toy promises explosive orgasms."

Leah, tipsy, pointed at it. "I need that! Like I always say, *an orgasm a day keeps depression away.*"

The women burst into laughter. The hostess then turned on some music, and the sultry sound of erotic spoken words filled the room. The women's attention shifted from the sex toys to the lyrics.

"Girl, turn that up!" one woman shouted. "Who is that?"

The hostess grinned and raised the volume. "This is from the new album *Lyrics and Lust* by the erotic poet Kareem. He's from Oakland. This song is called *Sweet Tooth*. Just wait until you hear his songs: *"You Deserve to Come First'* and *"What Happens in Vegas."*

The women shrieked. "Girrrrl, this song has me feeling some kind of way!" one shouted.

"What's his name again? I'm downloading this album now!"

"Kareem," the hostess announced.

Leah froze. *Kareem? It can't be Kareem Simmons from church.*

With no male strippers present, the party was boring, and Leah decided to leave early. She poured a glass of expensive Cabernet at home and opened Apple Music on her phone. She searched for *Sweet Tooth*. When the artist's photo popped up, her wine glass slipped from her hand, shattering on the floor. She knew that face.

Kareem…Kareem Simmons…is that you?

Leah googled his name, and numerous results came up. She clicked on the main link to his music website and could not believe her eyes - it was Kareem Simmons from church! He'd grown up so much since Leah last saw him. He was a scrawny teenager then, but now he had matured into a muscular, handsome man. *Damn, he's fine,* she thought to herself.

She saw his album release party for *Lyrics and Lust,* which was scheduled to take place at Yoshi's in Oakland. Without hesitation, she went to the website and purchased a VIP ticket. Leah couldn't take her eyes off the screen. I've finally found you after all these years!

Excitement bubbled inside her. She'd never forgotten her childhood crush. *Was he single? Married? Did he have any children?* Leah didn't care. She smirked.

Kareem will be mine; she smiled. Whatever Leah Banks wanted; she got!

8

A Poem for Maya

Kareem stood on his balcony, admiring the Oakland skyline from his high-rise condo. His strong arms gripped the railing as he reflected on his success. At twenty-eight, he'd come a long way from growing up in poverty in East Oakland.

His real estate career was booming. His keen intelligence and charisma helped propel him to become one of the top-selling realtors in the state of California. Specializing in luxury properties, he worked with sports stars and billionaire executives. He also owned multiple homes throughout the Bay Area.

Kareem stepped back inside his stylish condo, where the high ceilings and wooden floors added elegance. African art adorned the walls, and the living room featured expensive decor. On the end table sat a framed photo of his late grandmother, Carol Simmons. It was one of the few possessions he had left of her. He gazed at it and whispered, *I miss you, Granny.*

Kareem's thoughts drifted to Maya. They'd been dating for two months. He was happy she agreed to be his date for his album release and performance at Yoshi's Jazz Club that evening. Although he knew she wasn't a fan of his erotic poetry, the venue he selected for his live poetry performance release party was classy and sophisticated.

That evening, Kareem arrived at Maya's house with a bouquet of white roses. When she opened the door, he was captivated by her beauty. Her ivory dress complemented her melanin-rich complexion, highlighting her curves.

"You look gorgeous," he said, handing her the flowers. Maya thanked him for the flowers and placed them in a vase before they headed to Yoshi's.

***

A line had already formed outside Yoshi's an hour before showtime. Inside, local celebrities mingled. Maya ordered shrimp tempura, sushi rolls, and drinks for herself and Tasha as they made their way to their front-row seats.

Backstage, Kareem stood with Keith and some of the Bay Area's best musicians. "Man, this place is packed," Kareem said, peeking into the crowd. Keith smirked. "You've come a long way since performing in college."

Keith stepped onto the stage, taking his place at the keyboard. Tasha and Maya, having just finished their sushi, watched as he blew a kiss toward Tasha. The band began to play, setting the mood. Soon, the host took the stage.

"Ladies and gentlemen, welcome to an evening of live music featuring the lyrical poet all the ladies can't stop talking about! His erotic poetry has gone viral, and he's here in Oakland to celebrate the release of his new album, *Lyrics and Lust*. Give it up for Kareem!"

The band played the mellow intro to *Sweet Tooth* as Kareem walked onto the stage. The audience erupted in cheers. "Ladies, I have a sweet tooth," he announced. "Is there a lady out there who can satisfy my craving?"

A group of women screamed out *yes*, and Kareem began performing his poem, *Sweet Tooth*:

Sweet lady
I have a sudden craving for something sweet
I have a taste for a mocha treat

The only thing that can satisfy
My sweet tooth
is your tapioca pudding that I love to eat
Your body is my candy shop
I can't wait to suck on those two tasty gumdrops
you have on top

The crowd went wild. "I can satisfy your sweet tooth!" a woman with short blonde hair called out. "I taste like French vanilla, baby.

Kareem continued with his steamy lineup, performing *Go Deep, You Deserve to Come First,* and *Dim the Lights.* Kareem was a natural performer, and his lyrics flowed effortlessly from his lips. For his finale, he told the crowd he wanted to perform a love poem for someone special. The lights were dimmed, and the deep bass of his love poem *Intimate* reverberated throughout the room. He fixed his gaze on Maya, staring directly into her eyes while he recited the poem:

Intimacy
It means making love mentally
I want to be intimate with you
Just us two
Our intimate moment is not
to be confused with casual sex
Intimacy is cuddling,
caressing
emotionally undressing
allowing our souls to connect

Maya felt a wave of emotions as he serenaded her with his heartfelt words. She smiled as the audience erupted in applause. As the show ended, dozens of women rushed to the VIP section, eager for Kareem's attention. After greeting a few admirers, he made his way to Maya.

"Can I get you something to drink, love?" Kareem asked Maya. Maya smirked. "No thanks, Kareem. I'm not as thirsty as some women."

"There's only one woman I want," Kareem said with a wink, making her blush.

From across the room, Leah Banks watched closely. Dressed in a sleek black Prada dress with matching pumps, she exuded confidence. Once the crowd around Kareem thinned, she made her move.

"That was an amazing performance, Kareem," she said smoothly. "Your grandmother would be proud."

Kareem turned to the beautiful, brown-skinned woman with hazel eyes and big breasts standing behind him.

"Do I know you from somewhere?" he asked, his gaze dropping straight to the cleavage spilling out of her dress.

Leah smirked. "You sure do. We go way back."

Kareem stared at the beautiful woman for a moment. *She had to be a member of the Holy Tabernacle. But who?* Her face looked familiar, but he didn't recall a buxom, brown-skinned beauty with hazel eyes attending the church.

"I'm Leah…Leah Banks! We used to attend *Holy Tabernacle* when you were younger! You don't recognize me?"

"Leah!" Kareem shouted, startling everyone around him. He lifted her off the floor with a big hug. "Wow! You're all grown up now," he exclaimed after feeling her triple-D breast rub against his chest. "You look amazing!"

Leah was no longer the petite girl from church. She stood at five feet or ten inches tall and was top-heavy. Kareem remembered how she had a crush on him when they attended church together as children.

"Maya, this is Leah Banks, Kareem said, introducing the two women. "We used to attend church together when we were children." Leah stared enviously at Maya's natural beauty and bottom-heavy figure. *So that's what he likes. He's an ass, man.* Leah made a mental note to consult her plastic surgeon about getting a Brazilian butt lift.

"We've met," Maya said while extending her hand to Leah. "Leah manages the social media account for Holy Tabernacle." Leah reluctantly shook Maya's hand and followed with a fake smile, then turned her adoring eyes to Kareem.

"Anyway," Leah huffed, "Your performance was great, Kareem. I love your new album. Let's get reacquainted!" She handed him a business card with her number on it.

"Call me Kareem. We have a lot of catching up to do. I also have something to give you." Leah winked before rolling her eyes at Maya and strutting away.

Maya, irritated by all the attention Kareem was getting, offered to take an Uber home. But Kareem stopped her. "You came with me, and you'll leave with me."

As they walked to his car, Maya sighed. "I wonder why Leah had an attitude with me."

"What woman wouldn't be envious of you?" he asked, turning towards her and holding her hand. "Look at you! You wore no makeup and only minimal jewelry, yet you were still the most beautiful woman in the building."

Kareem's compliment made Maya blush. "Then again, what woman can't help but be jealous when standing next to *Kareem*, the poet!" Maya blurted out sarcastically, causing Kareem to chuckle.

"I don't love the limelight or the women," Kareem admitted. "Oh, you love it," Maya joked. "I Go Deep," she said, imitating Kareem's deep voice.

"What I love most is spending time with you," Kareem said, staring into her eyes, "and I'm happy you came tonight."

"Are you free Thursday afternoon?" Maya inquired. "I'm always free for you," he replied with a smile. "That's Good! I want to cook dinner for you."

Kareem's eyes widened. "Finally! After two months of dating, you're coming to my place?" Kareem was surprised because, during the two months they dated, she'd declined an invitation to his place several times to avoid temptation.

"When was the last time you had a home-cooked meal?" Maya asked. "It's been years," he admitted. "The last time a woman cooked for me, she tried to make beans and rice with cornbread."

"What happened?" Maya asked. "The food didn't taste good?"

"The beans were dissolved, the rice was burnt, and the cornbread was so hard that it nearly chipped my tooth."

Maya laughed and leaned in to play with Kareem's beard. "I'm going to cook you some Creole Jambalaya, and I'll make sure that my cornbread is fluffy and moist."

Kareem smiled and hugged Maya. *Finally! She's coming to my place!*

9

Predator on the Pulpit

Leah Banks flashed a fake smile at the church receptionist. "Good morning, Ms. Banks," the receptionist said. She pressed the intercom. "Bishop Banks, your daughter is here."

"Send her in," he replied.

"Good morning, Leah!" Bishop Banks hugged his daughter. "What brings you here today?" He already knew. Leah only came when she needed money.

"Daddy, guess who I saw last night?" Leah's voice bubbled with excitement.

"Who?" he asked, eyebrows raised. "Kareem Simmons! He's a famous poet now! His show at Yoshi's was packed with celebrities!"

"Invite him to our service," the bishop said. *More visitors meant more money,* he thought.

Bishop Banks glanced at his Rolex watch and reached into the top drawer of his credenza and pulled out a pill bottle labeled *Cialis.* These pills were his secret weapon.

"I'm glad you're taking your medicine," Leah said, watching him swallow a pill.

"This heart medication works wonders," he lied. "Do you need any money?" he asked, trying to get rid of Leah before his appointment arrived.

"I need $15,000. I want to go on vacation to Miami." The real reason Leah wanted the money was for a BBL. Bishop Banks wrote her a check for $20,000 and instructed her not to spend it all at once. Leah kissed his cheek and left.

Outside, Leah noticed a strikingly pretty teenage girl in the waiting area. The girl wore a faded coat, leggings, and worn shoes. She had a curvy shape. *She's pretty but poor,* Leah thought to herself as she sneered in the girl's direction before leaving.

"Hello. My name is Alexis Taylor," the teenage girl told the receptionist. The receptionist informed the bishop that Alexis Taylor, a new church member, had arrived for her appointment. "Send her in," he said, rubbing his hands together in anticipation. He had taken a Cialis pill earlier and was waiting for her to arrive.

Alexis Taylor was five feet four inches tall with smooth, light skin, full lips, and a curvy physique. She was also a high school dropout and unemployed single mother at sixteen. A survivor of domestic violence, her ex-boyfriend was serving a ten-year sentence for attempted murder. She joined Holy Tabernacle Church when she heard about their *Open Arms* program, which assisted single mothers and abused women.

After last Sunday's sermon, Alexis caught Bishop Banks's attention. He inquired about her and learned from the church's *Open Arms* program director that she was a sixteen-year-old single mother seeking financial, emotional, and spiritual support. He invited her to a *meeting.*

"Hello, Alexis. Sit down," he said, taking her coat. His eyes lingered on her curves.

Alexis gazed around his lavish office, which had photos of celebrities on the walls. His desk gleamed, and the carpet felt plush under her feet.

"Want a drink? Coffee? Water?"

"No, thank you," she said, tapping her foot nervously.

"Hearing about the trial and tribulations you've endured touched me," Bishop Banks said, trying to sound concerned as he sat at his desk. "I know that you've been facing financial hardships. If you don't mind me asking, where are your parents?"

She let out a heavy sigh as she spoke, "I never knew my father." Alexis lowered her head. "My mom is on drugs, and my baby daddy is in prison."

The bishop sneered as he thought. *She's an easy target!* he said to himself. *She's poor and desperate.* His smirk grew as he made his offer: "I have a job opening that pays $2,000 per week." All cash, under the table."

Alexis's eyes widened, and a single tear ran down her cheek as she heard the offer. She'd never made that kind of money. "But there is a cost," he said, lowering his voice and leaning closer. "The job needs to be done under the table. If word got out, it could jeopardize the church's financial standing. I need to ensure you can keep this a secret. Can I trust you?"

"You can trust me, Bishop Banks," Alexis whispered. "I put that on my son!" *The bishop is doing me a huge favor by allowing me to work under the table.*

"Good!" the bishop said, clapping his hands. "I want to hire you to clean my private condo in Walnut Creek twice a week," he said while leaning back in his leather recliner. "My former maid moved to Philadelphia, and I need someone reliable and trustworthy. Do you have any experience in housecleaning?"

"I'm a very clean person, and I know how to clean a house. It will be spotless," she assured. "I need a job. My baby needs formula, and my mom is behind on her rent."

"Let's go now," he said. "You can start today. I'll pay you upfront."

Alexis cried. "Thank you! You're a blessing!" Alexis got up to hug him, and the bishop felt the bulge in his pants growing.

He instructed his receptionist to forward all his calls to voicemail until he returned in a few hours. Then, he escorted Alexis through the back exit of the church to where his Bentley was parked. Alexis's eyes lit up in admiration of the Aegean Blue Bentley Continental GT coupe.

Alexis sank into the soft, sumptuous leather seats of Bishop Banks Bentley. They were much more comfortable than the hard and dirty seats on the bus she took every day to job interviews. She thought of her son, Odell. With this money, she'd buy him clothes and pay her neighbor, Janelle, to watch him.

Alexis gasped as she entered Bishop Banks' condominium, taking in the luxurious furnishings: a big-screen TV, a plush leather couch, and modern furniture. The condo featured marble countertops, stainless steel appliances, and expensive artwork on display. It was a palace compared to the cramped two-bedroom apartment she shared with her mother and son.

"Make yourself comfortable," Bishop Banks insisted. She sat on the luxury sofa while he went into the bedroom. He used his secret combination and opened the safe, removing a thousand dollars in cash.

Wearing a black silk robe several sizes too small, he emerged from his bedroom holding the money. *Why is he wearing a robe?* Alexis wondered.

He handed Alexis $1,000 and promised the rest after she finished the job. "Which area do you want me to clean first?" she asked, grateful for the opportunity. He led her to the primary bedroom, reached into the closet, and handed her an ivory-colored sheer lingerie set. Alexis looked at the lingerie set and lowered her head. She realized what was expected of her.

Alexis entered the bathroom, her heart heavy with the weight of what she was about to do. She changed into skimpy lingerie and entered the bedroom wearing the revealing outfit. Bishop Banks spread his robe wide, a smug grin on his face. "Get on your knees!" he barked. It's time to clean!"

Alexis sighed and kneeled on the floor. *I'm only doing this to keep the lights on and put food on the table for my son,* she reminded herself. She closed her eyes and choked back a sob. Bishop Banks was so lost in his own pleasure that he never noticed the silent tears that traced a path down her cheek.

10

Seeking Satisfaction

Atlanta, Georgia

Lisa Phillips plopped on her bed and opened the music app on her phone. She'd been anticipating the release of Kareem's spoken word album, *Lyrics and Lust,* and now it was finally available. She downloaded the album to her phone. She closed her eyes and listened to Kareem's deep and seductive voice over each track.

At forty-three, Lisa was ready to explore her deepest desires. She had an erotic fantasy that she wanted to come true. She was in her prime, confident, unapologetically sensual, and ready to experience true pleasure.

A week ago, she attended a pleasure party and heard Kareem's provocative poem, *Dim the Lights.* The lyrics in the song instantly aroused her. Listening to his erotic lyrics also allowed her to let go of all her inhibitions and fantasize about freaky things she'd never done before.

Lisa used her maiden name, *Phillips,* for her music account. She was divorcing her husband. Sadly, Lisa couldn't remember a time during her marriage when her husband put her sexual needs and desires before his own. As she stared at the screen, her mind wandered back to a decade ago when she met him at an active shooter response course.

He was a trainer; she was a cop. His charm, fit body, and smarts hooked her. They married quickly. But his constant travel chipped away at their bond. Over time, he grew distant.

Lisa often wondered why she married her husband in the first place. He wasn't romantic or affectionate. After tough days solving crimes, he never comforted her. Sex became a chore. Lisa was tired of being miserable and married, horny and unhappy.

Lisa closed her eyes and listened to Kareem's sensuous lyrics as she lay alone in her bed. His voice lulled her into a deep state of arousal. She imagined his hands caressing her curves, exploring every inch of her body, and taking her to heights of pleasure she'd never experienced.

The thought of him making love to her made her dripping wet with desire. *I need him*, she said to herself. She googled his name. Scrolling through the results, she discovered that he was a successful real estate agent in the San Francisco Bay Area. She clicked through his social media profile and admired his pictures, captivated by his extremely good looks.

After scrolling through his social media profiles, Lisa was surprised to see that he would be the featured poet at an upcoming Erotic event in Atlanta. *If you want something you've never had, you must be willing to do something you've never done*, she thought.

She knew that the best way to reach Kareem was through social media. She downloaded the Instagram app and decided to slide into his DMs. She noticed his profile had thousands of followers and decided to do something risqué to get his attention.

A month earlier, she had done a boudoir shoot - lace, corsets, sultry poses. The images were sexy and provocative, showcasing her curves. Lisa created a private Instagram profile and uploaded a dozen seductive boudoir photos and videos that would hopefully catch Kareem's attention.

Since her profile was private, only Kareem could see her pictures. She also sent Kareem a direct message, hoping he would notice. She wanted to meet the poet whose words had unlocked her erotic fantasies.

11

Celibacy Blues

Kareem took the elevator down to his lobby to meet Maya, who was coming over to cook dinner at his condo. Stepping outside, he spotted a sleek black Bentley approaching the condominium complex. He immediately knew who it was.

He walked over to the Bentley and out stepped a towering six-foot-four man with dreadlocks spilling over broad, muscled shoulders.

"What up, Tshaka!" Kareem yelled while embracing his friend in a brotherly hug.

"I just got back from Nigeria," Tshaka grinned. "It's good to be back home."

Despite being only thirty years old, Tshaka Akindele, the former world heavyweight champion, was regarded as a living legend. During his boxing career, Tshaka earned millions and retired undefeated. After he hung up his gloves, he became an activist and self-proclaimed freedom fighter, following in the footsteps of the great boxer Muhammad Ali. Kareem had become close friends with Tshaka after selling him a penthouse condo in their building.

Tshaka introduced Kareem to his girlfriend, Nina Wilson. Kareem stepped forward and greeted the beautiful, dark-skinned woman who exited the car. Nina smiled, revealing perfect, white teeth that contrasted against her flawless, brown skin.

Nina's luscious hair was braided into Bantu knots. She confidently strutted in form-fitting blue jeans, her feet adorned with stylish sandals. Her crisp white shirt proudly displayed the word *Genkinect,* printed in black, green, and red.

"Nina is the CEO of *Genkinect*, a DNA service that helps people of African descent trace our roots," Tshaka said as he leaned down and kissed her. "We've been spending the past month in West Africa collecting samples for the project," Nina added enthusiastically.

"Knowing our origins is important, especially since our ancestors were stolen from Africa and weren't allowed to carry on their languages or cultural traditions," Kareem said.

"Exactly," Nina agreed. "We must rediscover, reclaim, and reconnect with our ancestral roots!"

Out of the corner of his eye, Kareem spotted Maya walking towards them, carrying a bag of groceries. Kareem turned to Tshaka and said he wanted to introduce them to his girlfriend. Tshaka's eyes widened in surprise. "You have a girlfriend now?" he asked.

"You look gorgeous," Kareem said, leaning in to kiss Maya on the cheek before grabbing the bag of groceries. "Thank you, handsome," she replied, kissing him back. "Follow me. I want to introduce you to someone.

"Maya, this is Tshaka and his girlfriend, Nina." The two women hugged, and Maya shook Tshaka's hand.

"Tshaka! My father is a huge fan of yours," she said, eyes wide with surprise.

"I'm a big fan of your father," Tshaka replied. "Keith has told me great things about your church."

"Keith told me he knew you, but I didn't believe him," Maya said, glancing at Kareem. "And I had no idea you two were friends!"

"We've been friends for years," Tshaka said. "Kareem sold me my penthouse in this building." As the valet parked Tshaka's Bentley, they all headed inside.

"Let's meet up this weekend!" Kareem suggested. "Keith and I are renovating a house on Saturday. I'll text you the address. We can hang out by the fire pit in the backyard."

"We'd love to join you," Nina said. That way, Maya and I can spend time together." The women exchanged smiles as they entered the lobby.

Inside the elevator, Kareem noticed the book in Tshaka's hand.

"What are you reading?"

"*Of Water and the Spirit* by Malidoma Somé," Tshaka replied. "It's about African spirituality and how European colonizers tried to erase it." "Let's talk about it when you're done," Kareem suggested.

The elevator stopped at the top floor. The men bumped fists before heading to their penthouse suites.

Maya gasped as she stepped into Kareem's spacious condo. Sunlight poured in through skylights, highlighting the open space.

"Wow, Kareem," she said. "Poetry must pay well!"

Kareem laughed. "Poetry is my passion, but real estate is my profession. Poetry made me popular, but real estate made me wealthy."

"I like your place here," Maya said.

"Thanks! I bought it a few years ago," he said, placing a bag of groceries on his quartz countertop. "It has three bedrooms, hardwood floors, a fireplace for ambiance, skylights, and a brand-new kitchen with stainless steel appliances, "Kareem boasted.

"It's no wonder you're so successful in real estate, Kareem," Maya chuckled. "You sound like a realtor right now."

"Have I told you how beautiful your smile is?" Kareem asked, admiring Maya's dimples. "Yes," Maya's smile widened. "You tell me that often, Mr. Simmons."

Maya reached for the grocery bags, pulling out Andouille sausage, chicken breast, prawns, tomatoes, bell peppers, celery, and onions—everything she needed for jambalaya.

"Want something to drink?" Kareem asked.

"No, thanks," Maya said. "But show me where you keep the bowls and utensils."

Kareem handed her spoons and knives and pointed to the cabinet. As Maya opened a can of tomatoes, he grabbed a bottle of alkaline water from the fridge and took a long drink. He took several long swallows while watching Maya's hands chop up the celery, bell peppers, onions, and cayenne peppers.

"You look like you know what you're doing," he observed as Maya sautéed the vegetables. He eyed her lustfully, watching her ample hips sway while she cooked in the kitchen. Kareem came behind her, wrapping his arms around her waist. His bulging erection felt like a steel pole in his pants.

"Excuse me, love," she said, slipping out of his embrace to grab the Creole seasoning. She felt heat spreading like wildfire up her neck. And it wasn't just the jambalaya that was sizzling. Desire simmered beneath her skin, daring her to give to temptation.

"A beautiful lady with curves who can cook," Kareem complimented. "I could get used to this," he added.

Once the jambalaya was finished cooking, Maya served him a bowl with cornbread and sat beside him on the sofa. She blessed her food and watched as he took his first bite. "This is amazing," Kareem said, digging in.

"Are you excited about performing in Atlanta next weekend?" she asked.

"I am," Kareem said. "But I'd rather spend time with you—especially if you keep spoiling me with meals like this."

After dinner, Kareem put on a movie. When the credits rolled, they hugged and then started kissing. Kareem's lips moved gently over hers, teasing her bottom lip before deepening the kiss. His tongue explored her mouth, and after a few moments, his hands moved to her chest, massaging her hardened nipples.

This is happening too fast, Maya thought.

Kareem pulled off his shirt, revealing his tattoos and chiseled chest.

"Let's go to my room," he whispered, his eyes filled with desire. Maya's body responded, but her mind held her back. She placed her hands on his chest and pushed gently.

"Kareem, please… let's stop," she said softly.

He frowned. "What's wrong?"

"I don't want us to rush into sex. It's too soon. I want it to be right between us."

"Too soon?" Kareem said, exasperated. "We've been dating for months!"

"I know, but I want to…" Maya hesitated. "I want us to be married first."

Kareem sank onto the couch, rubbing his face with his hands. "Not this celibacy thing again," he muttered. "You're not even a virgin. You lost it in college, and now you expect me to wait?"

"I made a mistake back then - with a man who didn't love me. I won't make that mistake again." Her eyes locked onto his. "I told you from the beginning—I'm saved and celibate. Fornication is a sin, Kareem."

Tears welled up in her eyes. Kareem watched as her face shifted from shock to sadness, then to quiet tears. Guilt hit him. He reached out, gently wiping the tears from her cheeks. Then, he tenderly kissed them away.

"I apologize," Kareem said, his voice heavy with regret. "It's just that I want you. I've never felt this way about a woman."

Maya pulled away from his embrace. "I want you too, Kareem! But the thing I want most is for God to bless our union. Having sex is easy, but breaking a soul tie is hard."

"I guess this means I can't get a quickie, huh?" Kareem asked jokingly. Maya playfully punched him on the shoulder and cracked a smile even though she was still hurt that he'd brought up her past. "I like you, Kareem, and I want our relationship to work. Will you please be patient with me? Please?"

Kareem reached for her hand. "Come dance with me." He played a slow jam playlist on his smart speaker that he'd made just for her. Maya smiled as he pulled her close, wrapping his strong arms around her waist. She rested her head against his chest as they swayed to the music of Anita Baker, Kem, and Sade.

When Kareem tried to serenade her by singing a Raheem DeVaughn song, Maya shook her head. "Baby, please stick to poetry," she giggled.

She glanced at her watch. It was nearly midnight.

"It's late. I should go," she said reluctantly, pulling away from his embrace.

"Before I leave, let's pray together," she added, kneeling and reaching for his hand.

Kareem smirked. Usually, when women kneeled at his place, it wasn't to pray. Still, he sighed and joined her, lacing his fingers with hers. Maya prayed for strength, patience, and the ability to resist temptation. Kareem finished with a quiet *Amen*.

"I enjoyed tonight," Maya said, standing on her toes to kiss him. She grabbed her purse, and Kareem walked her to her car. As she started the engine, she rolled down the window.

"Thanks for dinner," Kareem said. "I know you're serious about this… and I'll be patient." His voice was softer now, more sincere.

Maya smiled before driving off. But as she gripped the steering wheel, all she could think about was how good Kareem felt. His warmth lingered on her skin, making her body ache with longing.

She turned up the car stereo. Jill Scott's *Celibacy Blues* played through the speakers.

"Jill, I feel you, girl," Maya sighed.

12

Southern Hospitality

After Maya left, Kareem returned to the lobby and pulled out his phone. He opened Instagram and checked his notifications. The video of him performing at Yoshi's had gone viral, racking up thousands of likes. As he scrolled through his feed, his phone buzzed with a new direct message.

While dating Maya, he usually ignored DMs from other women. But after months of no sex, he was feeling frustrated.

He opened the DM, and the profile picture caught his eye—a curvy, seductive woman posing confidently. *A thirst trap,* he thought, smirking. She'd posted the photo, hoping to get his attention, and it worked. He was intrigued.

Her message was short and direct: I'd like to share some private photos with my favorite poet. Check out my page.

Kareem sent a follow request, which was accepted immediately. As he browsed her photos, his interest grew. Each image showcased her thick body. Her breasts were barely contained in a lacy black bra, her hips spilling out from a cinched-waist leotard, and her thick thighs wrapped in lace.

There is nothing sexier than a curvy woman, Kareem thought to himself. Kareem replied to the DM, saying he'd like to get to know her.

Lisa smiled as she read his response to her direct message. A true Southern belle, Lisa promised to show him some genuine Southern hospitality during his stay in Atlanta. They exchanged numbers and agreed to text in the morning.

***

Just as Kareem drifted off to sleep that morning, his phone buzzed again.

2 a.m.? Must be Maya, he thought.

But when he looked at the screen, his eyes widened. The message wasn't from Maya—it was from Leah Banks.

Kareem frowned. *How did she get my number?* He was careful about keeping it private, only giving out his business number.

He opened the message. Leah's text was straight to the point. She wanted sex.

Kareem hesitated, his fingers hovering over the keyboard. Then, after a moment, he typed a response, inviting her over that evening.

Lying back in bed, Kareem stared at the ceiling. His thoughts drifted to Maya. He loved Maya. She was smart and loyal and possessed a natural beauty that didn't require make-up or filters. *But celibacy?* It was killing him.

Maya said she wanted to wait until marriage, and Kareem initially respected this. But weeks turned into months, and now he needed a release. Temptation was everywhere, and celibacy wasn't for him.

The spirit is willing, but the flesh needs fulfillment, he thought.

13

A Fling

Hair   done? Check! *Nails   freshly   manicured?* Check! *Giambattista Valli Dress with white Fendi leather tote bag?* Check!

Leah was feeling herself. Nobody could convince her that she wasn't looking sexy. She wore a pink silk-crepe dress with a plunging neckline and a tie that accentuated her cleavage. She jumped into her Lexus convertible and headed to Kareem's condo.

Kareem informed security to allow Leah onto his floor when she got there. After signing in at the front desk, she took the elevator to Kareem's penthouse. When he opened the door, he immediately noticed her ample cleavage spilling out of her dress.

"I love your place," Leah said as she stepped inside, her eyes drawn to the large skylights. Kareem gestured for her to sit and make herself comfortable while he microwaved popcorn for their Netflix and chill night.

"Oh…before I forget…I have something for you, but don't open it until after I leave." Leah reached into her bag, pulled out a box wrapped in shiny gold paper, and put it on his end table. Kareem was too busy with the popcorn to notice the gift.

"I want to let you know how proud I am of you, Kareem. I remember how you used to recite poetry at *Holy Tabernacle* when we were younger. My father always said you would grow up to become someone special." Kareem's jaw clenched at the mention of *Holy Tabernacle*. He still harbored resentment towards Bishop Banks and mentioned that church reminded him of her father's hypocrisy.

After microwaving a bowl of popcorn and opening a carton of Red Vines, Kareem plopped down on his sofa next to Leah to watch a movie on his big-screen television. He offered Leah a stick of licorice, and she took it in her mouth, imitating giving him fellatio. *Wow, she is truly a freak.*

A few minutes after the movie started, she pulled a Fruit Roll from her purse. "What's up with the Fruit Roll-up?" he asked. "You're about to find out," she replied, her voice seductive.

Leah placed her manicured fingers on the imprint of his slacks, using her fingertips to trace the outline of his manhood. She unbuckled his belt, unzipped his pants, and pulled out his well-endowed manhood.

Kneeling on her knees, she wrapped the Fruit Roll-up around the tip of his manhood and began sucking, using both hands to stroke him up and down. "This is my two-hand twist technique," she said between slurps.

She's a true blowfessional, he thought to himself. The veins in his manhood were bulging as he moaned in pleasure. Leah's slurping sounded like someone drinking the last drops of a Mocha Frappuccino from a Starbucks cup with a straw.

Kareem began gyrating his hips, and Leah eagerly increased her speed to match it. Minutes later, a wave of warm protein pulsed out of his groin and into her mouth. The sound of his screams of pleasure was music to her ears, and she continued to taste him until she milked every drop.

Kareem led Leah to his bedroom, where she began to undress. She unclipped the latch on her bra, exposing her large breasts. Kareem was immediately disappointed to discover that her breasts were not real. Both nipples were pointed in opposite directions, and he could see the surgery scars.

He reached into his drawer and pulled out a Magnum XL condom. "Why are you wearing a condom?" Leah whined. *I'm definitely wearing one now,* Kareem thought while putting the condom on.

"Wrap your arms around my neck," Kareem commanded.

He's so aggressive! I like that, Leah said to herself while wrapping her arms around the back of his neck. Kareem lifted Leah by her thighs and wrapped her legs around his waist. Leah was easy to lift since Kareem could easily bench press hundreds of pounds. While standing, he began to move with strong, steady motions.

"Oh shit," Leah screamed in pleasure, having never been with a man strong enough to pick her up and pound it in that position. His strength made Leah feel a rush of excitement.

"Kareeeeeem," she moaned, feeling the intensity of his deep thrusts, bringing her closer to a climax. After a few minutes, her body jerked uncontrollably, and a steady stream of fluid flowed between her thighs as she climaxed on the carpet.

Damn, I'm going to need to have my carpet cleaned! Kareem said to himself as he felt the flow of her juices ooze out and splash all over his manhood. He laid Leah on the bed and collapsed alongside her. Her body was still trembling after experiencing multiple orgasms for the first time.

"I love you, Kareem! I always have! I'm so glad I found you again!" she screamed, still gasping for breath as she lay on his bed.

Damn, she's mistaking multiple orgasms for love. Kareem already regretted having sex with her. They just had sex on the first date, and now she was talking about she loved him. As far as he was concerned, it was just a one-night stand, and he hoped she would realize that.

Kareem rolled over to avoid looking at her. She started rubbing his shoulders and back. "Do you mind if I stay the night?" she asked. The thought of being with him again made her want him more. Kareem felt annoyed by her question.

"Sorry, Leah, but I need to shower, wash my sheets, and pack for my trip to Atlanta," he said.

"I can help you pack," she pleaded. "Please, Kareem?" He glanced at her sideways. "Maybe next time," he lied. Kareem was frustrated and wanted her to leave. "Get dressed so I can walk you to your car."

Ahhhh, so romantic, she thought. *He's walking me to my car.*

Kareem walked Leah to her car, and when she tried to kiss him, he pulled away, saying that he needed to brush his teeth.

"Don't forget to open your gift," she reminded him as she drove away in her Lexus. "I won't," he lied. "Text me to let me know you made it home safe." *Ahhhh, he cares about me. Leah* smiled to herself. *He's going to make the perfect husband!*

Kareem's phone rang. It was Maya. "Hey love, how was your day?" he asked. "I didn't hear from you," she pouted. He could hear the disappointment in her voice and quickly lied. "I apologize. I was busy finalizing a real estate deal."

14

A House is not a Home

Kareem parked the U-Haul truck in front of the house he was renovating. The single-family home was at the end of a cul-de-sac on a quiet street in Oakland. When he purchased the property, the kitchen looked outdated, with Formica floors, white laminated countertops, and brown cabinets. Kareem hired a contractor to redo the kitchen and bedrooms himself. He installed stainless-steel appliances, replaced the old cabinets, and painted the house in colors that Maya had chosen.

The house looked brand new. It had fresh paint outside and a nicely landscaped front yard. After weeks of work, he was ready to sell it for a profit once he put the new quartz countertop in the kitchen.

"Uh, oh, we have a problem," Keith shouted after releasing the latch and opening the back door of the U-Haul truck. Kareem walked to the back and saw Keith, visibly upset. "We forgot the moving straps at the countertop store." Keith groaned in disbelief. "How are we going to lift this heavy countertop and move it into the house?"

"We can carry it in," Kareem replied confidently. "After all, aren't you the one who always says that with Christ, you can do all things?" he smirked.

Keith stretched out his long fingers and shook his head. "These hands were made for making music, not manual labor," he protested. "Do you want to risk damaging an eight-thousand-dollar countertop trying to carry it inside? We might as well drive back to Stockton and get the straps."

Kareem sighed. He was in a bind. He attempted to save thousands of dollars by installing the countertop himself rather than hiring a professional company. But Keith was right. The granite was heavy, and they didn't have moving straps to remove the countertop from the delivery truck.

"This thing must weigh at least eight hundred pounds," Keith groaned, his back sore from trying to lift the countertop. Then, Keith heard an Afrobeat song blasting from a black Bentley. He noticed Tshaka's car pulling into the driveway.

"Tshaka!" Keith shouted. "Give us a hand, man." Tshaka saw his friends struggling with the heavy countertop and hopped onto the truck to help.

"With all the weightlifting we do at the gym, you two can't lift a countertop?" Tshaka laughed, patting Keith and Kareem on the back. Tshaka easily lifted the countertop, hoisting it up in one go and carrying it into the house, leaving Keith and Kareem stunned.

"Did you just see him pick up the entire countertop and carry it into the house all by himself?" Keith asked Kareem in disbelief. "Tshaka's not human."

"How did you do that?" Kareem asked Tshaka once they were in the kitchen. "It's all those West African yams I've been eating," Tshaka joked.

In the kitchen, Kareem prepared to install the countertop. "Kareem, you're rich! Why not just hire people to fix up the house?" Keith asked.

"First, I'm not rich," Kareem said with a smile. "Tshaka is rich!" he said, pointing to Tshaka. "And second, paying someone to do what we can do ourselves takes away all the fun and profit from flipping a house." Kareem put on the construction adhesive, and all three men lifted the countertop and set it in place.

"Finished!" Kareem shouted. "We're done!" They all gave each other a high-five to celebrate.

From the kitchen, Kareem heard Maya explaining to Tasha and Nina why she chose neutral colors for the living room instead of plain white.

"You did a great job decorating this house, Maya," Tasha said while looking around. "Amazing job," Nina agreed. "I love the colors you picked. They're perfect," she praised.

"Thank you," Maya replied. "The living room gets a lot of natural light, so I chose cool neutrals like brown, cinnamon stick, tan, and grey."

Kareem paid Maya $ 20,000 to decorate the interior of the house. She picked out the color scheme and purchased a tan sectional sofa and loveseat for the living room, with brown throw pillows, and placed them near the fireplace as the focal point.

Kareem entered the living room and saw Maya in a Howard University sweater. He pulled her into a tight embrace. "I couldn't have asked for a better interior designer," he said before kissing her. Maya blushed, flattered by Kareem's compliment.

"Y'all did a good job flipping this house," Tasha said while admiring the fireplace. "Hopefully, the couple who buys it will turn it into a happy home."

"I hope so, too," Kareem said as he turned on his wireless speaker so everyone could relax and listen to music. "After a month of renovating, it feels good to be finished."

Nina took off her sandals, rested her head on Tshaka's chest, and listened to his heartbeat. "A lot of people don't know the difference between a house and a home," Nina said as she snuggled next to Tshaka on the sofa, running her fingers through his locs.

"You're right," Tshaka agreed in his deep voice. "A house is a physical structure made from wood, steel, concrete, and stone. It shields you from the elements and provides comfort. But a beautiful, lasting, and durable home is constructed on a strong spiritual and emotional foundation."

"Beautifully said, my love," Nina replied, kissing Tshaka's cheek.

Keith stood up and cleared his throat. "Luther Vandross said it best in his song, *A House is Not a Home,*" he said, then started to sing the song.

"Keith, don't sing!" Tshaka pleaded. "Please stick to producing because your singing is trash!" Everyone laughed.

"Tshaka, I never thought you were so down to earth," Maya said. "I remember watching your fights in college; your demeanor is so different outside the ring. You're funny and humble. Nothing like the menace that the media portrayed you to be inside the boxing ring."

"Thank you," Tshaka replied. "In the boxing ring, I was ruthless and relentless. I pummeled my opponents. However, now that I'm retired, I want to use my gifts to fight for our people."

Nina rubbed Tshaka's shoulders. "That's why I love him," she said. "He could have made millions more had he continued to fight inside the ring and *defeat* people. But he chose to step outside the ring and fight for millions of Black people who feel *defeated*."

Tshaka wrapped his muscular arm around Nina and drew her close. "It's such an honor to be in the presence of three beautiful and amazing Black women," Tshaka said.

"Oh Lord, here comes Tshaka preaching his *Black Women Rock* sermon," Keith joked, causing Kareem to spit out his water in laughter. Tshaka grinned. "I'm serious, bruh. We are blessed to have beautiful women committed to empowering our community."

"Ok, Malcolm X," Keith joked before conceding Tshaka's point. "All jokes aside. We're blessed to have such beautiful and intelligent girlfriends. I feel fortunate," Keith said as he began to serenade Tasha by singing the words *Fortunate* by the R&B singer Maxwell. "We aren't fortunate to hear you sing," Tshaka told Keith.

"The way you two go at it is hilarious," Nina giggled. "Ever since they met, they've gone at it," Kareem said, laughing. "You should see them at the gym. They act like siblings in a rivalry."

Keith connected his phone to the Bluetooth speaker and grabbed a paintbrush to use as a microphone. "Brothas, I need both of you to sing backup," he insisted.

"Oh no, not this again—Keith and his off-key karaoke," Tshaka groaned. He stood up and reluctantly joined Kareem. They positioned themselves behind Keith as his background singers. The old-school R&B song, *Before I Let Go,* by Maze, blared through the speaker. Keith began singing while Kareem and Tshaka danced in the background.

The women laughed, and Maya pulled out her phone to record. Halfway through the song, Keith handed Kareem the paintbrush and asked him to bust a freestyle:

Before I let go
I want to let you know
Keith is trying to sing this old-school jam
Tshaka likes to eat African yams
Rapping to this beat wasn't in my plans
Maya, please don't post this on Instagram

Everyone laughed hysterically after hearing Kareem's freestyle. Maya smiled as she posted the video to social media. "Don't put that video online," Kareem protested, aware that it might go viral. "Too late," she giggled. The women continued laughing as the video received hilarious reactions on social media.

Keith grabbed Tasha off the sofa and began singing another classic song by the R&B group New Edition. *Candy girl, you are my world,* he crooned while pulling Tasha close to him. He then tried to mimic New Edition's dance moves. When Keith attempted a spin, he lost his balance and fell to the floor. Laughter erupted. Keith got up, grinning at Tasha. He didn't mind the fall. Seeing her smile was worth it.

"Baby, I love you," Tasha said between giggles. "But Tshaka's right—you can't sing or dance!"

Kareem took a sip from his water bottle and watched his friends laugh. His gaze drifted to Maya. She was still laughing with Nina and Tasha, replaying the video of the men's performance. For the first time since his grandmother's death, Kareem felt like he was part of a family. Kareem's eyes met Maya's, and he felt a twinge of guilt. He'd slept with Leah and would be hooking up with Lisa in Atlanta. *What Maya doesn't know won't hurt her,* Kareem reasoned to himself.

Then, his phone vibrated. Leah's name flashed on the screen. He sent the call to voicemail. A minute later, a message popped up - a photo of Leah naked in bed, thighs spread. Kareem sighed, feeling irritated. Leah's constant texts were getting on his nerves. He deleted the message and tried to refocus his attention on his friends.

Maya popped open a bottle of champagne. "To the future homeowners," Tshaka toasted. "May they live happily in their new home." The glasses clinked.

15

A Ruby Ring

Keith drove Kareem to the airport for his flight to Atlanta. Kareem had planned to take an Uber Black, but Keith insisted on giving him a ride.

"You look hella tired," Keith said as Kareem rubbed his eyes. "Like you already have jet lag and haven't even boarded the plane yet."

Kareem slumped down in the passenger's seat. "I'm exhausted, bruh! Flipping houses and real estate deals make me sleep-deprived," Kareem lied. He'd been up late sexting Lisa, the sexy southern belle he planned to hook up with in Atlanta.

Keith smirked. "Looks like you and Maya are getting serious."

Kareem gazed out the window at a red light, his thoughts drifting to Maya. "I've never met a woman like her." But what he didn't like was Maya's commitment to celibacy. *We've been dating for months and still haven't had sex.*

Keith grinned. "It was me and Tasha's idea to set you two up." Kareem chuckled. "I should've known."

"I was tired of seeing you date different women. You've never been in a serious relationship."

Keith wasn't wrong. Kareem had never committed to one woman before.

"I was too busy chasing money, not women," Kareem boasted. "Like the saying goes, 'You'll lose a lot of money chasing women, but you'll never lose women chasing money.'"

Keith shook his head. "Well, according to the scriptures, man shouldn't be alone. You're getting older, fam. You're successful. Don't you think it's time to settle down?" He paused, then added, "Imagine how much you and Maya could do for the community. You're a real estate mogul. She's a social worker and activist. You two could teach the youth so much."

Kareem nodded. "Maya is the one. I've been waiting for a woman like her my whole life. I'm glad y'all hooked us up."

Keith smiled. "I'm simply returning the favor, my brotha. You introduced me to Tasha, remember?"

Kareem laughed. "Of course! Remember how we spent all night in the computer lab writing that poem? Only to find out the printer was broken?" Both men burst out laughing.

Kareem's smile widened as he remembered Keith's crush on Tasha in college. Plenty of women liked Keith, but it was Tasha—the thick, Southern girl with the Alabama twang—who caught his eye. Keith always stumbled over his words when talking to her. When he learned she loved poetry, he asked Kareem for help writing a love poem. After Keith read it to her, Tasha cried. They'd been together ever since.

As they pulled into the airport parking lot, Kareem looked at Keith, confused. "Why are you parking? I'm not checking any bags."

Keith grabbed a ticket from the machine. "I know. But I have to ask you a question. How much time do you have before your flight?"

"It leaves in two hours," Kareem yawned. "We've got time."

Keith parked, turned off the engine, and rolled down the window.

"For who can find a virtuous woman? Her price is far above rubies," Keith quoted. "Did you know rubies are more valuable than diamonds?"

"Yeah," Kareem replied. "I sold a house to a guy in Bodega Bay who bought his wife a $100,000 ruby ring."

Keith sighed. "I can't afford a hundred-thousand-dollar ruby, but I did buy Tasha this ring," Keith said before reaching into his glove compartment and pulling out a small velvet box. He opened it, revealing a pear-shaped ruby engagement ring set in white gold.

Kareem's eyes widened. "Congratulations!" He clapped his hands. "You're finally proposing!"

Keith grinned, running his thumb over the smooth ring. "Yeah. I'm proposing at church next Sunday."

Kareem stared at his best friend, stunned. It felt like just yesterday that they were writing that love poem in college. Now, Keith was about to get married.

"I'd be honored if you would be my best man." Kareem paused, taking a moment to process Keith's request. Finally, he nodded and extended his hand. "I'd be honored to be your best man," he said.

"Thanks," Keith replied. "Also, would it be possible for you to write a love poem for my proposal in church next Sunday?"

"I got you!" Kareem said as he gave Keith a fist bump. "I'll start writing a poem on the plane. I'll have it finished by Sunday."

"Thanks, fam! You're my best friend. Tasha and I love you, and having you be part of our wedding means everything to us."

"I love y'all also," Kareem said as his voice began to crack. "I never knew my parents, and I lost my grandmother when I was a teenager. So, you and Tasha are the closest thing I have to family."

Keith reached across and gave Kareem a brotherly hug. "I'm proud of your success, Kareem. You have a gift. Your poetry has the power to uplift people. I want you to use your talent to inspire others."

"Ok, Pastor Keith!" Kareem joked, causing Keith to shake his head. "I'm serious, bruh. That poem you wrote for Tasha brought us together. Imagine if your next album was a love album. You can call it *Lyrics and Love*. I'll produce it, and you can put your poem *Intimate* on it!"

Kareem knew that Keith wanted him to go back to writing political, life-changing poetry instead of erotica.

"Lyrics and Love," Kareem repeated. "I like the sound of that! Get started on the beats! We can start working on it when I get back! Kareem exited the car and walked into the airport terminal with a big smile on his face.

16

Kabul, Afghanistan

Thick smoke filled the air as Vincent surveyed the scene. His comrades lay dead, their bodies mangled from the brutal ambush. His fists clenched in rage. Minutes earlier, Taliban fighters in black turbans had fired a rocket-propelled grenade at their training base, killing five members of *Murky Waters*. With hatred in his heart and revenge in his mind, Vincent vowed to avenge their deaths.

Hours later, Vincent's Humvee screeched to a stop outside an Afghan village. His convoy was armed and ready with five wide-body Humvees and two tanks. They were looking for the bombers. As they searched the town, Vincent and his men entered a house suspected of harboring terrorists. Inside, a bearded man in a black turban spat at them and shouted threats in Arabic.

Vincent reacted instantly. He drove his Bowie knife into the man's chest—again and again.

A young woman wearing a blue burqa ran out of another room and began screaming *Baba*. She collapsed to the floor, sobbing. Her piercing green eyes were framed by thick black hair. She couldn't help but tremble as she stared at the bloody blade. Vincent grinned. He knelt beside her and ordered his men to wait outside. "Keep watch for insurgents," he said.

"You got it, Cutter," they replied, stepping out the door.

When they returned, their faces froze in shock. Blood covered the room. Both bodies lay lifeless. Vincent stood over them, smiling.

"Cutter, let's go!" one of his men shouted. "Insurgents are five kilometers away and closing in fast." Vincent turned without a word and followed them into the night. The next day, he watched the news from his barracks.

"Two headless Afghan civilians were found in southern Afghanistan," a CNN reporter announced. "The bodies were discovered in a remote village. No group has claimed responsibility, but sources suggest an American contractor may be involved."

Vincent's jaw tightened. He cursed the liberal media. They defended America's enemies instead of supporting those who fought for its interests.

The news sent Corporal Henson, commander of Murky Waters, into a rage. He summoned Vincent immediately.

When Vincent entered, Henson, a balding man in a crisp suit and glasses, sat behind his desk. He motioned to a leather chair, "Have a seat, Vincent." Vincent obeyed, his cold eyes locked on Henson.

"You've become a liability," Henson said, leaning forward. "You had no orders to attack civilians. Now, I'm under international pressure. Someone filmed the bodies your team left behind. CNN has the footage. The liberal media is having a field day with this!"

"Those terrorists attacked our compound and murdered our men," Vincent responded in a menacing tone. "I did my job," Vincent continued, an angry scowl on his face. He unsheathed his bayonet knife and began using it to clean the blood from under his fingernails.

Henson knew Vincent was one of the best assassins. He'd killed and tortured hundreds of suspected terrorists. However, his brutality was becoming a growing concern.

"Damn it, Thomas! The only reason you're not in prison is plausible deniability."

Vincent smirked. He knew the term well—it allowed mercenary groups to deny war crimes. Henson exhaled. "I'm pulling you out of Afghanistan. You're going back to the States. You need time to clear your head. And when you return to the States, you might want to go off the grid for a long time, Cutter," Henson suggested.

Vincent's jaw clenched in anger, and he shot the Corporal a threatening look as he marched out of the office.

17

Pleasure

Lisa could barely contain her excitement. After weeks of texting, she was finally meeting Kareem. She pulled out her favorite summer dress - a yellow, form-fitting design that accentuated her curves in all the right places. She usually dressed conservatively, but today was different. She wanted Kareem to notice every inch of her. First impressions mattered, and she planned to make hers unforgettable.

After one last glance in the mirror, she grabbed her keys and headed out.

Kareem's flight landed at Hartsfield-Jackson International Airport right on time. Lisa waited eagerly, hoping he wasn't too jetlagged. She had big plans for the weekend. After his poetry performance, she looked forward to a romantic weekend of lovemaking in his hotel room.

Kareem stepped through the automatic doors, tall and confident in a crisp linen outfit. His broad strides quickly closed the distance between them. Their eyes met, and she couldn't help but feel captivated by his handsome face and chiseled muscles. With her head held high, she walked towards him with purposeful steps, her thick thighs visible through her yellow sundress.

"The pictures don't do you justice," Kareem said, his voice smooth. "You're even more beautiful in person."

Lisa blushed. "Thanks, Kareem! You're not too hard on the eyes either." She winked, making him smile.

She drove them to the Ritz Carlton, where Kareem had booked a luxurious presidential suite overlooking Atlanta's skyline. The room had plush furniture, a fireplace, a wet bar, and a marble bathroom with a Jacuzzi. Lisa had brought everything he requested for their weekend: a bubble bath, candles, chocolate-covered strawberries, massage oil, and more.

After checking in, Kareem changed into linen pants and a light shirt, and Lisa took him on a quick tour of the CNN Center and the Martin Luther King National Historic Site. Later, they dined at Ray's in the City. Seated in a cozy corner booth, Kareem ordered Jumbo Lump Crab Cakes, while Lisa chose Crispy Shrimp and Grits. As they waited, he turned to her with curiosity.

"Why are you still single?" he asked. Lisa hesitated. She didn't want to reveal that she was still legally married. "The dating scene in Atlanta is trash," she said, frowning. "Plus, my job doesn't leave much time for relationships."

Kareem raised an eyebrow. He remembered she had mentioned law enforcement in their texts. When she pulled out her badge, his surprise deepened. "Don't forget to bring the handcuffs tonight," he joked.

Lisa looked up from her plate with a sly smile, batting her eyelashes playfully. "I won't... and won't press charges if you beat it up tonight."

Kareem leaned in. "What made you become a homicide detective?"

Lisa's playful smile faded. "My father was a cop. He was murdered when I was a teenager," she said quietly. "Then, years later, my niece, Brianna, went missing. The last time anyone saw her, she was being trafficked by a pimp here in Atlanta. I believe she was a victim of the GTS Killer.”

“The GTS Killer?” Kareem questioned, looking puzzled.

“GTS stands for *Gag, Torture, Streetwalkers,*” Lisa explained. “For over a decade, law enforcement has found murdered women in and around Atlanta. Many were tortured and left with a gag ball in their mouths, leading to the nickname. But not all of them were sex workers. Some were children forced into trafficking.” She sighed. “I joined the force because there were no leads in my niece’s case.”

Kareem’s expression softened. “I’m so sorry for your loss.” Kareem paused, recalling the staggering statistics Maya had shared with him. “I have a friend who told me there are over 90,000 missing Black women in this country.”

“Unfortunately, your friend is correct,” Lisa replied. “Almost half of sex trafficking victims in the United States are Black girls,” she said somberly.

Kareem’s thoughts drifted to Maya. He thought about the work she wanted to do with her *Safe Space* organization to help at-risk girls and protect young women from predators. Suddenly, he started to feel guilty for being with Lisa. Maya was devoting her life to *uplifting* women, and he was *lifting up* women’s skirts. Sensing a shift in Kareem’s mood, Lisa changed the subject.

“I’ve never really been sexually satisfied by a man, Kareem,” she confessed, her voice thick and sultry. “I have had sex with men, but I’ve never had a man make love to my mind the way you do in your poetry.”

His gaze locked onto hers. “Maybe that’s because men ignore your need to be mentally aroused,” he said smoothly. “A woman’s mind needs pleasure, too." Kareem knew the reason most women didn't have an orgasm during sex was because men often neglected her psychological need to be mentally aroused.

Lisa licked her lips. "You seem to know a lot about satisfying a woman. Do you have any sexual boundaries?"

Kareem hesitated. "I won't sleep with a married woman. I don't cross that line."

Lisa's heart sank. She was going through a divorce, but legally, she was still married. "Well, maybe you'll be the first man to satisfy me sexually," she suggested, her voice heavy with lust. Her mind drifted back to the first night she had fantasized about Kareem, and now he was seated at her table, only inches away from her. She couldn't deny the depths of her desire anymore.

At the hotel, Lisa changed into the sexy outfit she planned to wear during Kareem's performance. She looked in her full-length mirror and smiled at how the Maxi Dress she had ordered from her favorite designer, *Jibri,* fit her like a glove. Her dress featured a front-side split, which showed off her curves and thick thighs.

That evening, Kareem performed at an intimate erotic poetry showcase in downtown Atlanta. The venue was packed, the energy thick with anticipation.

A male poet opened the night with two sensual pieces. The first poem, *Room Service,* describes uninterrupted lovemaking in a hotel room. The second poem, *Painting Walls,* was about the art of pleasing a woman with his mouth. The mostly female audience was in a frenzy by the time he finished. The stage was set for Kareem.

The lights dimmed as Kareem stepped onto the stage, leaving only his silhouette. A live band played soft jazz, setting the mood. Then, his deep voice filled the room.

Kareem began his set with the poem, *You Deserve to Come First.* The women in the audience snapped their fingers in agreement. Kareem continued performing other erotic poems from his album *Lyrics and Lust.* He ended with *Dim the Lights,* a more intimate piece encouraging women to be comfortable with their curves when making love.

The audience gave him a standing ovation. After the show, Kareem waved goodbye and let Lisa drive him back to his hotel. When they arrived, he slid the key card into the reader and held the door open for her. He watched her hips sway, his anticipation building.

Kareem entered the bathroom and ran the water for a large soaking tub. Steam filled the air as he dropped in a vanilla-scented bath bomb. He lit small candles, casting a soft glow around the room. Then, he turned off the lights and scattered red rose petals on the floor.

While Kareem prepared the bath, Lisa had a plan of her own. She reached into her purse, pulling out a USB spy cam and a GoPro. She carefully placed them to capture the bed from the perfect angle—one hidden behind a pillow, the other propped on the credenza.

She knew recording their night without his consent was illegal in Georgia. But she convinced herself it was harmless. Kareem would be in town all weekend, and she wanted to relive their passionate nights once he left.

"Your bath is ready," Kareem said, stepping out of the bathroom. His eyes lingered on her.

Lisa undressed, letting her clothes fall softly to the floor, and eased herself into the warm, foamy water. Kareem placed a sleek bamboo bathtub tray across the tub, arranging a wine glass and a few vanilla-scented candles. He added a few drops of essential oils, filling the air with a sweet, calming fragrance.

As Lisa soaked, he tenderly washed her shoulders and back, his hands moving gently over her skin. After her bath, her skin glistening with moisture, he reached for a plush, velvety towel. After drying her off, he smoothed a generous layer of shea butter lotion onto her skin, leaving it soft and hydrated. Then, he led her to the sofa, where a chilled bottle of wine and a tray of chocolate-covered strawberries awaited.

He knelt and massaged Lisa's calves, his strong hands working their magic as the soft rhythm of *Sweet Tooth* played in the background. He then stood up and walked to the kitchen refrigerator, opened it, and returned with a can of cool whip. His tongue traced a slow, wet path from her hardened nipples down to her belly button, then lower. Lisa moaned softly in delight.

Finally, he entered her, staring into her eyes while slowly sliding inside her. He nibbled her neck, his hands gripping her hips, his rhythm steady and deliberate. As her wetness grew, his thrust quickened. Lisa's nails dug into his back. Her body arched, muscles tightening, the heat between them intensifying. A final thrust sent her over the edge, her moans filling the room as waves of pleasure ripped through her body.

Overwhelmed by the intensity of her orgasm, Lisa clung to Kareem. She'd never experienced anything so powerful before. Afterward, they showered together. The warmth of the water, combined with Kareem's gentle touch, felt soothing. As the steam rose around them, it hid the silent tears streaming down her face. For the first time in years, she felt truly loved and satisfied.

The following day, they left the hotel and went to Slutty Vegan. Kareem ordered a Super Slut burger, while Lisa chose crispy shrimp with buffalo sauce, fries, and coleslaw. For dessert, they shared sea moss banana pudding. It was so good that Kareem wished he had ordered extra. After enjoying their meal, they returned to their suite and made love multiple times, only taking a break to order dinner from room service.

By the next day, the linen sheets smelled of Kareem's sweat and Lisa's passion. Their marathon of lovemaking had exceeded her wildest expectations. Kareem had touched parts of her mind and body no man ever had. She woke up and watched him sleep, cherishing the moment. This weekend had been an escape from her harsh reality as a police detective—where death and violence were part of her daily routine.

Lisa quietly retrieved the spy cam and GoPro she had hidden on the dresser. She wanted to relive these moments whenever she had the desire to.

Suddenly, her phone buzzed, pulling her back to reality. It was her partner, Detective Collins. There was a homicide in Decatur. She had 30 minutes to change and get to the scene.

When she got dressed, Kareem was still in a deep sleep. She didn't want to leave him, but it was easier this way.

When he finally woke up, Lisa was gone. He reached for his phone and read the text she had sent:

> Thank you, Kareem, for everything. You fulfilled me in a way that no man ever has! Even though I know we can't be together now, I'll carry you in my heart until the day we can.
> I love you, Kareem, in a way that words can't express. I also have something to tell you: I'm going

through a divorce right now. I
didn't tell you because I know that
you mentioned not wanting to
sleep with a married woman.
Please don't hate me, Kareem.
Once everything is complete, I
pray that we can be together. If I
don't hear from you again, I'll
understand. Either way, I'll cherish
the memories we made this
weekend. I'll always be your
number one fan.

Love, Lisa 😘 😘 🖤

Kareem closed his eyes as a wave of guilt washed over him as he
gripped his phone. He would never have slept with her if he'd known
Lisa was married. On top of that, he'd also slept with Leah. And after
having sex with two different women within a week, he still he still felt
empty. Unhappy. Unfulfilled.

Kareem didn't love Lisa or Leah, and he was avoiding the
woman he did love. He could feel the heavy burden of shame and regret
weighing on him. He felt *dirty and disgusted*. Kareem paced around the
bathroom, desperate to take a hot shower to wash away his shame before
boarding his flight home. He dreaded returning to Oakland and facing
Maya, but he had no choice.

18

Relations and Revelations

"Good afternoon. Welcome to Oakland's International Airport. It is 1 p.m. local time, and the temperature is a pleasant 72 degrees," the captain announced from the cockpit.

Kareem rubbed his eyes, trying to shake off the exhaustion from his long flight from Atlanta. His body was tired, but the guilt from his affair weighed even heavier on his mind.

As passengers grabbed their bags from the overhead compartments, Kareem turned on his phone. He saw multiple texts from Leah and two from Maya. He frowned and deleted Leah's messages. It was time to end things with her. Then, he read Maya's texts. She said she missed him. He sighed, feeling guilty. They had talked every day since their first date, but he hadn't spoken to her in two days.

When Kareem met Maya, he thought he was ready for a real relationship. But after cheating on her with Leah and Lisa, he knew he wasn't. Regret filled his heart as he stepped off the plane and called Maya.

"Hey stranger, are you back in Oakland?" Maya asked.

"I just landed," Kareem said, trying to hide his guilt.

"How was Atlanta? I didn't see you post any pictures."

"It was fun. The performance went well," he muttered, trying to hide his guilt.

"That's good," Maya said. "I'm on my way to Holy Tabernacle right now to rehearse for the Gospel Fest, but I can pick you up from the airport if you need a ride."

"No, go ahead with your rehearsal. I'll grab an Uber. We could have dinner at Chef Smelly's downtown."

Maya smiled. That was one of her favorite places.

"Sounds good! I'll meet you there at 5 pm." She hung up, her mouth watering for fried lobster and garlic noodles.

Maya walked into Holy Tabernacle, her thoughts swirling. Something felt off about Kareem. He seemed distant, as if his mind were somewhere else. The past few months they'd been dating felt like a real-life romance. Before Atlanta, they talked every day. Now, she barely heard from him.

***

Leah Banks was taking a selfie when she spotted Maya entering the church. She narrowed her eyes, scanning Maya's denim dress and matching pumps.

This basic bitch has no sense of fashion, Leah thought. This basic chick has no style, Leah thought, clenching her jaw. She glanced at her phone. No messages from Kareem. *Maybe he's texting Maya instead,* she thought. Leah decided to confront Maya and let her know that Kareem was off-limits.

"Maya Rivers! We went to school together," Leah said with a smirk. "Weren't you at Kareem's album release?"

Maya raised an eyebrow. "Yes, I was."

"Your father runs that little church, *Agape,* right?" Leah sneered, shooting Maya an icy stare.

Maya kept calm, but Leah was testing her patience. "*Agape* has hundreds of members," she said calmly, before attempting to walk around, but Leah blocked her path.

"Well, Kareem and I had an intimate evening at his place last week," Leah hissed quietly, trying to provoke a reaction from Maya.

Maya kept her cool. *Not today, Satan!* she told herself, careful not to react emotionally. She knew that Leah liked Kareem and was trying to provoke her. Maya walked around Leah and began walking towards Keith, who was seated at the organ.

"Kareem does know how to satisfy a woman," Leah said with a grin.

Maya stopped dead in her tracks. *What did this heffa say?* She was shocked that Leah had the audacity to approach her in church and brag about sleeping with Kareem. She also hoped Leah was lying.

Maya walked back towards Leah, folded her arms, and narrowed her eyes. "Let me get this straight," she said, pointing at Leah and raising her eyebrows in disbelief. "You went to Kareem's place and had sex with him?"

Leah smirked. Maya shook her head in disgust before continuing. Kareem has taken me on several dates over the past two months. He's courted me, written love poems, and opened every door for me, and I didn't even have to open my legs."

Leah's jaw tightened. She put her phone back in her purse and reached for a knife. *No. Not here. Too many people,* Leah reminded herself.

Maya stepped closer. "You've got some nerve approaching me in church and boasting about having sex with Kareem," Maya whispered. "You need to take a seat, Leah. Better yet, take up an entire pew!" Maya suggested, pointing towards the rows of church pews.

A firm hand landed on Maya's shoulder. She turned to see Tahir, a teenage rapper from her church. He glared at Leah.

"Is there a problem?" he asked.

Maya sighed. "Everything's fine, Tahir," Maya said. "Leah was just about to leave, weren't you?"

Leah rolled her eyes. As she turned to go, she leaned in and whispered: "Kareem belongs to me now, bitch." Then, she stormed out of the church.

19

Regret

Kareem parked across the street from Smelly's, a popular seafood spot in Oakland. As he stepped inside, the delicious aroma filled the air. He spotted Maya's car pulling up. His chest tightened when he saw Maya step out.

When Maya stepped inside the restaurant, he went to hug her, but she pulled away. Kareem sensed that something was wrong, so he pulled out a chair for her to sit down.

"What's going on between you and Leah Banks?" she asked, looking him directly in the eyes.

"Nothing. We used to go to church together—"

"Don't lie to me, Kareem!" she snapped. "She approached me at rehearsal and told me she had sex with you." Kareem lowered his head.

"Is that why you didn't call me after our date?" Maya's voice was sharp.

"I'm not interested in Leah," he said, forcing calm into his tone. "She came over one night, and we kicked it, but that's it."

"What do you mean you kicked it? Did you sleep with her?" Maya asked, raising her eyebrows in an accusatory manner. Kareem was busted, and he knew it. He hesitated before responding, trying to think of a way to calm Maya down without admitting the truth.

"She came over and brought me a gift."

"What gift? The gift that keeps on giving?" Maya asked, looking disgusted.

"I haven't opened the gift yet," Kareem replied, remembering that he had left it on his end table.

"But I bet you had no problem opening her legs, huh?" Maya shot back.

Before Kareem could respond, the waitress arrived. He exhaled, hoping the food would lighten the mood. Maya ordered Dungeness Crab, Garlic Noodles, and Blackened Prawns. Kareem got Fried Red Snapper, Mac and Cheese, and Garlic Green Beans. As soon as the waitress left, Kareem tried to explain.

"She came over, and we had sex. It was a mistake that should never have happened. Maya clenched her jaw, hurt flashing in her eyes. "I don't get it. We talked every day for months. And then you just... go sleep with someone else?"

Kareem lowered his head. "I messed up—"

"And what about Atlanta?" Maya interrupted. "Is that why you didn't call me? Were you with one of your groupies?" Maya asked, shooting him another accusatory look.

Kareem turned to look out the window to avoid eye contact. During the months that they had been dating, Maya had gotten to know Kareem very well. She'd learned his mannerisms. She noticed he always hesitated and avoided eye contact whenever he wanted to avoid discussing something personal with her.

"Did you sleep with someone in Atlanta?" Maya asked, tapping her finger on the table. Kareem sighed and told Maya about his encounter with Lisa, explaining that he hadn't known she was married and regretted having slept with her. Maya listened to Kareem without flinching.

"I'm sorry, Maya," Kareem said, his voice cracking. Maya was numb with pain and disappointment. "I'm sorry too, Kareem. I thought you were serious about our future. You're not going to change until you_."

"Until I what? Go to church? Accept Christ into my life? Become celibate until marriage?" Kareem shot back. "Save it, Maya! I respect your celibacy, but I'm a grown-ass man with my own needs. I can't do this celibacy thing anymore." Kareem reached across the table and took her hand. "Baby, let's just go to my place and make love," Kareem pleaded. "I love you and don't want anybody else but you!"

Maya pulled her hand away and looked at Kareem as if he were crazy. "I'm not coming to your place, Kareem. *You're still living in the flesh!* I'm going home to pray that God delivers you from that demonic, lustful spirit that has a grip on you!"

"I enjoy sex, and I know I can make you enjoy it also," Kareem said. "As far as celibacy, this isn't the 1940s," he said with a smirk. "We've dated for months, and I can't do the celibacy thing anymore."

Maya sighed deeply and said, "You write all this erotic poetry because all you want is sex from women. You love all the attention you get from your female fans, but even after all the sex, you still feel lonely and unfulfilled, don't you?"

Kareem remained silent, his gaze shifting from Maya's face to the window outside. Deep inside, he knew she was right. All his life, he only had sexual relationships with women. Kareem had never been in love, so commitment never crossed his mind. But all that changed when he met Maya.

Maya sipped from her water and then continued. "You're more interested in a backstroke than being equally yoked! But keep using your poetry to feed your flesh instead of your spirit, and you'll always be spiritually hungry!" Suddenly feeling vulnerable and exposed, Kareem muttered, "I'm not going to sit here and argue with you, Maya. I made a mistake, ok? It won't happen again."

Maya straightened her posture. "Oh, I know it won't happen again," she said, lifting a brow. "No woman wants a man who wants every woman. I certainly don't!" Maya stared out the window. "I also know that the man God has for me won't hurt or cheat on me," she said, her voice cracking. "I can't blame you, though. You didn't see a man love a woman like my father loved my mother."

"Oh, so you want to go there?" Kareem exploded. "Ok, Ms. Saved and Sanctified. Do you think you're better than me? You're the one who gave up your virginity to some dude who cheated on you in college, yet you want me to wait until marriage before I can make love to you?"

"I won't make the mistake of having premarital sex again," Maya said, her voice growing louder. Maya felt the conversation becoming toxic. They were both using details of each other's past traumas to try and hurt each other. Kareem's mention of her ex brought back the memories of her dying mother's last words: *One day, you'll meet a man who will love you rather than lust after you. Until then, guard your heart, for everything you do flows from it.*

"I can get any woman I want!" Kareem said while waving his hand in the air. Maya clenched her jaw. She was hurt, but she was determined not to let it show.

"You can have your other women, Kareem. I don't *compete*; I *complete!*" Maya narrowed her eyes. "You'll keep changing partners to avoid changing yourself," she said, her voice low.

When the waitress returned with their orders, Maya requested a to-go box. "So, you'd rather eat alone than try to work this out?" Kareem asked, sounding regretful.

Maya packed her food. "A woman who knows what she brings to the table isn't afraid to eat alone."

As she reached for her purse, a book fell to the floor. Kareem picked it up. His eyes scanned the cover— "What's this?" The cover had a beautiful photo of Maya in a purple dress.

The book title read: *Single, Celibate, and Successful: Focusing on Your Purpose Instead of Waiting for a Proposal* by Maya Rivers.

He looked at her. "You wrote this?" Maya nodded. "I got the proof copy this weekend. I hoped we could read it together, but it's too late now." She swallowed hard. "Keep it. There's no need to walk me out," she said, her voice beginning to crack. She refused to let Kareem see her cry again. "Goodbye, Kareem."

He watched her leave, the sound of clinking dishes and low chatter filling the restaurant. His heart screamed at him to chase after her, but his pride wouldn't let him move. Instead, he slumped in his chair and asked for the bill.

20

Strings Attached

Kareem returned to his condo feeling miserable after his breakup with Maya. He put away the food from the restaurant because he'd lost his appetite. He collapsed onto his sofa and picked up Maya's book *Single, Celibate, and Successful: Focusing on Your Purpose Rather Than Waiting for a Proposal.*

The first chapter describes how Maya's mother passed away while she was also going through a painful breakup in college. She wrote about her grief, her struggles, and how faith and forgiveness helped her move forward. The second chapter encouraged women to set dating boundaries to protect their hearts. It warned against relationships with people who weren't equally yoked. The third chapter focused on finding life's purpose instead of losing oneself in relationships. One quote struck a nerve: *A man who lacks a purpose in life will become preoccupied with lust and sexual pleasure.*

The book had Kareem questioning himself: *Am I working towards finding my life's purpose or just searching for sexual pleasure? Am I ready for a committed relationship? Why do I still feel unfulfilled after sex?*

Guilt gnawed at him. He'd betrayed Maya. She didn't deserve his dishonesty or lack of respect. Right then, he decided he needed to become a better man before he could have a better relationship.

Kareem's thoughts were interrupted by a soft knock on his door. Startled, he tensed up.

Who the hell is knocking on my door?

Lobby security had a strict policy of not allowing anyone access to his penthouse condo without prior notice.

The pounding came again, even louder this time.

Kareem put the book down and cautiously crept towards the door, feeling his anxiety build as he peered through the peephole. He was shocked to see Leah Banks standing there.

"Surprise!" Leah beamed. "I brought you—"

"How the hell did you get up here?" Kareem cut her off, his voice seething with anger. Leah took a step back, her eyes wide. "Security, let me up," she said, surprised at his reaction.

Kareem clenched his jaw and made a mental note to contact the security director about the lax security in the lobby. Leah's showing up at his place without calling confirmed that he needed to cut her off.

"First of all, don't ever show up at my place uninvited. Second, why did you tell Maya we 'kicked it'?" He pointed at her, his frustration rising. "What's wrong with you?"

"Look, Kareem. It wasn't even like that," Leah said, trying to find an excuse for confronting Maya. "Can I please come in and explain?" Leah begged.

Kareem reluctantly stepped aside. She strolled in, slipping off her jacket, making sure he had a full view of her curves. Sensing his anger, she tried a different approach: "I just told her I brought you a gift."

"You had no right to approach her, especially in church," Kareem snapped. "You're not my woman!"

Leah's stomach twisted. *Why is he so mad at me?* She lowered her gaze, batting her long, fake lashes. She wasn't used to men speaking to her this way, but strangely, she liked his dominance. It reminded her of how he took control in bed. She longed for that feeling again.

"You sound stressed, Kareem. Let me help you relax," she purred, stepping closer.

"Nah. I'm good," Kareem said firmly. Regret weighed heavy on him—his fling with Leah had caused him and Maya to break up.

"Are you sure?" Leah's voice dripped with disappointment. "I can make you feel good."

"Leah, what happened between us shouldn't have happened. I have feelings for Maya," Kareem admitted. "And thanks to you, we broke up."

Leah's face hardened, jealousy flaring in her chest. She wanted to lash out but forced a sweet smile instead.

"I've always cared about you, Kareem. Since we were kids at church."

Kareem said nothing. His eyes drifted to Maya's book on the table. Leah followed his gaze and picked it up.

"Maya wrote a book?" She glanced at the title *Single, Celibate, and Successful*, then raised an eyebrow. "Wait—Maya's celibate?"

"Yeah," Kareem answered. "She wants to wait until she gets married."

Leah smirked. "And how do you feel about that?" She tapped her manicured nails on the counter, her tone teasing. "Wouldn't you rather be with a woman who can satisfy you?" She shot him a playful wink.

"I love Maya," he said, grabbing the book from Leah. "I need more than sex. Reading Maya's book makes me realize the importance of being patient. She quotes a verse from Song of Solomon that teaches not to arouse or awaken love before its time."

Leah stiffened. His devotion to Maya angered her. She forced another smile. "Did you open the gift I gave you?"

Kareem sighed. He just wanted her to leave. "No, Leah."

Leah walked over to the end table and grabbed the box. "Please open it, Kareem," she pleaded.

Kareem reluctantly unwrapped it. Once he removed the wrapping, he stared in disbelief. It was his grandmother's Bible - the same black Bible he had left on her grave at the cemetery after her funeral.

"Wow," Kareem whispered, running his fingers over the worn leather cover. "This is my grandmother's Bible."

Leah beamed. "I picked it up after her funeral and kept it for you, hoping I'd see you again.

Leah softened her voice. "I'll apologize to Maya at Gospel Fest. I can tell you care about her. But if you ever need anything, I'm here. We have history, Kareem. I love you."

Kareem barely heard her. He mumbled, "Yeah, ok, Leah," still staring at the Bible.

"Leah cleared her throat. "Speaking of Gospel Fest... maybe you should perform a poem—something inspirational, like the ones you did as a kid."

Kareem hesitated. This could be a chance to see Maya and make things right.

"Alright. Sign me up."

Leah grinned. "Good. And if you ever need a little stress relief, no strings attached."

Kareem opened the door, signaling for her to leave. Leah's heart sank. She wasn't used to being rejected. But she wouldn't give up. She'd already scheduled a Brazilian Butt Lift in Miami. *Once I get my body done, no woman—including Maya—will be able to compete with me,* Leah grinned.

Kareem would be her husband because whatever Leah Banks wanted, Leah Banks got.

Leah left Kareem's condo and drove straight to her father's church, hoping he'd fund a shopping spree to cheer her up. Bishop Banks noticed her pout.

"What's wrong, sweetheart?"

"I feel angry, Dad."

Sensing a meltdown, Bishop Banks pulled out his wallet. "Here's my Platinum Visa. Go treat yourself."

Leah smirked. There's a Gucci purse calling my name. She dialed a friend and planned an all-day spree through Bloomingdale's, Nordstrom, and Prada.

"Oh, by the way, Dad," she said casually. "Kareem agreed to perform a poem at Gospel Fest."

Her father smiled. "Great! Add him to the lineup."

Leah did as she was told, but she was already plotting. Kareem might love Maya now, but that wouldn't last. Leah always got what she wanted.

And she wanted Kareem.

21

What's Done in the Dark

After a year of working with special forces and training elite U.S. military units in Iraq and Afghanistan, Vincent was glad to be back home. He looked forward to hunting again. For decades, he had been kidnapping and killing unsuspecting Black women across the South to feed his bloodlust.

His wife had no idea he was back in the States. He hadn't called her, so she would be surprised to see him. He took a taxi from the airport, and upon arrival, he noticed her car wasn't there. It was early morning, so she was probably at work. That gave him plenty of time to settle in, unpack, and rest before she returned.

He tried to unlock the front door, but his key didn't work. *Damn. She must have changed the locks.* Frustrated, he walked to the side of the house and used his Bowie knife to break the weak padlock on the crawl space. He squeezed through the cold air return, removed the screen, and kicked out the cover. Once inside, he disarmed the alarm, opened the front door, and brought in his bags.

As he entered the primary bedroom, his eyes landed on a photo of his wife:

Lisa Thomas

Vincent took a deep breath, taking in his familiar surroundings. Everything looked the same except for one thing. The computer in the bedroom was still on.

Curious, he noticed a flash drive plugged into the USB port. The words GoPro adapter was engraved on it. He had used a similar device in Afghanistan to record the confessions of tortured terrorists. Intrigued, he clicked on the files and downloaded them onto the computer. A video popped up. He pressed to play.

The screen showed his wife, Lisa, walking around a hotel room. She spoke to someone in the bathroom, where the water was running. "You're so romantic," she said.

Vincent's chest tightened. He fast-forwarded the video. A man walked up behind Lisa and began massaging her shoulders. Moments later, she knelt before him. *She never did that for me*, Vincent thought, his jaw clenching. His stomach twisted as he watched Lisa moan the man's name:

Kareem.

Anger and something else—something darker—boiled inside him. He had always finished quickly with Lisa. But Kareem? He lasted much longer. Vincent's eyes darted to a flyer on Lisa's desk.

Lyrics and Lust: An Erotic Spoken Word Showcase featuring *Kareem*. He flipped the flyer over and read the back:

"To my #1 fan, Lisa. Thanks for your love and support! Kareem."

Vincent slammed the flyer back onto her desk. He searched through her desk drawers to find a sealed yellow envelope. He ripped open the seal and discovered her divorce petition. Vincent seethed as he placed the divorce papers back in the envelope. His eyes darted to the clock. It was almost noon. He only had a few hours to prepare before Lisa arrived home. Vincent sprinted to his backyard shed, gathering the tools he would need for that evening.

22

Vengeance

Lisa pulled her SUV into her driveway. She was mentally and physically exhausted. After spending the entire day in Southwest Atlanta investigating a homicide, all she wanted was a long bath, a glass of wine, and the soothing hum of smooth jazz. Kareem hadn't texted since leaving Atlanta, so she assumed she'd never hear from him again. But she had memories, including the erotic video from their weekend together.

As she stepped inside her house, Lisa sensed something wasn't right. Her cop senses kicked into high gear; the alarm was on, but she sensed someone was watching her. She drew her weapon and scanned the rooms. "Who's there? Hands up!"

She crept toward her bedroom, pushed the door open, and froze. Her computer was on. *I turned this off this morning,* she thought.

She inched towards the monitor but felt the strange presence of someone standing behind her. Her eyes widened in terror as she turned around and faced the menacing figure behind her.

"Vincent…what are you doing here?" she stammered, her voice shaking.

"This is my home! I'm your husband! Or have you forgotten that?" he growled.

Lisa forced a hesitant smile onto her face. "But …I haven't heard from you in over a year!"

He narrowed his eyes. "It's hard to call home when conducting covert operations in Afghanistan."

"I missed you!" she lied, steadying her aim.

Vincent's voice seethed with rage. "Did you really miss me? If so, then why are you holding that gun like you're going to shoot me?"

She raised her chin defiantly and kept her gun aimed at him. "You need to leave, Vincent. You're creeping me out!" Lisa kept her weapon trained on Vincent.

His eyes flashed with rage. "I found the divorce papers."

Lisa shivered and tightened her grip on the gun. "A divorce is the best option-"

"What the hell do you mean divorce is the best option?" Vincent roared as he slammed his fist into the wall. "I told you when we got married that I don't believe in divorce! My parents got divorced, and it ruined me! When we got married, it was till death do us part! Do you know what that means?"

Vincent angrily tossed the manila envelope with the divorce papers to the floor. Distracted by the divorce papers being thrown, Lisa took her eyes off Vincent long enough for him to use his leg and kick the gun out of her hands. In a swift movement, he pulled out a hunting knife from behind his back and grabbed her from behind. She felt the cold, sharp edge of the hunting knife press against her throat.

"Vincent, what are you doing?" she gasped in terror. With every breath she took, the blade of the knife pressed tighter against her throat.

"I also found the video," he said through clenched teeth, grinding the serrated blade into her skin. "You've been screwing other men while I've been defending our country? You're just like my stepmother!"

Lisa remembered that a dangerous lover had killed Vincent's stepmother. She had to act fast, or she'd end up dead. The knife around her neck was too tight to attempt a reverse headbutt, so Lisa stomped down hard on his left foot, but it was no use because Vincent was wearing steel-toed boots. He retaliated with lightning speed, delivering a vicious blow to her temple and knocking her unconscious.

When she regained consciousness, Lisa found herself bound and gagged to her bed. The cold steel of her handcuffs was tearing into her wrist. A ball gag was pulled tightly over her mouth, making it difficult to breathe.

Moments later, Vincent entered the bedroom. She noticed that he had her phone. He moved forward, and Lisa's eyes widened as he lifted the phone to her face and unlocked the device using facial recognition.

He leaned in close, his voice low and menacing as he spoke, "Here's what I want you to do," Vincent ordered. "I'm going to remove your gag, and you are going to call your partner, Detective Rashad, and tell him that you just had a death in your family, so you'll be taking two weeks off from work," Vincent demanded. "Make it sound convincing, or I'll slit your throat," he threatened, holding the blade of his hunting knife to her neck.

Vincent removed the gag ball from her mouth, and Lisa called her partner, Detective Rashad Collins. Lisa's voice quivered as she spoke, "Hey, Rashad, my Aunt Gracie in Louisiana passed away. I need to fly out for the funeral and attend to her estate."

Rashad's voice thickened with worry. "Are you ok?" Tears streaming down her face, Lisa mustered a response. "I'll be alright. I just need a few weeks off."

After saying goodbye, Lisa turned back to Vincent. "I'm sorry, Vincent. Please forgive me. I love you," Lisa pleaded, her voice trembling. She was hoping to gain a psychological advantage. If she could get him to remove the cuffs, she might have a fighting chance against him.

"What's the password to your email?" Vincent asked, seething. Lisa reluctantly told him her password: **Kareemsfuturewife10!**

Vincent slapped her face and then placed the ball gag back in her mouth.

"All these years, I treated you with respect when I should've treated you like those other whores I killed," he said in a low voice. Lisa's face grimaced.

What did he mean whores that he killed? What is he talking about?

Lisa stared at her husband in sheer terror, her heart racing as she took in the sinister smirk on his face. "You see, Lisa, I know where all the skeletons are hidden. Because I'm the one who buried them." He laughed.

Lisa's eyes widened in disbelief as the truth of Vincent's identity was revealed - her own husband was the GTS Killer, the serial killer she'd been hunting for over a decade. Vincent Thomas, the man she married, was the same monster who had killed her niece and countless other women. She felt her blood run cold in terror as the realization sunk in.

Vincent's face contorted with rage as he whispered, "Do you remember the case of the missing girl from Decatur a few years back? It haunted you that you could never find her body. Remember that?" Vincent asked with his nostrils flaring. "I buried her body in our backyard! Not far from your beloved garden."

Lisa fought frantically to free herself from the cold metal cuffs, but it was useless. Tears streaked down her face as her screams for help were muffled by the gag in her mouth. She watched as he pulled out her phone and started scrolling through the messages she had sent Kareem.

"You know, in the country I just served in, they stoned women for infidelity," Vincent said with an evil smirk on his face.

His eyes darkened with rage. "I'm going to kill him! I'll find your friend Kareem, slit his throat, and watch him bleed to death!"

Bound and gagged, Lisa did the only thing that she could do: She prayed. She asked God to protect Kareem and his loved ones from Vincent.

"You'll never get the satisfaction of having my ring," Vincent sneered, his voice dripping with venom. He snatched the blade off the dresser, and in one swift motion, he took Lisa's life.

Now, Vincent had a new mission—to kill Kareem. Usually, when he killed, emotions didn't enter the equation. But this time, it was personal.

Flying would leave a trail, so Vincent chose to drive. The Atlanta police would soon come looking for Lisa, and he had to move fast. He packed a bag, made a few calls on his burner phone, and climbed into Lisa's SUV. Vincent merged onto the interstate, California-bound.

23

Heavy Lifting

Kareem gasped for breath as he finished his final bench press rep. As Keith spotted him, sweat dripped from his face and chest. Kareem lifted the 300-pound barbell with ease. The air inside the private gym was tense as they pushed themselves to the limit. After an hour of intense exercise, Kareem's chest and biceps burned with exertion. He'd been pushing himself hard, but no amount of physical strain could keep his mind off Maya.

With gritted teeth, Kareem got off the bench and prepared to spot Keith as he began his set. Across the gym, Tshaka pounded the heavy bag with sharp, controlled punches. "You ok, bruh?" Keith asked as he lifted the bar from the rack.

Kareem helped guide the weight as Keith started his reps. "I messed up with Maya," Kareem admitted, shaking his head. "It's been over a week since we broke up, and I miss her." He missed her smile, their late-night conversations, the sound of her laughter, and their walks around the lake. He had tried to convince himself that he would get over her, but he knew that was a lie. Maya was irreplaceable.

"Leah Banks ruined it for you, huh?" Keith asked, finishing his set.

"Did Maya tell you?" Kareem asked, helping him rack the barbell.

"No. Tahir and I were at the church when Leah confronted her. Maya was upset."

Kareem sank onto the weight bench opposite Keith. "I can't even be mad at Leah, though, because, honestly... it's all my fault," he admitted. "I slept with Leah. And another woman I met in Atlanta."

Keith wiped his face and neck with a towel. "You hooked up with a woman in Atlanta, too?" He shook his head, chuckling. "You're a wild boy, Kareem. Let me guess—she was thick, huh?" He playfully placed a hand on Kareem's head as if praying. "Dear God, hear my prayer. Please help save Kareem, the player. His weakness is a woman with a big derrière."

"C'mon, bruh. You don't have to go all T.D. Jakes on me," Kareem said, standing up.

"I tried to warn you about messing with too many women. Maya is rare. When a woman is rare, you can't treat her like she's regular," Keith said.

Kareem put his head in his hands, feeling the weight of his mistakes. Keith clapped a firm hand on his shoulder. "I'm only preaching to you because I care. As Proverbs says: *As iron sharpens iron, so one man sharpens another.*"

Tshaka walked towards his two friends, wiping sweat from his forehead. "So, what happened in Atlanta?" he asked, taking a seat.

Kareem sighed and told them about Lisa. He admitted her bombshell body had him making all kinds of bad decisions.

"Kareem, you need to enroll in AA: Ass-a-holics Anonymous," Keith joked. All three men laughed, but the humor faded when Kareem told them about Lisa's text, in which she admitted to being married.

Both men shook their heads in disbelief. Keith met Kareem's gaze seriously. "Lust takes. Love gives."

Kareem had heard that before, but coming from Keith, it hit differently.

"I thought you liked Maya?" Tshaka asked, raising an eyebrow.

"I do like her," Kareem admitted. "I knew she was the one the first moment I met her. But she's celibate. I can't wait until marriage to have sex. It's all this testosterone in my body."

"C'mon, bruh. Don't blame your *testosterone* level for failing the *test* of temptation," Keith responded.

"Testosterone fuels our sex drive, but as men, we've got to be disciplined. Self-control is what separates boys from men. Lack of discipline is a liability," Tshaka said seriously.

"I agree," Keith added. "Proverbs 25:28 says, 'A man who lacks self-control is like a city without walls."

Tshaka sat on the edge of a weight bench, his gaze steady on Kareem. "There is an African proverb: *Haste has no blessing.* Lust craves that quick fix. However, rushing things in a relationship can lead to mistakes. When was the last time you were in a serious relationship?" Tshaka asked.

Kareem shifted uncomfortably, rubbing his beard. "I've never been in one. I've been focused on making money, not finding a fiancée." He hesitated, brows furrowing. "To be honest, commitment scares me."

Keith and Tshaka exchanged knowing glances. "Uh-oh," Keith said, grinning. "Tshaka's about to unleash ancient African relationship wisdom on you, Kareem! Go ahead, Iyanla—fix his life."

Tshaka smirked. "Sometimes, we allow past pain to prevent us from building real connections. We'd rather be alone than risk getting hurt, so we sabotage our happiness by cheating or leaving, even when things are good. Maybe you avoid commitment because you fear losing people you love."

"Boom! That's it," Keith said, standing up.

"My father's a psychologist," Tshaka continued. "He taught me about the power of the subconscious mind. If you believe love leads to loss, you'll avoid it. Take Maya, for example. She wants commitment, but your fear of losing her might be causing you to self-sabotage the relationship."

Kareem nodded in agreement. He never really thought about it that way, but Tshaka was right. He'd never been in a real relationship and only had casual flings. Before dating Maya, he'd never been emotionally attached to any woman.

"That explains why you're so successful in Real Estate, Kareem," Tshaka continued. "You work hard so you never have to live in poverty again. You fear failure."

"He has a point," Keith agreed. Tshaka stood up and softened his voice. "None of us are perfect. We all have struggles. We, as Black men, face trauma every day in this country. We've all been tempted and made mistakes. But the first step towards change is being honest with ourselves." He paused, letting the words sink in, then continued, "Own up to your mistakes, Kareem. Learn from them. Don't let past pain stop you from future happiness. You deserve a good woman."

"Thanks, fam," Kareem said, shaking his head. "That really hit home. You broke it down better than any psychologist ever could. I'm going to be celibate. Maya's book made me realize some things I need to work on."

Tshaka tossed his towel over his shoulder. I've got to go, brothas. I have a date with Nina." Kareem gave both men dap. "I appreciate y'all for helping me out with this."

Keith smiled. "The Bible says, *Wounds from a sincere friend are better than many kisses from an enemy.* I'll always keep it real with you."

"Enough about me," Kareem said, changing the subject. "Are you ready for tomorrow?"

"Bruh, I'm so excited! Tasha has no idea I'm proposing in church," Keith said, grinning. "Did you finish the poem?"

"I'll finish it tonight. I won't let my best friend and his fiancée down."

Back at his condo, Tshaka's words replayed repeatedly in his mind. *Why am I so scared of love? Why have I always slept with women and avoided commitment?*

Kareem dropped his keys on the side table and reached for Maya's book. He opened it to the final chapter called *Friends First, Lovers Last*. To his surprise, the last chapter of the book talks about their relationship:

> Months ago. I met someone special. We ate at a waterfront restaurant on our first date and then took a gondola ride around Lake Merritt. He's a wonderful man who was raised by his grandmother. He's not in church right now because of the church hurt that he suffered as a child. But I pray for him daily. I ask God to guide him. I've grown to love and respect him. He's a provider and protector, but most importantly, he's patient with me. I pray that God blesses our union because he's everything I've ever desired in a husband.

Kareem felt the weight of guilt pressing in on him. The realization of why Maya had been celibate for so long, out of respect for God and to build a bond of friendship before marriage, only made it worse. He'd cheated on her, betrayed her trust, and broke her heart.

How could he make things right again? He knew that forgiveness wouldn't come easy, but if he wanted to salvage their relationship, he had to try. He'd leveled up financially, but now he needed to level up emotionally and spiritually.

24

Gruesome Discovery

Detective Rashad Collins arrived at the scene, immediately assaulted by an unpleasant stench. "The body is in the bedroom," the uniformed officer said grimly, leading Collins down a narrow hallway.

"The victim is Lisa Thomas," the CSI tech said. Patrol found her this morning when she didn't show up for roll call. A welfare check led them here. They noticed the smell before they even knocked."

Detective Rashad Collins felt nauseated while listening to the details of Lisa's death. The medical examiner, kneeling beside the bed, glanced up. "She's been dead for several weeks, judging by the decomposition."

Collins, a broad-shouldered man with graying hair and a neatly trimmed goatee, had seen more homicides in his twenty-three years with the Atlanta Police Department than he cared to count. But this... this was different. This was his partner, Lisa. *Lisa...Oh God.... Lisa!!!*

Detective Collins looked at her corpse and shuddered. The bed was soaked in blood. Even a hardened criminologist like Collins wasn't ready for the morbid sight.

"The primary suspect is Vincent Thomas, her estranged husband," a uniformed officer said. "A neighbor saw him driving her SUV a few weeks ago. He works for a private security firm overseas. We found divorce papers, so this could be a crime of passion."

Collins barely registered the officer's words as he scanned the scene. His eyes locked onto something on the bedside table. Duct tape residue clung to her wrists and ankles. A ball gag lay discarded on the floor. And then, Collins noticed a blood-spattered flyer.

To my #1 fan, Lisa. Thanks for your love and support!
Kareem

The flyer advertised *Lyrics and Lust,* a spoken-word event featuring Kareem, a poet from Oakland, California.

"You ever heard of this guy?" Collins asked one of the younger officers.

"Yeah," the cop said. "Some poet from the West Coast. He performed here a few weeks ago. Supposedly, his spoken word is off the charts. The ladies love it."

A voice behind Collins broke the uneasy silence. "Severing the wedding finger isn't part of his usual modus operandi."

Collins turned to see a young man with blond hair dressed in a navy blue FBI jacket. He was probably in his late twenties. He was lean but muscular. He flipped open his badge and introduced himself.

"Special Agent Drew Nelson, FBI." Nelson," the agent said after putting his wallet back in his pocket and extending his hand. Collins shook the agent's hand with a firm grip.

"My condolences, Detective," Nelson said solemnly. "I understand you and Lisa were partners."

Collins nodded, trying to suppress the lump forming in his throat. "For over a decade," he said. "Worked cold cases together, interviewed witnesses, built cases." His voice faltered as he stared at Lisa's corpse.

"This isn't just any murder," the FBI agent continued. "It's *erotophonophilia* - a lust murder. At Quantico, we analyze this type of behavior. Offenders get sexual gratification from torture, mutilation, and ultimately, the kill."

"So, Vincent is the GTS killer?" Collins asked the agent, trying to hide the pain in his voice.

"Yes," Nelson confirmed. "GTS stands for *Gag, Torture, Streetwalkers*. We gave him that name after discovering multiple victims in Georgia—all strangled, all gagged. Until now, we thought he only targeted prostitutes."

"We've been after this serial killer for over ten years," Collins muttered. "Over a decade of hard investigative work, and the killer was right under our noses," he said in disgust. "He was difficult to trace. We would find victims, and the trail would go cold for years. Now it makes sense that when he was overseas, the murders would stop."

Collins narrowed his eyes. *The perfect cover. No one ever suspected a serial killer would be married to a homicide detective.* The detective rubbed his temples, trying to make sense of it all. "What intel does the Bureau have on him?"

Agent Nelson's gaze flicked toward the forensic team before motioning Collins toward the front door. "Let's talk outside." They stepped into the cool morning air, the stench of death finally fading.

"I know Lisa was your friend, and I promise you that we will catch the monster who did this. But Vincent Thomas isn't just a killer. He's a predator. A trained mercenary who murders for pleasure."

"How many victims do you think he's killed?" Collins asked.

"At least twenty that we've documented. All Black women." Nelson's jaw tightened. "We believe some of his victims may be buried on this property."

A sharp voice cut through the tense air.

"We found something!"

Detective Collins and Agent Nelson rushed toward the backyard, where crime scene investigators had been digging near a tool shed. Cadaver dogs had led them to a specific patch of dirt. One of the forensic techs stood over a shallow hole, his gloved hands trembling. Collins and Nelson stepped closer and stared down into the earth.

A human skull. Its empty eye sockets stared back at them.

Agent Nelson's jaw tightened, and his eyes narrowed. Atlanta to Oakland was approximately a 37-hour drive, and Lisa had been murdered weeks ago, meaning that Vincent was probably already in Oakland. He needed to move fast. If Vincent Thomas were already in Oakland, he could have been hunting his next victim.

25

The Proposal Poem

Kareem pulled his Mercedes into the parking lot of *Agape* Church, a white stucco, two-story building located in West Oakland. Dr. Mark Rivers, Maya's father, was the pastor of the church. *Agape Assembly* had a membership of 500 and was well-known for its community work.

Kareem felt slightly apprehensive. It had been over a decade since he had set foot in a church— not since his grandmother's passing. Taking a deep breath, he opened the car door.

As he approached the entrance, Kareem was greeted by a woman in a wheelchair. Her warm smile and deep brown skin radiated kindness. "Happy Sunday! I'm Sister Jones. Welcome to Agape Assembly Church."

Kareem smiled, feeling an immediate connection with her.

Above the sanctuary entrance hung a sign that read, "Above all, love each other deeply because love covers a multitude of sins." 1 Peter 4:8. The moment Kareem stepped inside, he felt a sense of love and spiritual peace that he hadn't felt since he was a child.

Across the room, he spotted Keith standing near the grand organ, arms folded as he chatted with Tahir, whom Kareem recognized from the recording studio. Keith had been producing Tahir's gospel rap album. As soon as Keith saw Kareem, he rushed down the aisle and pulled him into a warm embrace.

"Man, thank you for coming! It took all this to get you to come to church," he laughed. "Are you ready?" he asked.

"I'm ready. I finished the poem last night." Kareem placed a reassuring hand on Keith's shoulder. "Are you ready?" he asked with a grin.

Keith nodded. "As ready as I'll ever be. I'm nervous, but I've got to do this. And what better place than the Lord's house?"

Just then, Keith pointed toward the entrance. "Look who just walked in!"

Tshaka and Nina entered, draped in vibrant African attire, looking like royalty. Keith ran over to greet them while the congregation buzzed with excitement at Tshaka's presence.

"Look at you two, coming in like the cast of *Coming to America*," Keith joked, hugging them both.

Maya was shocked to see Kareem walk into the church. He stood in a blue Armani suit, looking extremely handsome and stylish. He was the last person in the world she expected to see at her church, but there he was. Even though she was still angry at him, part of her wanted to run up to him and hug him. Maya quickly averted her eyes to keep from staring at Kareem.

The service began at noon. Kareem, Tshaka, and Nina sat in the third pew beside Tasha. Kareem watched as Pastor Rivers ascended the pulpit, accompanied by his ministers. Tall and distinguished, with dark skin, salt-and-pepper hair, and a regal air, he reminded Kareem of Idris Elba. He was tall, dark, and slim, with salt-and-pepper hair. Pastor Rivers looked regal and distinguished in a double-breasted grey suit.

Before beginning his sermon, Pastor Rivers scanned the congregation. "Would all of our visitors please stand?"

Kareem hesitated, then slowly rose to his feet, feeling the weight of every gaze upon him. Pastor Rivers smiled warmly. "Welcome to Agape Assembly. Would you like to introduce yourself to the congregation?"

Kareem glanced at Keith before speaking. "My best friend has been inviting me to church for years, and today felt like the right day to come."

"I hear you're a poet, son," Pastor Rivers said, his smile deepening. *He's obviously in on the proposal,* Kareem thought.

"Yes, Pastor, I am," he replied.

"I also heard you recited poems in church as a child. Would you be willing to share one with us today?"

Tshaka and Nina beamed as Kareem exited the pew and went to the pulpit, where the Pastor handed him the microphone.

Tasha and Maya exchanged curious glances, sensing something was happening.

Kareem cleared his throat. "I started writing poetry as a kid in church, though most of my work these days isn't exactly church-appropriate," he admitted, earning a few chuckles from the congregation. "But today, I'd like to dedicate this love poem to Keith and Tasha."

Keith stood and took Tasha's hand, guiding her toward the front of the church. "I love you so much," he whispered as tears glistened from her eyes, sensing that Keith was about to propose to her.

Kareem waited until they were standing at the front of the congregation and then began reciting the proposal poem that he had written for Keith called *Godsend:*

When did I know I loved you?
It was the moment I stopped referring to you as my girlfriend
and began to call you my Godsend
Because your love
has been such a blessing to me

I don't believe that we met by accident
Our first conversation was confirmation
that you were heaven-sent

Before I met you
I'd grown weary of sleeping with lust
And waking up to loneliness
So, one night
I kneeled on my knees
and prayed to God
asking him to please send me a woman to love

A woman who was loyal, supportive, and loving
Someone that I could pray with every night
That woman was you
because it felt like forever at first sight

A good woman is rare
and you're the embodiment of a Proverbs 31 woman
so I'm convinced that you're my answered prayer

Halfway through the poem, Kareem looked up at the church ceiling to prevent himself from becoming emotional and messing up the poem during Keith's proposal:

When did I know I loved you?
The moment I stopped referring to my ex-girlfriends as past mistakes
and started viewing them as lessons
Their mouths were multiple choice questions
And I kept selecting
the wrong one
until the day I discovered
the correct answer in your kiss

I've taken time to court you
I wanted you to know that I will always be here to support you
I made a promise to God
That I would cherish your heart
before kneeling on bended knee
And asking for your hand in marriage

When did I know I loved you?
When your name started to sound like a wedding bell
When I wanted you to be the woman who walked down the aisle
So, I could see your beautiful face underneath the wedding veil

The scriptures say
He who finds a wife
Finds a good thing
You've been the greatest blessing
to walk into my life
So, I pray that you accept this wedding ring

And if you accept my proposal
I promise never to treat you improperly
Because even as my wife
I know that heaven holds the patent for creating such a beautiful prototype
You are also God's property

All my life
I've searched for you
And now I've finally found you
I knew that I loved you
From The Moment
I first stared into your eyes
and my soul said I do

Will you marry me?

As Kareem finished reciting his poem, he saw tears streaming down Tasha's face. Her parents, who Keith had flown in from Alabama, made their way to the front of the church. Tasha ran to them, embracing them with a tight hug. Then, with tears still glistening, she turned to see Keith kneeling on one knee, holding out a ring and asking for her hand in marriage. Kareem stepped back and handed Keith the microphone to begin his proposal:

Natasha Aryn Jennings. From the first moment I saw you, I knew you were my perfect match. You've become my best friend, prayer partner, and bowling buddy. I love you so much that I even let you beat me in bowling once or twice this year.

The congregation erupted in laughter. Keith was a comedian, and a wedding proposal wouldn't be the same without him telling a few jokes.

I thank God every day for bringing you into my life, and I know my life would not be complete without you by my side. So, if you can tolerate my morning breath for the rest of your life, I'm asking if you'll become my wife. Natasha Aryn Harris. Will you marry me?

Keith slowly opened the black velvet box, revealing a sparkling ruby ring. Tasha smiled through her tears and nodded. "Yes," she said, "I'll marry you!!"

As Tasha and Keith embraced, the congregation erupted in cheers and applause. Across the aisle, Kareem saw Maya wiping away tears. He closed his eyes and took a deep breath, praying for the strength to resist his lustful desires and become a better man. Opening his eyes, Kareem felt a sense of peace. He knew it would take time and effort, but he was determined to earn Maya's forgiveness and make things right between them.

After the proposal, everyone congratulated the couple. As everyone returned to their seats, Pastor Rivers resumed the service, his voice booming with passion and conviction as he preached about the true meaning of love - agape love.

26

After church service, Tasha couldn't contain her excitement. "He put a ring on it," she gushed while showing her ring to Maya. "I'm so happy for you," Maya said while hugging her best friend. "You two were made for each other."

Keith's proposal was the most romantic and beautiful thing she'd ever seen. Maya couldn't hold back tears as she watched Keith propose to Tasha while Kareem recited a poem. She wanted to compliment Kareem on his poem, but her rational side remembered her mother's advice: *Guard your heart.*

Tasha invited Maya to join them for dinner, but Maya declined. She didn't want to see Kareem and had work to do on a grant for her foundation.

"Can you at least come with me to the bridal store on Tuesday to look at wedding dresses?" Tasha pouted. Maya agreed, and the two friends hugged. As Maya exited the church, she noticed a small group of women vying for Kareem's attention. The longer she looked at him in his navy blue Armani suit, the quicker her defenses began to crumble. *Why does he have to be so fine?* She thought.

Maya still loved Kareem but no longer wanted to be with a man who couldn't stay faithful. She'd seen many marriages fail because women assumed that their husbands cheating ways would *change* after they *exchanged* their wedding vows. She'd seen her mother console heartbroken married women in the church who realized the marriage *altar* did not *alter* their husbands unfaithful ways.

Over the next twenty minutes, people exited the church. Kareem went looking for Maya, but she was nowhere to be found. He was hoping she would give him a chance to apologize. *Would she forgive me for cheating? Would she give me another chance?* Kareem wasn't sure. But he did want to tell her that reading her book had changed his perspective on dating.

As he scanned the parking lot, searching for Maya, a hand on his shoulder made him turn around. Pastor Rivers was standing there. "Your proposal poem was beautiful," the Pastor said. Kareem gave him a firm handshake. "Thank you, Pastor Rivers. I haven't stepped inside a church in years, but the love and fellowship I felt in your church was real."

I'm looking forward to coming back soon." He paused for a moment. "I feel like I need to get right with God," he said sincerely.

Pastor Rivers warmly welcomed him to join them anytime. Kareem felt guilty for not attending *Agape Assembly* sooner. Kareem liked Pastor Rivers immediately. He noticed the Pastor still wore his wedding ring even though Maya had told him that her mother had passed from cancer years ago.

"Dope poem," Tahir said to Kareem after he finished speaking with the Pastor. "I liked the metaphors you used!" He flashed a beaming smile, revealing his perfectly white teeth. "Thanks, Tahir," Kareem said before embracing him in a brotherly hug. Kareem couldn't help but notice how tall and imposing Tahir was at only sixteen years old.

Kareem congratulated Tahir on his success with gospel rap. Tahir nodded and thanked him, giving credit to Keith's beats. The same woman in the wheelchair that he'd seen earlier wheeled up to Kareem. "That was a beautiful poem, young brother," she said with a warm smile, clapping her hands together. "I'm Sister Jones, Tahir's mom." Kareem crouched down to meet her eyes, smiling at her.

"You should be proud of your son, Tahir," Kareem said. "With so many rappers today glorifying violence, death, and the destruction of our community, he uses positive lyrics to inspire people."

"I'm proud of him," Sister Jones replied as Tahir pulled her in for a side hug. "I hope you'll join us for service again," she said warmly. "Alright, let's go, son. Our bus is coming."

Kareem made a mental note that Sister Jones was in her wheelchair taking the bus home after church. *The church didn't have a van?* Watching Tahir walk to the bus stop with his mom reminded him of his childhood with his grandmother.

Kareem watched everyone slowly file out of the church. Tshaka and Nina had their arms linked with Keith and Tasha as they celebrated the occasion. The moment was bittersweet. Kareem was disappointed that he didn't reconcile with Maya but was happy that Keith and Tasha were engaged. Kareem joined his friends, and they all went out for dinner.

27

The Tollers

The next day, Kareem pulled up to the North Oakland house he'd renovated. After months of manual labor, it was finally ready for potential buyers. The Bay Area real estate market has been booming lately, with high demand for housing and limited availability. So, when the Tollers – an elderly couple hoping to become first-time homeowners - contacted Kareem about purchasing a property, he agreed to show them the home before it went on the market.

Kareem sat in his car, watching a silver sedan pull into the driveway. A couple emerged, both with salt-and-pepper hair. Mr. Toller's black Kangol cap and turtleneck were perfectly coordinated with Mrs. Toller's blazer and black slacks. They looked familiar, but Kareem couldn't remember where he had seen them before. He greeted the couple and handed them a property brochure and business card.

"We're excited to see the house," Mr. Toller exclaimed, massaging his wife's hand.

"Let me show you the interior," Kareem suggested, ushering the Tollers into the newly painted home. Maya had tastefully decorated it in neutral colors, maximizing the natural light.

"This home is so beautiful," Mrs. Toller exclaimed, covering her mouth with her hands.

"This three-bedroom house features a gourmet kitchen with premium quartz countertops, top-of-the-line cabinets, two newly remodeled bathrooms, and a large backyard. You get all these perks in a quiet, desirable neighborhood just minutes away from the Oakland Zoo, Downtown Oakland, and Lake Merritt," Kareem said.

"I love that we wouldn't be too far from the lake, Daryl," Mrs. Toller said while admiring the backyard. "We could still go on our walks."

Suddenly, Kareem remembered where he had seen them before.

"You mentioned Lake Merritt! I think I saw you both there a while ago. You were wearing matching blue sweatsuits!"

"That was us," Daryl beamed. "We walk the lake at least twice a week."

How likely was it that he would sell a home to the same couple he and Maya saw on their first date? Was this a coincidence, or was God sending him a sign?

Denise leaned in. "Why didn't you say hello?"

Kareem looked away, his eyes fixed on the floor. "I was on a date with my ex-girlfriend."

"Ex-girlfriend? If you don't mind me asking, what happened?"

Mr. Toller interrupted, placing a hand on his wife's shoulder. "Denise, that's none of your business." He turned toward Kareem. "I'm sorry, Kareem," he said apologetically. "My wife is nosy."

Denise ignored her husband, placing a hand on her hip while awaiting an answer.

"I don't mind telling you," Kareem admitted, feeling a lump in his throat. He told the Tollers how Maya was celibate and wanted to wait until marriage before having sex and how he hadn't felt the same way. He confessed to making the mistake of cheating on her with other women and how he hadn't spoken to her since.

"My grandmother always told me that if you give a person too much too soon, they'll end up falling in love with your hand and not your heart," Mrs. Toller said.

"That's a deep quote, Mrs. Toller," Kareem replied. "I've never heard that before."

"Do you love her, son?" Mr. Toller asked, his voice filled with concern.

Kareem's thoughts drifted to Maya. She was the first woman he had ever met who stirred something deep inside him. He could picture himself coming home to her for the rest of his life.

"I do! I've never met a woman like her."

Mr. Toller smiled. "Send her a bouquet of flowers."

Denise shook her head. "Flowers are nice, but if you want to convey your feelings, send her a handwritten letter. Don't hold back your feelings either."

"How long have you two been married?" Kareem asked.

"Thirty-six years," Mr. Toller beamed, turning to his wife. "It hasn't been perfect, but it's been worth it."

"My two best friends just got engaged," Kareem said. "If you don't mind me asking, what's the secret to your marriage?"

They both turned to each other, smiling. "We started as best friends," Mr. Toller added, reaching for his wife's hand. Then, he looked directly into Kareem's eyes. "Don't marry the woman you can live with; marry the woman you can't live without. Cherish the woman whose friendship and love bring out the best in you. And remember, change is the first step toward getting a second chance."

Those words resonated with Kareem. *Change is the first step toward a second chance.* Kareem was working on becoming a better man.

"I love this house. I'm just not sure we'll be able to match the other offers," Mr. Toller said, a look of concern crossing his face.

Kareem understood. The Bay Area housing market was brutal. Many African Americans were being priced out due to rising costs and gentrification.

"The market is very competitive," Kareem said. "I sold a similar home in this neighborhood for over a million dollars last year. How much would your preemptive offer be?"

Mr. Toller sighed. "We were preapproved for an $800,000 loan with a locked-in 6% interest rate."

Kareem knew that the Tollers would be overbid. He did the math in his head. He purchased the home for $400,000 cash, and after all the expenses on the amenities, holding costs, and eventual closing costs, he would still make a small profit if he sold the home to the Tollers.

Mrs. Toller anxiously wrung her hands and took a deep breath. "I'm putting my trust in God that we will get this home."

Kareem was convinced God had called him to sell this home to the Tollers. Money didn't matter anymore. He wanted to put this couple in their dream home.

"Welcome home, Mr. and Mrs. Toller," Kareem said, pulling out the deed from his sleek attaché case and placing it in their hands. Mrs. Toller's wide eyes scanned the deed with disbelief as she clutched it tightly. "I'm the owner of this home," Kareem admitted. "I'll have my attorney draw up the purchase agreement this afternoon. If everything falls through, I'll sell you this home for your loan amount and pay the closing cost myself."

Mrs. Toller's brown hand trembled against the cool granite kitchen countertop. With her other arm raised to the sky, tears streaming down her exhausted face, she shouted a loud prayer of thanks.

Kareem felt pure joy as he watched the couple celebrate in the kitchen. He'd sold homes worth millions and celebrated those successes, but nothing had ever made him feel as fulfilled as watching the Tollers rejoice in their new home. He wished Maya was there with him to witness their celebration.

Kareem took a picture with the couple and shared it on Instagram. He tagged Maya in the post, hoping it would get her attention:

> I went on a special date with Maya Rivers a few months ago. While on a gondola ride, we saw this beautiful couple, The Tollers, holding hands at Lake Merritt. Today, I was blessed to sell them a house that Maya helped renovate. I wish she were here to celebrate with me. #MissingMaya

Maya scrolled through her social media feed and froze when she saw Kareem's post. She zoomed in on the photo and saw that it was the same couple they saw at Lake Merritt on their first date.

What were the odds of the same couple buying a home she and Kareem helped renovate? She felt her eyes welling up as she stared at Kareem beside the couple. Maya had to admit that she missed him also.

28

The Blade

Vincent arrived in Oakland after four days on the road. He'd only stopped once - at a rest stop - to sleep before continuing his drive. He knew it was only a matter of time before local authorities discovered Lisa's body, and once they did, the FBI would be on his trail.

When Vincent reached Oakland, he stole a California license plate from another SUV to replace the ones on Lisa's Navigator. If everything went as planned, he would already be off the grid when the owner reported the plates stolen.

Dressed in a military flak jacket and combat boots, Vincent checked into a cheap hotel near the airport, paying cash for the room. He didn't want to leave any paper trail. Around midnight, he headed down International Boulevard in East Oakland, an area infamously known as *The Blade,* where thousands of underage girls are trafficked each year. He was on the hunt, and Oakland was notorious for sex trafficking. While deployed in Afghanistan, he remembered seeing a news report about Oakland police officers being sued for soliciting a teenage prostitute and forcing her to have sex.

Driving along International Boulevard, he spotted at least a dozen streetwalkers congregating around a single intersection. One brown-skinned, pretty, and petite young girl stood off by herself. She wore a blue miniskirt with a matching blouse and stilettos. Vincent parked and watched her from the SUV in silence, his steel-blue eyes following her every move as she waved at passing cars. The longer he stared, the more his bloodlust grew. He scanned the street for a few more minutes, ensuring no police were in sight, before making his move.

I'll abduct her, he decided.

He pulled his SUV up to the curb where the girl stood and rolled down the window.

"Hey, baby, you wanna date?" she asked, bending over and giving him a clear view of her hardened nipples through her blouse.

"Sure! I'm on leave and looking for a good time," Vincent replied, flashing a smile and pulling out a thick roll of twenties.

"A military man," she noted, eyeing his green combat fatigues. "A man in uniform is so sexy."

Vincent asked how much it would cost, still scanning the street. She answered seductively, and he agreed to pay a hundred dollars for everything. He unlocked the passenger door, and she climbed inside. Vincent checked his surroundings one last time before driving away.

"I have a place," the girl said, grinning. "A vacant house nearby." This was her third trick in two hours, but she always carried her phone for safety.

"My name's Janelle," she said, trying to make small talk.

"My name is Chris," he lied. Vincent followed her directions to the back of the house, where she switched on a dim bedroom light.

"Turn off your phone," Vincent ordered. "I don't like being disturbed when you're on my time."

Janelle hesitated, explaining that she always kept her phone on for protection. Then she pulled out a condom.

"You won't be needing that. I don't want to have sex with you," Vincent said with a mischievous smile.

Janelle frowned. "You don't want to have sex with me? Then what do you want?"

"I want to see you suffer," he snarled.

In an instant, Vincent grabbed her from behind, applying a rear chokehold to cut off oxygen to her brain. Janelle lost her balance and quickly felt herself fading as his bicep tightened around her neck. He released her seconds later, letting her collapse to the floor, gasping for air.

Tears welled in her eyes, and she began to whimper. There was something evil in Vincent's gaze that chilled her. Vincent drew a large Bowie knife and slashed her miniskirt. Janelle burst into terrified sobs.

"Please don't hurt me…" she pleaded.

Vincent gave a cruel smile and pulled out a ball gag.

"Oh… I intend to do more than hurt you," he sneered. "Much more!"

29

Flowers and Forgiveness

Maya smiled as she watched Tasha twirl in the white wedding dress she'd chosen. Tasha looked radiant. Angelic. Her skin glowed, and her white teeth gleamed like pearls against her warm brown complexion.

"You look beautiful, Tasha," Maya said. "Your wedding is going to be amazing!"

Maya had always admired Keith and Tasha's relationship. The two had been inseparable since they first met at church years ago.

"I'm excited, too," Tasha said, trembling with anticipation. She turned to the mirror, admiring herself. "Ever since I was a little girl in Alabama, I've dreamed of getting married. And now, I'm finally going to be Mrs. Hicks."

"The institution of marriage is beautiful," Maya said. "Knowing that God has handpicked someone to be your closest friend and partner for life—it's a blessing."

Tasha nodded in agreement. "And that poem Kareem recited during the proposal? That was beautiful."

"Girl, I was shocked when I saw him walk into the church," Maya said with a laugh. "And when he got up to say that poem, I just knew something was up!" She chuckled. "My father was in on it, too!"

Then, Maya's laughter faded. Her voice softened. "It was beautiful," she said, lowering her head.

Tasha immediately noticed the shift in her friend's demeanor. The usual brightness in Maya's eyes had been replaced with sadness. Tasha sat beside her, still wearing the wedding dress, and wrapped an arm around her shoulder.

"What's wrong, Maya? Please, tell me."

Maya sighed. "The whole breakup with Kareem," she admitted. "I thought he was the one."

"Girl, you know doggone well Kareem loves you."

Maya frowned. "If he loved me, he wouldn't have cheated on me with Leah Banks."

Tasha's face hardened. "I still can't believe that Heffa had the audacity to approach you in church and brag about sleeping with Kareem. In the Lord's house, of all places!"

"Remember when we saw her at Yoshi's?" Tasha grimaced. "She was doing too much!"

"I was raised differently," Maya said with a shrug. "My mama made me wear a satin slip and a skirt below the knee to church."

Tasha clapped her hands and laughed. "Same here, girl!"

Maya exhaled. "I'm not the type to use my body to seduce a man, either. But maybe that's what Kareem likes."

Maya had been avoiding talking about her breakup, but now, anger bubbled to the surface. "Kareem also slept with some woman in Atlanta!"

Tasha shook her head. "He knows he messed up. When we went to dinner on Sunday, he said he regretted it." She paused. "He also said that Leah is crazy."

"Leah is crazy!" Maya replied. "She stabbed this girl back in High School who she saw talking to her boyfriend.

"What?!" Tasha gasped.

"Bishop Banks had to pull some serious strings to keep her out of juvie," Maya continued. "He hired a high-profile attorney and paid off the victim's family. Then, he sent her to some fancy boarding school."

"Keith never told me any of that!" Tasha shook her head in disbelief.

"Keith never went to our school, so he wouldn't know. Plus, it was kept under wraps because of who Leah's father is," Maya said. "This is my first time seeing her since we were teenagers."

Maya took a deep breath. "Women make the mistake of thinking we can change a man. But no matter how good you are, you'll never be enough for a man not ready to commit."

"I think Kareem is ready," Tasha said.

Maya looked at her skeptically. "What makes you think that?"

"Sunday after church, we all went out to eat—me, Keith, Tshaka, Nina, and Kareem. And girl, Kareem wouldn't even eat!" Tasha shook her head. "I have never known that man to turn down food. Then, get this—he told us he's on a seven-day fast."

Maya's eyebrows lifted. "Kareem? Fasting?"

"Right? I didn't even know he knew what fasting was!" Tasha laughed. "And he wouldn't shut up about your book."

Maya blinked in surprise. "My book?"

"Girl, he kept going on about how it changed his perspective on dating and marriage."

Maya was stunned. "Are you serious?"

"Mmm-hmm," Tasha smirked. "And he said he's coming back to church on Sunday." Tasha squeezed Maya's hand. "The Bible says to pray without ceasing. Just pray on it, girl. If anyone can change a man, God can."

***

When Maya got home, her father greeted her in the living room.

"Something came for you today," he said, nodding toward the kitchen table.

A beautiful bouquet of two dozen long-stemmed roses sat there. Maya read the card attached to the flowers:

> Maya, the worst mistake I ever made was cheating on you. I messed up, and I apologize. Please forgive me. I miss you so much! I read your book, and I'm focused on getting right with God. If you never talk to me again, I want to thank you for helping make me a better man.

Maya placed the card on the kitchen table. *He can send me all the flowers he wants, but I'm not forgiving him!*

Even the thought of him kissing Leah Banks made her stomach turn. She asked God for the grace to forgive Kareem, but her anger was still raw.

Pastor Rivers watched his daughter closely. "What's wrong, Maya?" he asked, his voice filled with concern.

"Kareem is what's wrong," she said, shaking her head. "He slept with two different women while he was dating me. We broke up because he said that he was tired of being celibate. Now he's saying that he wants to get right with God. I don't know if I can trust him."

Her father sighed. "Well, he sounds sincere in the card."

Maya looked at the card and then gazed at her father. "Daddy, did you read my card?" Pastor Rivers held up his hands in a defensive stance. "I thought the flowers were for me," he laughed. Maya playfully shook her fist at her father.

"Maya, you don't have to trust him, but you must let go of your anger and forgive him. Forgiveness doesn't change the past; it changes the future. And just because you forgive him doesn't mean you have to rebuild a relationship. Be forgiving, but don't be a fool."

"I know, Daddy, but that's easier said than done. I want to forgive Kareem, but he hurt me. I thought he was different from the rest of these triflin' men in Oakland, but he isn't."

"We can't ask God for forgiveness if we're unwilling to extend it to others. No man is perfect, Maya. We're all flawed. If you love someone, you have to look past their mistakes to build a future together."

Maya hesitated. "You and Mama set the standard for what I want in a relationship. You never cheated on her."

Her father took a deep breath. "Maya... our relationship wasn't always perfect."

She frowned. "What are you saying?"

He lowered his head. "I had an affair."

Maya's eyes widened in shock. "What?"

"It happened when your mother was running for Oakland city council," he admitted. "She was so busy with her campaign that I felt neglected. I had an affair with a co-worker. She found out and threatened to file for divorce."

Maya's mouth dropped open. "Mama never told me about that!" she said in disbelief.

"This happened before you were born," her father replied, his voice heavy with regret. "I was so caught up in my anger and resentment towards your mother and what was *wrong* in our marriage that I failed to realize what was *wrong* with me. I ended the affair, and we attended marriage counseling with a Christian pastor."

The Pastor stood up and began to pace the floor. "During counseling, I learned I needed to quit being self-centered and egotistical. I learned about *Agape* love, and to truly love her, I needed to accept God and love her as Christ loved the church. Eventually, your mom forgave my infidelities. We renewed our vows, and you were born," he smiled. "I never desired another woman again, and we grew closer our entire marriage."

"If your mother hadn't forgiven me...you wouldn't be here right now," Pastor Rivers said while pointing at Maya. "God still loves us despite our mistakes, and we must learn to forgive even those we don't think deserve it," he continued.

"Mama used to say the past is just something to reflect on, not somewhere to stay," Maya recalled.

"You are your mother's daughter," he laughed. You are stubborn just like her but also beautiful, brilliant, and amazing."

Maya watched her father's eyes turn misty. "She was the strongest woman I've ever known. She fought cancer with every breath that she had. Not a minute goes by that I don't miss her." Maya stood up and hugged her father.

Pastor Rivers turned to walk towards his study. Before he could leave, Maya's phone screen lit up with a breaking news alert. Her scream stopped him in his tracks.

"Oh, my God!" Maya screamed, causing her father to rush back. He saw Maya covering her mouth in shock as she held up her phone for him to see.

"Look!" She gasped. "I just got a news alert. A young girl was murdered in East Oakland, just a few blocks from the church!"

30

Candlelight Vigil

Kareem sank into the plush leather of his oversized office chair and loosened his tie. He swiveled around to look at the Oakland skyline through the high-rise windows. His real estate firm occupied the top floor of a downtown building, and he was working late to close a few deals. His receptionist had already gone home.

A news alert buzzed on his smartwatch. He glanced at it and opened a local news app on his phone.

> "This is KRON4 News. Police made a gruesome discovery: the body of a 17-year-old girl was found murdered inside a vacant home in East Oakland last night."

Kareem watched in horror as the reporter described how the victim had been killed—multiple stab wounds, with a ball gag still lodged in her throat. He felt a deep sense of sadness as he watched. He thought of Maya and how passionate she'd always been about helping at-risk girls.

He recognized the area shown on the broadcast; the victim's body had been found only a few blocks from *Agape* Church. Checking social media, he saw that a candlelight vigil was scheduled near the crime scene at sunset. Kareem decided he would attend to pay his respects.

When he arrived, he parked a block away from where about a dozen people had gathered, many leaving flowers and cards. He soon locked eyes with a young woman holding a small child standing by herself. Her face was a mask of grief and shock.

Kareem approached her. "Did you know the victim?" he asked softly.

"Yes, her name was Janelle," the girl sobbed. "She was my best friend and neighbor. She even watched my son a few times. She was the nicest person you'd ever meet," she added, wiping tears from her cheeks. "She'd give you the shirt off her back."

Nearby, someone mentioned Janelle had been trafficked on "The Blade." He asked if this was true, and her friend confirmed Janelle had been forced into prostitution by a local pimp and had also suffered sexual assault during childhood. Hearing Janelle's life story was heartbreaking.

Kareem studied the young mother. She was beautiful. Although she was dressed conservatively, he couldn't help but notice her curvy figure and worried she might also be caught up in life on the streets. Too many young girls in Oakland had fallen victim to *The Blade*.

"Thank you for telling me Janelle's story," Kareem said gently. "I'm going to pay for her funeral expenses and help raise awareness." He knew which poem he wanted to recite at the upcoming Gospel Fest.

The young girl sniffed and looked up at him with red eyes. She told Kareem that she had been looking for a place to stay but was having difficulty finding a sitter for her son. Kareem's eyes lit up at the chance to help.

"I know someone who can help," he said, trying to offer comfort. "She's starting an organization for young women and is passionate about social justice."

Kareem pulled out his phone and dialed Maya's number. He hadn't spoken to her since they broke up but didn't hesitate. After a few rings, Maya answered.

"Hello, Maya. I hope I'm not disturbing you."

"Not at all, Kareem," she replied. "I was just about to call and thank you for the flowers."

He paused, relieved she was no longer avoiding him. "I'm at a candlelight vigil for the girl who was murdered in East Oakland."

"Oh my God," Maya said. "I saw that on the news. It's heartbreaking."

Kareem sighed. "Her best friend needs a place to stay. Can I send her your way?"

"Absolutely," Maya answered, then gave him her phone number. "Have her call me tonight."

"Thanks, Maya. I'll get back to you in a few."

Kareem hung up and handed the young woman a slip of paper with Maya's number. "By the way, what's your name?" he asked.

"My name is Alexis," she said, shaking his hand. "Alexis Taylor."

31

Gospel Fest

The crowd began arriving for the Gospel Fest early in the evening. In addition to thousands of church members, many families brought sick and ailing relatives, hoping for a healing miracle from Bishop Banks. Around 6:00 p.m., Bishop Banks arrived in a limousine.

Numerous gospel singers and choirs were backstage, preparing to perform classic and contemporary gospel pieces. Kareem stood backstage with Keith and Tahir. "This place is packed!" Kareem caught a glimpse of Maya backstage. He saw her on her knees, praying before her performance.

Leah sat in the first row. She turned around and was surprised to see the same girl she had seen walking into her father's office a while back, sitting directly behind her. The young girl was no longer wearing cheap leggings. Now, she was dressed in a stylish outfit. *She's upgraded her style,* Leah thought to herself. *Good for her.*

Leah frowned when the hostess announced Maya Rivers would be performing first. She glared at Maya and crossed her arms as Maya stepped onto the stage in a shimmering gold dress and opened her mouth to sing *Call on God.* When Maya finished, the audience rose to their feet in thunderous applause.

The music stopped, and the host approached the microphone to introduce Tahir. Tahir took the stage and performed his powerful rap song, "You're Gonna Make It." The congregation sang along with the hook:

I know it's hard with the drama life brings
But with God, you can do all things
When times get tough
And you feel like you can't take it
Have faith
Because You're Gonna Make It

Tahir's performance received loud applause. The song was so inspirational that many people began chanting, *You're Gonna Make It*, throughout the church. After a few moments, Kareem slowly approached the microphone to address the crowd. He waited until there was complete silence before speaking.

"The other day, a young girl was found murdered in East Oakland. As men, we must love and protect our women rather than be predators. We need to pray for our women rather than prey on our women. So, I dedicate this poem to Janelle, the young woman who was killed:

Janelle grew up with no one to love her
She was raised by an abusive mother
Grew up with no family stability
Her father was locked up in a prison facility

At the age of twelve
She met a pimp
Who told her that she was too pretty
To have sex with boys for free
He said she should charge them a fee

The pimp became her father figure
She smiled whenever he called her cute
But what she didn't realize was that he
Grooming her to become a prostitute.

The pimp's charisma and charm
Turned to death threats and bodily harm
He told Janelle that she would have to sell her body for sex
To pay off her debts

Her childhood was tragic
Her pimp was psychopathic
Using teenage girls as slaves for sex traffic

Alexis listened to Kareem perform, and tears welled in her eyes. She felt as if he were speaking directly to her. Leah looked at the girl crying behind her. *What is this bitch crying for?* she asked herself. *She probably wants Kareem!*

A pimp will tell a teenage girl
That she's sitting on a gold mine
But it's my job as a poet to remind you
That your body is divine
Your soul is more precious than gold
It's time to stop casting your pearls to the swine

After Kareem ended his poem, the congregation erupted in applause. The words touched Alexis, moving her to tears; a woman beside her handed her a tissue.

Then, Bishop Banks took to the stage and was welcomed with rousing applause. He acknowledged Kareem for his powerful poem. Even though the message unsettled him, Bishop Banks used it to his advantage. "You know, Kareem used to recite poems in *my church*. I'm so proud of him," he said, flashing his signature smile.

Things have changed since then. Bishop Banks was now the world's most popular prosperity preacher. He was worth millions, thanks to revenue from his books, speaking engagements, television broadcasts, and sales of his healing oils.

Bishop Banks began his sermon slowly, clearly articulating each word. "Church, turn with me to James, chapter five, verses fourteen and fifteen," he directed. "Once you find the scripture, give me an Amen."

"Amen!" one member shouted. The bishop continued, "The Bible says, 'Is anyone among you sick? Let him call for the church elders, and let them pray over him, anointing him with oil in the name of the Lord. And the prayer of faith will save the one who is sick, and the Lord will raise him up.'"

Bishop Banks's voice boomed over the congregation as he called for the sick to come forward. Kareem watched as droves of people shuffled to the pulpit to receive Bishop Banks's anointing oil. *Sheep*, he thought. He rolled his eyes as the spectacle unfolded.

When the ceremony ended, Bishop Banks wiped the sweat from his brow. "Now, the Lord has told me to tell you: If you sow into this ministry, God will bless you abundantly! If you sow a seed offering of a hundred dollars, He will bless you with double that amount!" His baritone voice boomed throughout the church. "Turn to the person next to you and say, 'Invest and be blessed.'"

The congregation repeated, "Invest and be blessed."

The Gospel Fest couldn't end soon enough for Kareem. Bishop Banks's sermon was about money, focusing on tithes rather than faith. Finally, as the event concluded, Kareem rushed into the parking lot, hoping to find Maya. Instead, he was startled to see a familiar face.

"Thank you for that poem, Kareem," said Alexis Taylor, the woman he had met at the candlelight vigil.

"Alexis, we meet again! I didn't know you'd be here tonight. Do you attend Holy Tabernacle?" Kareem asked.

"Yes, but I don't know how much longer I'll be attending this church," Alexis said, glancing at the ground before meeting his gaze. "I just wanted to tell you that your poem touched me like no poem ever has. It helped me realize my worth as a woman."

Leah's blood boiled as she watched Alexis talking to Kareem. *This bitch is trying to flirt with Kareem.* Rage surged through her veins like wildfire, threatening to consume what little self-control she had left. She crept closer, attempting to eavesdrop on their discussion. When she couldn't hear, she decided to intrude on their conversation.

"Hi, Kareem," Leah said, reaching for a hug and rudely interrupting his conversation with Alexis.

Kareem pulled away. "Excuse me, Leah, but I'm talking to Alexis," he said abruptly. "Why are you here?"

Leah stepped back, her face twisting in anger. Her eyes burned with rage and humiliation as she shot daggers at Alexis. Before she could respond, her father, Bishop Banks, approached.

"Kareem Simmons! It's good to see you after all these years!" Bishop Banks said, extending his hand towards Kareem. Kareem smirked and shook his hand reluctantly. The bishop's gaze shifted quickly to Alexis, suspicious about what she was talking to Kareem about.

"Leah tells me you've been very successful with your real estate ventures," he said.

Kareem nodded. "Yes, I have. Business has been good."

"God is blessing you financially. I hope you remember to bless the Lord by tithing. You still believe in paying your tithes, right?" Bishop Banks asked, sounding like he was expecting a donation from Kareem.

"The Bible also says to build your treasures in heaven, not on earth. And judging from the size of your watch and rings, you've amassed quite a fortune here." Kareem replied.

Alexis giggled. The bishop's face darkened with rage, his eyes flashing. He tugged at the lapels of his suit jacket and tapped the diamond-encrusted gold Rolex on his wrist. "A man of God deserves to be blessed," he said through gritted teeth.

"Jesus rode on a donkey. He didn't drive a Bentley," Kareem shot back. "I have a problem with prosperity pastors who cruise past homeless people in luxury cars on their way to multimillion-dollar homes in the hills."

Resisting the urge to say more, Kareem turned and walked away with Alexis, shaking his head. Bishop Banks, fuming, walked off to greet some of his clergy.

"C'mon, Alexis. I want to introduce you to Maya." Kareem spotted Pastor Rivers standing near a car with Maya.

Pastor Rivers turned and smiled warmly. "Good to see you again, Kareem! That was a powerful poem you performed tonight," he said, extending his hand.

"Thank you, Pastor," Kareem said, shaking his hand. Unlike Bishop Banks, he respected Pastor Rivers as a true man of God.

"Thank you for that poem. Kareem," Maya said. "I'm glad to hear your poetry is becoming more spiritual." Kareem bowed in appreciation.

"You've inspired me to become a better man, Maya," Kareem confessed. "Before I met you, I didn't realize how many Black women have endured psychological, physical, and sexual abuse."

Kareem introduced Alexis to Maya. They shook hands warmly and then walked away to talk in private.

From ten feet away, Leah stood watching. Her gaze followed Kareem's every move, then flickered to Maya and Alexis, who had embraced and begun speaking in hushed tones. Leah's eyes narrowed. *What are those two talking about?* she wondered. Whatever it was, Leah wanted Maya out of the picture as soon as possible.

32

Flawed

The next day, Kareem arrived early at Keith's recording studio. He had stayed up most of the night writing a poem called *Flawed* that he wanted Maya to hear. Keith began setting the words to music, but Kareem decided against using any instrumentation. He wanted Maya to catch every word.

When Maya and Tasha arrived, Kareem opened the door with a wide grin. "Thanks for coming," he said. "I've written a poem called *Flawed* that I want to spit for you."

Maya giggled while Tasha leaned in, smirking. "Good morning, Kareem," Tasha chuckled. "You're definitely flawed, my brotha! You need Jeeeeesus!" She looked him up and down. "And what's up with that extra 'shmedium' shirt? Are you trying to show off your little muscles?"

Everyone laughed, including Kareem. He wore the snug shirt because Maya liked how it emphasized his arms and chest.

"You look beautiful," he said to Maya, his voice deep and soothing. She smiled at his compliment but stayed cautious. Kareem was a charmer, and she was still guarded about opening her heart to him.

"What's up with you and that word *spit*, Kareem?" Maya asked, laughing. It was the first time he'd heard her laugh in weeks, and it reminded him how much he missed it.

"I'm being brutally honest in this poem," Kareem admitted.

"An honesty poem, huh? This should be interesting," Maya said.
"OK, spit it."

Kareem stepped into the recording booth, and Keith began
recording:

Hurt people, hurt people
And for most of my life
I've been one of the walking wounded

My parents were murdered when I was a baby
My grandmother died in my arms
I grew up believing
that anyone who loved me
would eventually leave me

So, I closed my heart
And used my tongue as a crowbar
to pry open the thighs of women

I had no direction in life
I was lost in a land called lust
Wandering down a dangerous path of promiscuity
Navigated by a broken compass of casual sex

I've struggled with lust
I had to learn that being a man
requires developing the strength and discipline
to manhandle temptation

I subconsciously sabotaged our relationship
Because being in love scared me
I always felt that
Love was something I should avoid
but now my heart feels like an empty void

without the woman I love

I'm flawed
Instead of sleeping with women
I should have called on God
All I can do now is pray
Work towards becoming a better man every day

Kareem's voice trembled, and he choked up on certain lines as he continued the poem. Maya looked into his eyes as he poured out his heart in the booth, and she could tell he meant every word. His vulnerability moved her. She had sworn never to let his words affect her again, but seeing him so raw and honest, she felt tears welling up. He continued:

Hurt people hurt people
And for most of my life
I've been one of the walking wounded

So, I poured my pain into my pen
And I wrote this poem using the tears from my eyes
I apologize
Maya,
I apologize

After listening to Kareem's poem, Maya knew he was sincere. She dabbed her eyes with a tissue and silently whispered, *"I forgive you, Kareem. I release all anger toward you."* She stepped into the booth and felt Kareem's strong arms wrap around her waist in a tight hug. Tears flowed again as he pulled away and gently held her hands, gazing into her eyes.

"Maya, I love you. I've loved you from the moment you stepped into this recording studio," Kareem said, pausing. "I apologize for cheating on you. You didn't deserve that," he added softly. "I'm asking for your forgiveness. I want us to attend church together. I want to get right with God and become a better man."

Maya wiped away her tears and looked into his eyes. "Kareem, I love you too! I've missed you so much," she said, gently stroking his cheek.

"I've missed you too," he replied. The two kissed deeply. Kareem thought he would never reconcile with Maya after weeks of being separated, and now she had forgiven him.

"As far as your poem, we're all flawed. None of us are perfect," Keith said. "Tasha complains about me snoring all the time." Tasha punched him lightly on the shoulder, and everyone laughed.

"Who would've thought the same studio where y'all met months ago would be the place where you finally admit you love each other," Tasha said.

"Don't mess this up," Keith warned.

"Don't worry, fam," Kareem assured him. "I won't do anything to lose my woman again."

Kareem felt like a teenager with a high school crush. It felt so good to have Maya back in his life. They agreed to meet up for lunch at Vegan Mob on Grand Street, across from Lake Merritt.

***

Kareem drove back to his condo to shower and change clothes. His heart felt good for the first time in weeks - Maya was back. As he dried off, he closed his eyes and started singing an old-school song, *Forever My Lady,* by Jodeci. Then he stepped into a pair of jeans, pulled on a clean T-shirt, and began moisturizing his beard.

Suddenly, he heard loud banging on his front door, followed by an unsettling silence.

Bang! Bang! Bang!

The noise startled him. Who the hell is banging on my door? Lobby security had strict orders not to allow anyone to come up without his permission. He tiptoed toward the entrance and peeked through the peephole—but it was covered. Then the banging started again.

Bang! Bang! Bang!

Kareem jumped away from the door, his heart thudding against his chest. This time, the banging was louder, more urgent, more forceful.

Bang! Bang! Bang! Bang!

Sensing danger, he ran to his bookshelf and retrieved the gun he kept hidden inside a hollow storage book. He had purchased a Beretta 92 Compact a few years earlier after a neighbor fell victim to a home invasion robbery. He kept the bullets locked and loaded in the chamber.

Bang! Bang! Bang! Bang! BANG!!!!

Gun in hand, Kareem crept back toward the door, heart hammering. He yelled, "Who is it?" keeping his weapon pointed at the door. The banging stopped. "Who the fuck is at my door?" he asked again, muscles tense and ready to shoot. The banging stopped.

A minute passed before he cautiously opened the door, gun drawn, and peered down the hallway. No one was there. He walked to the elevator; still nothing.

Kareem called the lobby, but security didn't answer. *Damn it!* He swore under his breath, hanging up. Quickly pulling on a pair of black jeans, a black hoodie, and Air Jordans, he grabbed his gun and raced down the stairs. When he reached the lobby, the security officer was nowhere to be found.

I'll have to talk to building management about this, he thought, hurrying out the door. For now, he needed to meet Maya at Vegan Mob.

33

Confrontation

Leah sat in her Lexus across the street from Kareem's condo. Slumped low in the driver's seat, she peeked over the dashboard with binoculars, watching the front entrance like a sniper tracking a target. Kareem was in there—she knew it. His car hadn't moved. Yet, he wasn't answering her texts. He was avoiding her.

Kareem, can't you see we belong together? She crooned, making up lyrics to a song. Leah wondered why Kareem was avoiding her. *Hadn't I given him everything a man wants in a woman? Hadn't I made him scream in ecstasy that night at his condo?*

Leah thought back to the first time she was exposed to sex. She was just eight years old, lying in bed when she heard moans coming from her father's room. Curious, Leah got out of bed and saw the church secretary on her knees, giving him oral pleasure. Even though her father never married his secretary, he gave her money and lavish gifts. From that experience, Leah grew up believing that men only needed to be satisfied sexually for a woman to get whatever she desired.

As a teenager, Leah developed a pattern of explosive temper tantrums whenever she didn't get what she wanted. Over time, her outbursts got worse. One day, she stabbed a girl at school for talking to the same boy she had a crush on. After that incident, Leah was diagnosed with *High-Anger Rejection Sensitive Dysphoria* (RSD). Her therapist prescribed medication to help manage her condition, explaining that individuals with *High-Anger RSD* often experience uncontrollable outbursts when they feel hurt or rejected.

Her father, hoping to avoid triggering her rage, frequently gave in to her demands, buying her whatever she wanted. This led to Leah having a series of short-lived relationships that ended as soon as her boyfriend said something that upset her. But Kareem was different - he was her first crush, her first love, and the man she wanted to marry.

Every time Kareem ignored her call, it felt like a physical punch to her gut. Each rejection felt like a razor blade slicing her heart. She could hear Maya's laughter echoing in her mind as if she was taunting her. Leah's blood boiled with hatred at the thought of them kissing.

Suddenly, she saw Kareem's Mercedes pull out of the condo parking lot. She grabbed her oversized Gucci sunglasses from the dashboard, put them on, and followed him. When he parked at Vegan Mob, she also pulled over, preparing to confront him.

"Hello, Kareem," Leah purred, sashaying toward him in a dress accentuating her cleavage and flaunting a Cartier diamond Love Bracelet.

Kareem was already on edge from the earlier incident at his condo. His jaw tensed as he turned to face her. "Did you bang on my door earlier?" he asked, trying to stay composed.

"No!" Leah's palms began to sweat, and tension rose inside her. "Why haven't you called me back, Kareem? I thought we were friends." Kareem sighed, his patience wearing thin.

"Look, Leah, I'm not interested in you. I already have a girlfriend—a woman I love. We're about to go on a date."

"A date with who?" Leah demanded, crossing her arms, her jaw tight.

"A date with me," Maya said, appearing behind them, her eyes locked onto Leah's. Kareem wasn't sure how much of the conversation she had overheard.

Leah watched as Kareem's frown turned into a smile when Maya approached. He pulled her into a tight embrace and lifted her off the ground. "Hey, love," he murmured before kissing Maya on the lips.

Leah's face twisted with rage. "Are you serious? You're choosing this fat, basic bitch over me?" she spat venomously.

"Don't you ever disrespect my woman!" Kareem snapped.

"No, Kareem, I've got this!" Maya said firmly, pushing him aside. She narrowed her gaze and looked Leah directly in the eye. "Leah, where you messed up is thinking that the way to a man's heart is through his dick!" Maya said, piercing Leah with a hard stare. "You're the daughter of a pastor. You should try being *holy* instead of being a *ho*. And God made all this," Maya said as she ran her hands over her ample hips and thighs. "I'm a proud plus-size and don't need a BBL."

Leah was stunned because she'd scheduled a Brazilian Butt Lift appointment in Miami the following month.

"She's not worth it, baby," Kareem said, holding Maya back. "Leave us alone, Leah!" he shouted, the veins in his neck bulging. "This is my last warning!"

Leah looked Maya up and down with a death stare. She wasn't used to rejection. She always got what she wanted. Raw anger pulsed in Leah's chest. Her fingers twitched at the edge of her tote. She wanted to grab the knife inside and stab Maya to death. One quick motion and Maya would regret ever crossing her.

Instead, Leah glared at Maya and raised a freshly manicured index finger, slowly sliding it across her throat in a menacing, throat-slitting gesture. Then, with an angry scowl, she turned on her heel and stomped off.

Kareem turned to Maya, staring into her eyes. "I'm sorry you had to deal with that," he said softly, kissing her forehead.

Maya nestled into his chest and sighed. "It's OK," she murmured. "Let's go enjoy the movie."

34

Shadow Ops

Vincent gritted his teeth in rage and pulled his Oakland A's baseball cap low over his eyes as he watched Kareem and Maya walk away. He'd stalked Kareem for seven days, a silent shadow fueled by a thirst for revenge. He wanted to wait for the perfect time to kill the poet who'd slept with his wife.

Vincent had considered shooting him earlier at his condo when he'd heard him walking towards the door. He could've killed him with a single shot. But that would have been too merciful, too quick. Instead, Vincent wanted Kareem to break before he bled. He wanted Kareem to suffer a slow, agonizing death.

Today, a new plan took root as he followed Kareem to a vegan restaurant and watched him and his girlfriend argue with a fiery woman named Leah. After witnessing the argument, Vincent devised a new plan.

Kareem would die only after being forced to deal with the deaths of the people closest to him, the people whose deaths would devastate him the most.

Vincent smirked as he slowly slid his sunglasses onto his face and watched Leah walk away.

35

Kareem called Keith from his phone with the speaker on. "Bruh, Maya and I are about to go to the movies. Do you and Tasha want to join us?"

"I just booked a four-hour session today," Keith sighed. Some guy wants to record a Christian audiobook. We're free afterward, though."

"OK, Cool!" Kareem said. "Let's all get together tonight."

"Fam, the price for this wedding is no joke!" Keith grumbled over the phone. "Caterers, limos, hotel rooms, and the wedding photographer." Keith paused for a moment. "Hey Kareem, you have an iPhone. What do you think about taking some pictures at the wedding?"

Tasha cut Keith off immediately. "Kareem will not be using his iPhone to take our wedding photos! What's wrong with you?" Tasha asked. Kareem and Maya chuckled on the other end of the line.

"I'm just joking," Keith chuckled before speaking again. "Yeah, bruh, this wedding costs a lot, but Tasha is worth it. I couldn't imagine my life without her."

"Awwww....thanks, baby," Tasha said in the background.

"But baby, I didn't know the wedding would cost this much. Keith continued to whine. "Do we have to pay hundreds of dollars for a wedding cake? Can't we get Sister Myers to bake one for us? She made a delicious lemon cake last week at the church's bake sale!"

Tasha rolled her eyes. "Three hundred dollars is nothing for a wedding cake! Stop being cheap! And no, Sister Myers will not be baking our cake!" she said, barely containing a laugh. Kareem and Maya continued to laugh while listening in on the conversation.

"Ay Keith, don't trip about the wedding cost because I'm paying for everything!" Kareem announced. "And I'm paying for your honeymoon also. Go anywhere you both want."

The phone went silent, and Maya stared at Kareem in complete surprise. "Are you serious, bruh?" Keith asked, still in shock. "Man, thanks, Kareem," he finally managed to say.

"No, thank you, Keith! You're my best friend and brother. And because of both of you, I found the love of my life. Paying for your wedding is the least I can do. Let's meet for dinner after the movie," Kareem suggested.

"That sounds good, bruh. I hope you two enjoy the movie, and thank you!" Keith said before ending the phone conversation.

Maya reached across the center console and held Kareem's hand while he was driving. "That was very generous of you, "she said, kissing his fingers in response.

"Kareem, can I tell you something?"

"Of course," he replied.

"Your grandmother did an incredible job raising you." Kareem reached for her hand and kissed it as he drove to the movie theatre. He smiled and was happy that the woman he loved was back in his life.

36

A Surprise Session

Vincent pulled his car into the parking lot of *Inspirational Sounds* Recording Studio. He scanned the exterior and spotted a surveillance camera near the entrance - exactly what he expected, given the studio's website boasted about its expensive recording gear. Although Vincent hadn't done thorough surveillance of the building, he was sure there would also be cameras inside. He walked toward the door, pulling the brim of his Oakland A's cap low, when he noticed the Ring Video Doorbell. Pressing the buzzer, he angled his face away so the camera wouldn't get a clear profile.

"May I help you?" Keith asked, narrowing his eyes suspiciously.

"Hello. I'm here for the four-hour session," Vincent replied.

Keith buzzed him in. When Vincent entered the studio, Tasha felt a chill run down her spine. Something about him was off, sending a rush of fear through her veins. His eyes pierced into hers like a predator eyeing its prey.

"Do you have an idea of what you want to do?" Keith asked, still wary.

"Yeah, I have some material written down," Vincent said, pulling a crumpled sheet of paper from his pocket. "I want to record some Christian poetry - acapella."

Keith nodded, motioning Vincent into the recording booth. Vincent took a deep breath and began:

> *For by your words, you will be acquitted*
> *And by your words, you will be condemned*
> *Death to the poet*
> *Who promotes lust and sin*

Keith and Tasha exchanged uneasy looks. "Okay… Clearly, you didn't like that one," Vincent said. "How about this one, then?"

> *Today is a day that you should dread*
> *A day that the poet will end up dead*
> *Closed-casket funeral because I shot him in his head*

"Did you like my poem?" Vincent sneered, glaring at Tasha. Keith jumped to his feet, chest heaving.

"All right, I've heard enough," Keith snapped. "You need to leave the studio now." He pointed to the door.

Vincent, noticing Keith's imposing frame, chose not to fight. But then a sadistic smirk crossed his face. "I'm not going anywhere." He drew a black handgun fitted with a silencer and aimed it at Keith's temple. His gaze flicked to Tasha, who crouched beside Keith, and he growled, "Get over here now."

Tasha stood frozen, terror keeping her from moving. When she didn't move, Vincent pulled a Bowie knife from his waistband. Tasha had always feared any man with a knife since she watched that Halloween movie about the knife-wielding Michael Myers as a child. But the man standing before her was no Hollywood creation; he was a real-life monster, and he was standing in the studio, threatening to kill them both.

Keith lunged in front of Tasha, shielding her. He refused to let anything happen to his fiancée. Acting on pure instinct, he tackled Vincent like a linebacker, sending a bullet grazing his left shoulder. The pain was immediate, but Keith didn't let it stop him.

"Run, Tasha!" he roared, adrenaline spiking through his veins. She hesitated, but she bolted from the studio when he shouted again.

Vincent, however, was no match for Keith's brute strength. Keith wrestled the gun away and bulldozed Vincent into the recording booth. Even as blood trickled from his shoulder, Keith drove a punishing left hook into Vincent's jaw, flooring him with an earsplitting crack. Then came another fist and another until he felt bones snapping beneath his knuckles.

Keith was fighting for his life. His body burned with adrenaline as he remembered a childhood nightmare about a fire-breathing dragon trying to kill him. His mother had assured him monsters weren't real. But this monster was living proof that monsters did exist, and Keith was fighting one right now, determined to save the life of Tasha, his damsel in distress.

I've got to make sure he never gets to Tasha, Keith thought. Standing over Vincent, he stomped on his shoulder and face. In desperation, Vincent yanked the Bowie knife from his waistband and drove it into Keith's calf, sending lightning-like pain through Keith's leg. Keith retaliated with a crushing elbow to Vincent's face, finally knocking him unconscious.

Keith staggered away, blood oozing from multiple wounds. Vincent's face was a hideous mess, and his arm hung limply from its socket. Keith limped to the door, stepping through his blood as he reached for his phone to call 911.

Keith was dialing 911 but didn't notice Vincent stirring in the corner. Vincent had regained consciousness and pulled another gun from his waistband. He squeezed the trigger, shooting Keith in the back just as Keith touched the door.

Keith felt his strength slipping away. Darkness crept in. Heaven was calling him home. In his final seconds, he saw himself playing the church organ and heard the congregation's applause. His late mother was clapping. He had performed well, and now God was closing the curtain.

"I love you, Tasha…" he whispered before his eyes closed for the last time.

Vincent pushed himself upright, staggering and dripping blood. He stumbled out of the studio, tumbled into his car, and sped out of the parking lot.

37

Too Late

Detective Ronald Murphy, a seasoned veteran of the Oakland Police Department, ducked under the bright yellow perimeter crime scene tape. His tall, lean figure moved with purpose as he approached the music studio. In his early fifties, Murphy had seen it all - from petty theft to brutal murders. Unfortunately, this was Oakland's second homicide within two weeks. His mind replayed the gruesome image from a week ago: Janelle, a young girl whose lifeless eyes stared up at the ceiling, with a ball gag stuffed into her mouth. In all his years as a homicide detective, he'd never seen anything that matched the savagery of that murder.

Detective Murphy entered the recording studio, carefully avoiding the blood trail. Inside, he was briefed on the murder by his fellow Detective, Andy Cho. Cho was a prodigy in the department, and Murphy had taken him under his wing, admiring his sharp mind and determination.

"The victim's fiancée said the suspect was a Caucasian male who came into the studio and killed Keith Hicks," Cho said. "She said the suspect was recording a poem about killing a poet. We have video footage of him entering the studio as well." But why would he kill a music producer, Murphy wondered.

FBI Agent Nelson stepped out of the unmarked car wearing his FBI coat and cap. His eyes scanned the area until they locked onto a group of crime scene techs at the entrance of the recording studio. Photos were taken, and fingerprints were collected as a crowd of media and curious onlookers waited behind police lines. Nelson was directed to the lead detective and strode over to introduce himself.

"I'm Special Agent Drew Nelson out of Quantico, Virginia," he said, extending his hand to Detectives Murphy and Cho. Murphy's eyebrows shot up in surprise as he asked, "Is the FBI involved in this investigation?" Agent Nelson nodded. "Yes, we are. We have reason to believe that Vincent Thomas, the GTS Killer, committed this murder."

Detective Murphy's eyes narrowed as he processed that information. "The GTS killer?"

"GTS stands for Gag, Torture, Streetwalkers," Agent Nelson explained. "Vincent Thomas likes to leave gags made from rubber balls in his victims' mouths. His fixation with gagging is known as *paraphilia*. It arouses him to see women suffer before they die."

A chilling realization crept over Detective Murphy. A deranged serial killer was still out there. He turned to his partner, Detective Cho, with a grim look. "We have to catch this monster before he strikes again," he warned, knowing that the press would go into a frenzy over this case. Together, they briefed Agent Nelson on the disturbing video evidence from the studio.

***

Kareem and Maya left the movie theater, unaware of the drama that awaited them. When Maya turned on her phone, it buzzed with a series of frantic messages from Tasha. Puzzled, Kareem checked his cell phone to discover a chilling line from Tasha - "Kareem ...CALL ME!! IT'S URGENT!!!!"

Kareem called Tasha's number, only to hear her muffled cries on the other end. "What's wrong, Tasha? Is everything alright?" he asked, genuinely concerned.

"Kareem..." Tasha paused. "Keith is... Dead!"

38

The Profiler

"This is KTVU news in Oakland. We're coming at you live from the recording studio of music producer Keith Hicks. Police have informed us that he was found brutally murdered this afternoon. So far, investigators have not revealed if they have a suspect or motive for the killing."

Kareem's fingers clenched the steering wheel as he watched the news alert on his phone - homicide at Inspirational Sound Studios. He floored the gas pedal, the engine roaring as he sped through the Oakland streets. He slowed down his Mercedes as the recording studio came into view. The sidewalk was ablaze with lights from local Bay Area news vans. Yellow crime scene tape stretched across the entrance.

Kareem parked his car and raced towards the studio. This can't be happening, he muttered, shoving through the crowd with Maya close behind. Kareem ducked under the tape, but a police officer stopped him. "That's my studio," he yelled at the officer.

"I'm sorry, but this is a crime scene."

Kareem stared at the CSI agents as they took photos and dusted for fingerprints. Tasha was speaking to a detective when she spotted Kareem arguing with a police officer near the studio entrance.

"Kareem, I'm over here!" Tasha shouted. Kareem and Maya ran to her, and he wrapped his arms around her.

"Kareem!" she sobbed. "Keith is dead. Somebody killed –"

"It's okay, Tasha," he whispered, pulling her head to his chest. He rubbed her back as she wept, her gut-wrenching sobs wracking her body. Her tears soaked his shirt, and when her legs buckled, he held her up to keep her from collapsing.

"Make sure this scene remains secure," Detective Murphy ordered, walking toward them with Agent Nelson.

"Are you Kareem Simmons?"

Kareem turned to see a stern-looking man in a blue FBI jacket.

"Yes," Kareem replied, still in shock.

"I'm Agent Nelson. This is Detective Murphy from the Oakland Police Department." Nelson's tone was formal. "I wish we were meeting under better circumstances. I'm sorry for the loss of your friend. Would you mind answering a few questions in private?"

"I'll be right back," Kareem told Tasha, his voice unsteady.

Nelson led him toward a patrol car and handed him a thick manila folder packed with official-looking documents and photographs. Detective Murphy stood by, holding a small recording device, ready to capture every word.

"Do you recognize this man?" Nelson asked, showing him five photos of Vincent Thomas. Kareem examined them carefully. "No."

"The information I'm about to share with you is disturbing," Nelson warned. "It may impact your loved ones and family."

"I understand," Kareem said, shaking his head.

Nelson pulled out another photo. "Do you recognize this woman? Her name is Lisa Thomas."

Kareem's body stiffened. Seeing Lisa's face sent a rush of memories flooding back—memories of their passionate weekend together. He took a deep breath. "That's Lisa. I met her in Atlanta."

"Can you tell us, in your own words, what happened between you and Lisa Thomas?" Nelson pressed.

Kareem hesitated but spoke carefully. "She picked me up at the airport and took me on a tour of the CNN Center. We had dinner. She attended my poetry event and spent the weekend with me at my hotel." He omitted the more intimate details.

"Did Lisa Thomas tell you she was married?"

"Yes," Kareem admitted reluctantly. "She texted me after she left the hotel, saying she was married but filing for divorce." His brow furrowed. "What does any of this have to do with Keith's murder?"

Agent Nelson and Detective Murphy exchanged glances.

"Lisa Thomas was found murdered in Atlanta," Nelson said grimly. "Her estranged husband, Vincent Thomas, is the primary suspect. We also have evidence linking him to your friend's murder."

Kareem gasped. His heart pounded in his chest. "What?!" *This can't be happening!* His brow wrinkled in disbelief as he tried to process what he'd just heard.

This was a nightmare. His affair with Lisa had led to his best friend being murdered. Kareem began to wish he could back the hands of time and never respond to Lisa's DM on Instagram.

"I'm sorry, Kareem," Detective Murphy said. "My deepest condolences to you."

"How do you know that he's a serial killer?" Kareem asked, still in shock and disbelief.

Nelson met his gaze. "Vincent Thomas is the GTS Killer. Initially, we believed he was responsible for at least a dozen murders throughout Atlanta and other areas." He exhaled. "But when we brought in cadaver dogs, we found the remains of twelve more victims buried in his backyard. We now suspect he may have killed over thirty women in the past fifteen years."

Kareem's jaw tightened. "You mean to tell me this man has been murdering Black women for decades, and the FBI never caught him?"

"Vincent Thomas was never a suspect," Nelson said flatly. "Plus, he married Lisa Thomas - an Atlanta homicide detective. You'd think she would've figured out her husband was a serial killer."

Kareem narrowed his gaze on the FBI agent, picking up on his indifferent attitude.

"Bullshit!" Kareem exploded, locking eyes with Nelson. "The FBI didn't prioritize this case because he was killing Black girls!" Kareem knew that Black women who went missing didn't receive the national spotlight or get the same media coverage as other women. "If those girls were Caucasian, the entire damn FBI would have been on his trail," Kareem seethed.

Nelson held up a hand. "Let's not make this about race, Mr. Simmons."

"It's always about race in this country!" Kareem shot back.

"I'm not here to argue," Nelson said solemnly. "We all want this killer caught. But we're dealing with the deadliest type of serial killer. We've already linked him to another murder out here a week ago."

"You're telling me he killed Janelle too?" Agent Nelson nodded. "Yes."

Kareem shut his eyes and rubbed the back of his neck. Keith and Janelle would still be alive if he'd never gotten involved with Lisa.

Nelson's voice cut through his thoughts. "Vincent Thomas is a highly trained mercenary—and he's targeting you and your friends."

Kareem's head snapped up. "Are you saying my girlfriend, Maya, is next?"

"She's a target," the FBI agent responded. A tense silence lingered between them. Detective Murphy intervened, hoping to diffuse the tension.

"We're reviewing the security footage from the studio," Murphy said. "We have the suspect on video. He's injured. Keith put up one hell of a fight."

Kareem's emotions raged back and forth between disbelief and paranoia. He'd gone from creating a song with his best friend that morning to mourning his death. Shit like this only happens in movies, Kareem thought. He massaged his fingers on his temples. It felt like his head was about to explode.

"Do you have any more questions?" Kareem sneered at the FBI agent. "I need to check on my friends and ensure they're safe since the FBI can't do their damn job!"

Detective Murphy's voice was heavy with regret. "I'm sorry for your loss." He handed Kareem his card, a number scrawled on the back. "I'll be in touch."

As Detective Murphy watched Kareem walk away, his brow furrowed. The name Kareem Simmons tugged at something in his memory. *Kareem Simmons. Where had I heard that name before?*

Then it hit him.

Twenty-seven years ago, Murphy had been a rookie cop when he responded to a shooting in East Oakland. Gunshots had echoed from a small house. When he entered, he found a man and a woman dead on the floor. A baby was crying in a crib.

That baby had been Kareem. And now here they were again, reunited during a tragedy.

Detective Murphy wondered if he should tell Kareem that he was the cop who had found him in the crib —orphaned and alone, after his parents' murder. He decided against it. The case was still a cold case, and the revelation might open wounds in Kareem that had closed too long ago.

Where the fuck are you hiding? Detective Murphy asked while staring at Vincent's photo.

39

Lust Takes

The first stage of grief is denial. Kareem had been in denial until seeing the paramedics wheel out Keith's lifeless body on a gurney. His best friend had been murdered. He ignored questions from the reporters, rubbing his hands over his face in disbelief. This can't be happening! But it was—his best friend was dead.

There were no family members to notify. Keith's mother had passed away, and he had no siblings. He spent most of his time with Tasha at the studio, the gym, or church. Kareem spotted Tasha and Maya standing near an ambulance, Tasha's cries muffled against Maya's shoulder.

Suddenly, Pastor Rivers appeared on the scene and rushed toward Tasha with open arms. She clung to him, sobs wracking her body, her shoulders trembling as she cried harder.
"Pastor, this man… he killed… Keith," Tasha sobbed as he held her close.

"It's okay to cry," Pastor Rivers said gently. "Crying is cleansing."

"I just spoke to the FBI and Detective Murphy," Kareem said, his head lowered. "They told me the man who killed Keith also murdered that young girl, Janelle." He swallowed hard. "And he's after me too."

Everyone froze, turning to stare at Kareem.

"There's this woman I met in Atlanta—Lisa. She was married to a killer named Vincent. He's the one who killed Keith." Kareem's voice trembled. "The FBI says he's a serial killer. He's been murdering Black women for decades."

"Oh, my God!" Maya gasped, covering her mouth. She stopped for a moment, trying to process what she had just heard.

Kareem's eyes darted around the parking lot. The killer was still out there, and he had to protect Maya at all costs. His jaw tightened with rage, and he clenched his fist in anger. "I'm going to find Keith's killer," Kareem vowed, remembering that his gun was locked away in his car.

"Kareem, please... listen to me!" Pastor Rivers pleaded, his voice beginning to crack. "There's a nationwide search for this killer. I saw it on the news. I want justice too, but becoming a vigilante isn't the way."

Pastor Rivers stepped forward and embraced Kareem. The tears Kareem had been holding back finally spilled over. Both men stood there, crying in each other's arms. Maya watched from the side, her tears falling. She hadn't seen her father cry since her mother's funeral.

Detective Murphy approached Pastor Rivers and gave him a brotherly hug. The two men had known each other for decades and were close friends. Murphy pulled out a small notepad and pen from his coat pocket, scribbling down everyone's names and contact information.

He assured them, "I'll have one of my officers follow you home and keep your place under 24-hour surveillance until we catch the suspect. "

Pastor Rivers nodded, grateful for the added protection. He knew Vincent was still out there. However, with Detective Murphy on the case, they had their best chance at catching the killer.

40

Off the Grid

The FBI has announced a nationwide search for Vincent Thomas, a serial killer suspected of murdering up to 30 women across the country. Authorities urged the public to assist in locating the fugitive, warning that Thomas was considered armed and dangerous.

Vincent seethed as he watched the news from his hotel room. He was angry with himself. He'd always been methodical in his kills, but this time, he'd underestimated his target. Kareem was still alive, and now the FBI was closing in on him. Even worse, his shoulder and jaw were both broken, pain radiating through his body. If he hadn't played possum during the fight with Keith, he would have been killed or captured.

Determined to avoid recognition, he shaved his head and beard and wore cheap reading glasses to appear older. He had to leave Oakland immediately.

A sharp, burning pain tore through him, reminding him that he needed time to recover. Pulling out his burner phone, he called an old friend who owned a secluded cabin deep in Six Rivers National Forest - the perfect place to go off the grid and heal while planning his next move. The drive would take hours. He needed to move fast.

Years of military training had honed his survival instincts. He fashioned a makeshift sling from a pillowcase to secure his broken arm, but he still needed help loading his supplies into the stolen SUV parked a few blocks away. Limping outside, he made his way toward a nearby homeless encampment.

"Any change, bro?" a homeless man asked, holding out his hand.

Vincent offered the man money and a hot meal in exchange for help carrying boxes from his hotel room to the SUV. When the job was done, Vincent handed over the cash and bought the man fast food from a McDonald's drive-thru before hitting the highway toward Six Rivers National Forest.

An hour into the drive, he saw flashing red and blue lights in his rearview mirror. Damn it, he thought to himself. A California Highway Patrol car tailed him on Highway One. It would only take a moment for them to scan the stolen plates. Once they linked the SUV to the murders, backup would be on its way.

Moments later, Vincent heard the police siren scream. Vincent clenched his teeth and slammed his foot on the gas. The SUV roared forward. It was dark outside. He couldn't see the beautiful coastal views of California's Highway One. But he knew there was a deadly steep drop-off from the cliffs into the ocean.

The patrol car pursued him relentlessly, weaving through traffic with expert precision. Vincent, equally skilled, swerved between lanes, determined to maintain his lead.

Up ahead, he spotted a van in his peripheral vision. Without hesitation, he swerved right, slamming into the van's rear bumper. The vehicle spun out, careening into the next lane —directly in the path of an oncoming patrol car. Sounds of collisions and shattering glass roared in the background. Vincent smirked. That should buy me some time.

Vincent continued accelerating during the high-speed chase, even though he could no longer see the flashing blue beacons on his tail. I need a little more time, he said through gritted teeth, his broken arm in excruciating pain.

He knew the police would deploy spike strips ahead, and helicopters would soon take up the chase. He put the SUV into stealth mode, turning off all lights and blending in with the darkness of night.

He was still hours away from reaching Six Rivers National Forest, so he accelerated to over 95 mph on the winding coast.

Twenty minutes later, the unmistakable thump of helicopter blades echoed overhead. Vincent glanced up to see a police chopper, its powerful spotlight scanning the road. Soon, news helicopters would be broadcasting the chase to the entire country.

His heart pounded as he neared Devil's Slide. One wrong move, and he'd be dead. But he knew one thing for sure: He would not be taken alive.

With a final burst of speed, Vincent jerked the wheel hard to the right. The SUV skidded, tires screeching, before it veered off the highway. The vehicle plunged off the cliffside, tumbling down the rocky terrain and disappearing into the ocean below.

Sirens wailed as the California Highway Patrol arrived at the crash site. A police helicopter hovered above, its spotlight illuminating debris floating on the water's surface. The Coast Guard was called in to assist.

By the time Special Agent Nelson and Detective Murphy arrived, the scene was already swarming with law enforcement. Investigators confirmed that Vincent's SUV had gone over the cliff. A diver reported seeing a body in the driver's seat, but treacherous conditions forced the Coast Guard to suspend recovery efforts.

Agent Nelson turned to a Coast Guard officer. "When can we resume the search?"

"It'll take a few days," the officer replied.

Nelson exhaled sharply, deepening the frown lines on his forehead. It would be at least a week before they could confirm the body's identity.

"We should declare Vincent Thomas dead," Nelson suggested, glancing at Detective Murphy. "No criminal record in Georgia. No DNA match from the family. The forensic dental results will take weeks."

Murphy shook his head. "We need positive identification," he said firmly. Just then, a Coast Guard diver emerged from the cliffs, holding up a pair of doggie tags engraved with Vincent Thomas's name. He handed them to Agent Nelson.

Nelson smirked and dangled them in front of Murphy. "Is this enough identification for you, detective?"

Murphy narrowed his eyes but said nothing. Agent Nelson turned away, gripping the dog tags. This was the highest-profile case of his young career, and he wasn't about to blow it. He walked toward the press, preparing to deliver the news.

"The Coast Guard has recovered evidence confirming the suspect's identity," Nelson announced. "Vincent Thomas is dead."

41

It's So Hard to Say Goodbye

Maya grabbed two porcelain teacups from her late mother's fine China cabinet. She poured steaming hot water over chamomile teabags in both cups and added two teaspoons of local honey. Maya remembered how her mother often made chamomile tea to calm her nerves. Now, she was doing the same for Tasha, who was shocked and grief-stricken after Keith's murder.

She carried both cups into the living room and handed one to Tasha. Pastor Rivers had insisted that she remain at his house until Vincent was captured. Maya sat on the sofa next to her best friend as she sipped the hot tea.

"I keep re-reading all the texts he sent me," Tasha said softly. "I can't believe Keith is gone."

Suddenly, Pastor Rivers called everyone to the living room. "It's on the news." The newscaster's voice filled the room:

A man's body was discovered this evening after a vehicle plunged down an embankment on Highway One. The body is believed to belong to Vincent Thomas, the suspected serial killer wanted for multiple homicides across the nation. The van he was driving careened off a cliff during a police pursuit.

Despite the news of Vincent's death, the closure Kareem expected to feel was absent. Even though the serial killer was gone, the regret and remorse inside him remained.

Coping with Keith's murder was difficult for everyone. Kareem was especially worried about Tasha. Just two days ago, she had been twirling in her wedding dress. Now, Tasha was planning her fiancé's funeral. Keith's insurance policy listed Tasha as the beneficiary, but no amount of money could make up for losing the man she loved.

The trauma weighed heavily on Kareem as well. He looked like a man whose world had been destroyed. Dark circles rimmed his eyes; he hadn't slept or shaved in days. He felt a deep, familiar pain - the kind he hadn't experienced since his grandmother's death. Maya helped Kareem through it, insisting that he stop blaming himself.

Weeks later, Keith's funeral was held at Agape Church. Thousands gathered to offer their condolences. Tasha sat in the front pew, a black veil draped over her head, sunglasses shielding her from the sight of Keith in his casket. Kareem stepped up to the podium, his voice thick with emotion, recalling how he and Keith had met in college and bonded like brothers. Tahir also spoke, his voice trembling as he remembered how Keith had been more than a music producer but also a big brother, always there to guide him.

Pastor Rivers took the podium to deliver the eulogy. "John 15:13 says, 'There is no greater love than to lay down one's life for one's friends.' We witnessed a moment of that love during Keith and Tasha's proposal in this very church. When a man understands the power of God's love, it transforms how he loves others. Keith died a hero, protecting the woman he loved."

"I know we are mourning right now," Pastor Rivers continued, his voice full of emotion, "but the scriptures say that God will wipe away every tear." He looked at Tasha with sympathy. "We love you, Tasha," he said softly. "We are praying for you."

"Somebody said we lost our musical director when Keith was killed." Pastor Rivers shook his head. "We didn't lose Keith. Something is lost when you don't know where it is." The congregation rose to their feet. "To be absent from the body is to be present with the Lord!" His voice rose to a crescendo. "Keith is not lost because we know where he is! He's in heaven! He's in heaven! He's in heaven!"

"Glory to God!" someone shouted. "Hallelujah!" Praises filled the sanctuary as the Pastor's words moved mourners.

After the service, Kareem, Tahir, a minister, and several musicians from the church carried Keith's casket to the waiting hearse. Kareem wished Tshaka had been there to help carry it, but he hadn't been able to reach him. Tshaka was in Africa, and Kareem wasn't even sure if he knew that Keith had been killed.

The church members followed the casket to Rolling Hills Cemetery, where a private burial ceremony was held. Tasha couldn't bear to watch the casket lowered. Instead, she placed her hand on the smooth wood, whispered a silent goodbye, and walked away.

Kareem followed and joined Tasha in the waiting limo. He stopped Tasha, his voice heavy with guilt. "I'm at fault for all this. If I hadn't gotten involved with Lisa, none of this would've happened," he said, lowering his head in shame. I'm so sorry, Tasha. I'm so sorry for everything."

Tasha placed a gentle hand on Kareem's shoulder. "Stop blaming yourself! You had no idea any of this would happen." She hugged him tightly. "I know how much you loved Keith. You were his best friend. You two were like brothers."

"Keith left me the recording studio in his will," Tasha said, her voice heavy with sorrow. "I can't step foot in that studio again. We had some of our best memories there, but I'll never forget what happened that night."

Nightmares still haunted Tasha - Vincent's sadistic grin, the gun aimed at Keith, the moment he gave his life to save her.

"I want you to have the studio, Kareem," Tasha said softly. "Use it however you want, but something positive would be good. Keith would've loved that." She hesitated before continuing. "I'm leaving tomorrow morning. I need to go back home to Alabama and stay with my parents. I need to be near my family. Keith was the only thing I had keeping me out here."

Tears streamed down her face as she spoke of Keith. "He gave his life to protect me. He fought that killer off so I could escape," she whispered, her voice breaking. "He was my soulmate," she sobbed. "I've lost my soul mate," she sniffed, "don't lose yours, Kareem," Tasha said in a low voice while staring at Maya.

Maya approached and embraced Tasha. "I love you, best friend," Maya whispered.

Tasha squeezed back with all her might. "I love you too, friend. I'll miss you so much. I'll be praying for you and Kareem every day."

42

A Gift for Tahir

Kareem relaxed in the passenger's seat of his Mercedes, watching Tahir as he drove them to the recording studio. The bond between Kareem and Tahir had grown stronger with each passing day. Kareem looked at Tahir as the little brother that he never had. Both had lost their fathers at a young age, leaving them with a void that could never be filled. Both were hustlers, constantly fighting for survival in a world that seemed to be against them.

Tahir was excited about going back to the studio, but Kareem couldn't help but feel a sense of remorse as he remembered that this was the same place where Keith had been killed only a few weeks ago. Kareem hired a bioremediation specialist to disinfect the studio once the police informed him that it was no longer a crime scene. It would be their first time entering the studio since then, and neither knew what to expect.

When they stepped inside the studio, Kareem looked around, and his gaze settled on the photograph of Keith and him that hung on the wall. A wave of guilt washed over him. Kareem couldn't shake off the thought that he should have been the one who died instead of Keith. As much as people tried to console him, Kareem knew that he would never be able to forgive himself.

The studio felt empty without the sound of Keith's laughter or the rhythms of his fingers tapping on the keyboards and drum machine. When Keith opened the studio, Kareem remembered how he would freestyle raps on topics ranging from politics to police brutality. Kareem cherished those memories.

Tahir turned on the computers and loaded the Pro Tools session to view the hundreds of music tracks Keith had created. Tahir was familiar with Pro Tools, and he'd watched Keith enough times to know how to open a folder and import sounds into it. "I didn't know Keith had so many beats. There are hundreds of tracks in these folders. He could've made so many albums from all this," Tahir said, shocked. "He was a true musical genius." Kareem nodded in agreement as he watched Tahir sift through the beats.

Tahir opened Kareem's sessions and found two folders, one titled Lyrics and Lust and another labeled Lyrics and Love. Kareem recalled how he and Keith discussed recording an album called Lyrics and Love. He had no idea that Keith had been producing music for an album. Kareem's albums contained instrumentals without titles, so Tahir played each track. The beats sounded like a mix of R&B love songs. Kareem felt himself vibing to the soulful melodies.

Kareem smiled and said, "I'm going to record a song for each track." Writing poetry had always been therapeutic for Kareem. It allowed him to express his pain, problems, dreams, and desires. He wanted to honor Keith's memory by finishing the albums that Keith had wanted him to create.

Kareem and Tahir spent long hours in the studio for the next few days, mixing tracks for their upcoming albums. Tahir was funny and constantly joking, providing Kareem with much-needed comedy relief.

One day, after Tahir had spent hours mixing down the Lyrics and Love album, Kareem pulled out a plastic access badge and a set of keys and handed them to Tahir. "Tahir, this is your studio now. Keith left it behind for Tasha, but she doesn't want it," Kareem said. Tahir stared in disbelief at the access badge and keys, his eyes gleaming with gratitude. He looked up and hugged Kareem. "I love you, big bro! I promise to make you proud of me!" Tahir was now the proud owner of Inspirational Studios.

43

An Old Poem

Kareem and Maya stood in the Agape Church parking lot, handing the homeless plates of hot food. The tables were covered with paper plates, plastic utensils, and a juice dispenser. The church hosted an outreach program Pastor Rivers and his late wife started every fourth Saturday, providing meals and necessities to low-income seniors and homeless people. Over forty church members had shown up to help.

Keith had always invited Kareem to join him in feeding people experiencing homelessness, but he'd declined, choosing instead to donate money for socks, toothpaste, and other essentials. Back then, he had thought that was enough. But now, volunteering helped ease his guilt. It gave him a sense of purpose. He found solace in volunteering and peace with every plate he served.

It had been weeks since the FBI confirmed Vincent's death, yet Kareem's heart still mourned the loss of his best friend, Keith. Spending time with Maya and working on his album helped, as did volunteering at the church. He'd grown close to Pastor Rivers, who, in many ways, had become the father figure he never had.

Kareem watched Sister Jones maneuver her wheelchair through the crowd, handing out plates while her son, Tahir, served alongside her. He couldn't help but admire her strength. Despite having been burned in a fire that killed her husband and burned down her home, she'd dedicated her life to serving others. He turned to Maya, who was scooping spaghetti onto a plate.

"It's beautiful how much love and compassion Sister Jones has," he said.

Maya nodded, smiling. "She's got a heart of gold."

After feeding the homeless, Maya led Kareem to an abandoned house next to the church. She pointed to it, her eyes gleaming with excitement.

"This is it," she said. "The future home of A Safe Space."

She'd already paid a holding deposit, and the landlord had given her the keys early, expecting her to sign the lease soon. Maya unlocked the door and ushered Kareem inside.

The house was spacious - four bedrooms, two bathrooms, a small kitchen, a dining area, a laundry room, and an open space perfect for meetings and classes. An olive-colored sofa and two overstuffed chairs sat opposite each other in front of a stone fireplace. The large backyard would be perfect for children to play in.

Maya gently squeezed Kareem's arm. "What do you think? Wouldn't this be perfect for A Safe Space?"

Kareem smiled. "It's perfect."

"I'm signing a two-year lease tomorrow," she said. "Alexis will be the first girl to stay here. We can house four girls with children at a time."

Kareem nodded, proud of her. This wasn't just a dream for Maya - it was her calling.

After touring the house, Kareem returned to the church and spoke with Pastor Rivers in his office. The weight of guilt pressed heavy on his chest.

"I've been feeling guilty, Pastor," he admitted, his voice low. "Keith would still be here if I hadn't hooked up with Lisa in Atlanta."

His jaw tightened as his thoughts shifted to Vincent—the serial killer who had brutally murdered innocent women and stolen Keith's life.

The Pastor rose from his desk, walked toward Kareem, and placed a firm, supportive hand on his shoulder. "Guilt is a gun you need to stop aiming at yourself," he said gently. "You're not at fault. Vincent Thomas was a monster. The police have linked him to over twenty murders. Who knows how many more women he would have killed if Keith hadn't injured him and helped the police capture him?"

Pastor Rivers paused, choosing his words carefully. "Guilt drains the joy from our souls, but God's grace replenishes it." Kareem exhaled, his head still heavy with guilt.

"What the enemy meant for evil, God used for good," the Pastor continued. "The devil thought Keith's death would break this church, but look around. Tahir's music is bringing more young people in. Maya's organization is about to change lives. Our homeless ministry is thriving."

Kareem took a moment to gather his thoughts before changing the subject. "Maya is so passionate about helping the community. Where does she get that from?"

The Pastor smiled and walked over to his desk. He picked up a framed photograph and handed it to Kareem. In the picture, a younger version of Pastor Rivers stood beside Maya's mother. Maya's mother also wore a black beret adorned with a cat head patch. Maya stood in front, dressed in all black, with her fist raised high, reminiscent of the Black Panther Party.

"We took this when Maya was a child—a tribute to the Black Panther Party," the Pastor said. "My wife's family were Panthers. Maya's grandmother volunteered for their free breakfast program for children. That's what inspired me to start these food drives."

Kareem studied the photo and then handed it back.

"My wife later went into politics," Pastor Rivers continued. "She served on Oakland's city council for over a decade. She fought hard to protect children and create a better future for them. And Maya? She's her mother's child—out here trying to save every little Black girl from the streets."

The Pastor's voice softened. "When we couldn't find a church home that felt right, we started Agape Assembly. We began by feeding the homeless, and before we knew it, we had built a family."

Kareem smiled and stood, shaking the Pastor's hand. "And thank God you did."

***

The next day, Kareem shuffled into church, his heart still heavy with grief. He slid into the second pew next to Maya and kissed her hand. He'd been fasting all week, abstaining from food until evening, focusing on prayer and cultivating inner peace.

When Pastor Rivers stepped up to the pulpit, he instructed the congregation to open their Bibles to the Book of Job.

Kareem reached for his grandmother's Bible. A small, folded paper fell to the floor as he flipped it open. Kareem picked it up and unfolded it. As he opened it, he was amazed to find it was his poem Spiritual Warfare, which he'd read at church on the day his grandmother passed away. She must've placed the poem in her Bible.

Kareem closed his eyes and began reminiscing about seeing his grandmother sitting in the church pew while he read his poetry. He remembered how she nodded her head after hearing every word he said. Kareem read part of the poem:

Don't be fooled by lies and deceit
The devil wants to drag you to defeat
Stand firm in your faith

Because the enemy won't cease
There can be no peace in your life
Without the Prince of Peace

Kareem had turned his back on God following his grandmother's death. But now, more than ever, he was beginning to realize how much he needed God. Kareem looked up as Pastor Rivers paced back and forth across the pulpit, his ministers cheering him on.

"If you didn't have a calling on your life, the enemy wouldn't be coming after you!" the Pastor declared. "If your life had no purpose, the enemy wouldn't be plotting against you!"

Something inside Kareem stirred. Before he knew it, he was on his feet. "Preach!" he shouted.

After the sermon, Pastor Rivers began the altar call. He invited anyone who wanted to accept Christ as their savior to the altar. "Come on now!" Pastor Rivers shouted with outstretched hands. "Jesus loves you, and we love you!"

The organist began playing, and Maya made her way to the front of the church and began singing a moving rendition of Le'Andria Johnson's gospel song *Deliver Me.*

The lyrics hit Kareem in his core. The song that Maya sang brought back a childhood memory for Kareem. He remembered his grandmother catching him one day talking to an invisible friend while walking home from school.

"Do you have an invisible friend?" she asked.

"No, Granny," he had said. "I was talking to God. I leave space on the sidewalk for Him to walk beside me." His grandmother's eyes filled with emotion as she hugged her grandson, reminding him that God would always walk beside him.

For years, he had turned his back on God. But now, holding his grandmother's Bible, listening to Maya sing, and hearing the Pastor's words, something inside him broke. Kareem needed God back in his life. Kareem stepped into the aisle. His chest heaved. His vision blurred.

"I need You now, Lord!" he cried, his voice echoing through the sanctuary. "Please forgive me!"

Maya's voice cracked with emotion as she watched Kareem walk toward the altar.

He dropped to his knees, lifting his arms in surrender.

Pastor Rivers knelt beside him, placing a firm hand on his head. As the ministers joined in prayer, a wave of peace washed over Kareem, and he felt God's love, forgiveness, and grace washing away all his pain and guilt. When he opened his eyes again, everything felt new.

44

To Catch a Predator

Tahir swerved the Mercedes S600 in and out of the traffic while Kareem bobbed his head to Tahir's latest song. Since Tahir had recently received his learner's permit, Kareem had allowed him to drive his Mercedes almost every day. Tahir's hands gripped the steering wheel, his lower back pressed against the leather, and his eyes focused on the road. "I appreciate you letting me drive your car for the driving test tomorrow," Tahir said, steering the car through a sea of red brake lights.

"No problem. I appreciate you helping me deliver these computers," Kareem replied. They'd just left the Apple Store to pick up the iMacs Kareem had purchased for A Safe Space. "Are you ready for your driving exam tomorrow?"

"Fa sho!" Tahir said. "After I get my driver's license, I'm going to buy a van to drive my mama around. No more waiting for wheelchair lifts on the bus." Kareem directed Tahir to park at the curb outside of the Safe Space house. As they pulled up, Kareem noticed Maya step down from the porch and give him a wave hello.

Kareem popped the trunk and helped Tahir unload the iMacs. "I wasn't expecting all this!" Maya said with a surprised look on her face. Kareem smiled and said, "Well, if you're going to empower and educate at-risk girls, you need the best technology." He handed Maya the stack of computers,

"Thank you so much, baby," she hugged Kareem. "Alexis is inside with her son."

The two then walked inside the Safe Space house, and Kareem marveled at how Maya had transformed it within a week. It was now full of vibrant colors, paintings, and furniture.

Maya led Tahir to the back of the house, where the computers would be used as a learning center. When Tahir entered the room, he was taken aback by the beautiful girl who stood before him. Although she wore her hair in a ponytail and had a slight belly from giving birth, she was still breathtaking. Tahir couldn't take his eyes off her.

"Hello. I'm Tahir," he said, barely able to take his gaze away from Alexis long enough to extend his hand to shake hers. Alexis's hand was warm and soft. "I saw you perform at the Gospel Fest," she said with a sparkle in her eye as she remembered seeing him at the concert.

"Is this your baby?" Tahir asked while reaching down to play with the toddler, who was walking around with a pacifier in his mouth. "This is my son Odell. He's ten months old." Alexis smiled as Tahir's strong hands gently scooped up her son and brought him close. He ticked Odell's tiny belly, and the baby gurgled with laughter. As Alexis watched, she felt a wave of emotion wash over her – one that filled her with affection for the man now playing with her son.

Kareem and Maya looked at Tahir and Alexis at the computer, laughing and joking. "I think they like each other," Kareem joked.

After Kareem and Tahir left, Alexis sat with Maya and reviewed her career goals. For Alexis, meeting Maya had been a blessing. Now, she had a mentor who could help her get a job and a diploma and open a world of new opportunities. They were looking up job openings until Alexis felt her phone vibrate. She reached into her pocket and saw Bishop Banks's name on the screen. She'd ignored him since the Gospel Fest and wanted nothing to do with him anymore.

Maya noticed that Alexis was disturbed by her phone. "What's wrong?" Maya asked.

"I cut him off, and he keeps calling me." Maya reached out to grasp Alexis's shoulder. "Who keeps harassing you?" she asked, her face creased with worry.

Alexis sighed before replying. "He made me sign a confidentiality agreement," she mumbled, looking away shamefully. Maya lifted Alexis's head with her index finger and looked her in the eyes. "No confidentiality agreement can stop you from telling the truth. If someone is bothering you, please don't hesitate to let me know. I'm here to help you. But you have to trust me."

"I know," Alexis whispered under her breath. She knew she had to stop Bishop Banks from preying on other young women. Alexis told Maya how Bishop Banks had been paying her money in exchange for her silence about their sexual relationship.

Maya grew wide-eyed with shock as soon as the words left Alexis's mouth. Tears began to well in Alexis's eyes, and Maya gave her some tissue to wipe them away. "Alexis, we need to go to the police," she said gently. "He can't be allowed to do this to anyone else - you're only seventeen! You're still a minor!"

Maya called her father, Pastor Rivers, and explained the situation with Alexis and how Bishop Banks had manipulated and abused her. Without hesitation, Pastor Rivers contacted his friend, Detective Ronald Murphy. Within minutes, Detective Murphy arrived at A Safe Space and sat with Alexis to take a detailed police report. As she spoke, Murphy scribbled notes onto his pad, listening intently as she revealed how Bishop Banks had paid her thousands of dollars to keep their relationship hidden and had forced her to sign a nondisclosure agreement.

Detective Murphy sat across from Alexis, his tone gentle but firm. "You don't have to be afraid anymore," he said. "As a minor, that nondisclosure agreement is illegal and will not hold up in court." Maya praised Alexis for speaking up about her trauma, and Alexis agreed that it was hard but necessary.

"I'm extremely sorry for what you've suffered," Pastor Rivers said to Alexis, his voice cracked with emotion. "The church is supposed to provide safety and security to all, particularly women and vulnerable children. We have a responsibility to promote love and protect you. The church is not supposed to hurt you, molest you, or do anything vile that violates you."

"Thank you for coming so quickly," Pastor Rivers said with a grim tone. "There's going to be a huge fallout from this. *Holy Tabernacle* is one of the largest churches in the country," the detective warned.

"The church isn't a building; it's the people," Pastor Rivers told the detective. "In all my years of preaching, I've never protected anyone who intentionally harmed anyone, and I'm not going to start now. As the scriptures say, *Woe be unto the pastors that destroy the sheep of my pasture.*"

"You've always been a good man," Murphy said, his voice filled with admiration. "I'm going to have to pay your church a visit again, It's been too long."

A warm smile spread across Pastor Rivers's face. "Please do, Ronald. We would love to have you!" After the detective left, the Pastor bowed his head and prayed for his friend's safety, knowing the dangers of being a detective in Oakland.

45

What's Done in the Dark

Kareem sat on the sunny deck of Sam's Chowder House, enjoying a breathtaking view of the Pacific Ocean. He'd just finished showing a multi-million-dollar home in Half Moon Bay, a small but wealthy city an hour away from Oakland. The property was expected to fetch millions from the buyer, which meant another large commission for him.

It was a beautiful sunny day, so he invited Maya for brunch. Maya loved seafood, and the restaurant menu included lobster rolls, clam chowder, crab cakes, and spicy shrimp appetizers. While waiting, he ordered an Iced Tea and scrolled through the news app on his phone. Suddenly, an alert caught his attention:

Oakland Bishop Arrested on Sex Charges

He clicked on the breaking news story. The newscaster reported that Bishop Banks had been arrested for allegedly misappropriating church funds and engaging in an inappropriate relationship with a minor. His gaze fixed on the reporter standing in front of the bishop's home:

"We are coming to you live from the home of Bishop Banks, the head of *Holy Tabernacle* church, who was taken into custody today," the newscaster said. "Authorities allege that Banks has been accused of sexually assaulting a minor multiple times within the past year. According to court documents, he is also charged with misusing church funds. Banks is currently in jail awaiting a bond hearing."

Kareem sighed and shook his head. *What's done in the dark will come to light,* he said under his breath. He spotted Maya walking towards him, her sundress swaying in the breeze. Her braids bounced, and her oversized sunglasses blocked her face from view. He noticed her furrowed brow and missing smile and could tell something was wrong. He quickly rose from his seat to greet her.

"Hey love, did you hear about Bishop Banks? He's been arrested for a sex crime." Kareem asked, motioning for her to take a seat at the table. He sat across from her and reached for her hands, noticing the worry lines forming on her forehead. Maya took a few breaths before responding. "I'm the one who encouraged one of his victims to come forward.

"Was it Alexis?" Karem asked.

"This is between us, but yes," Maya said, her voice cracking with emotion. "She was one of his victims."

Kareem rubbed his beard, and his jaw tightened in anger. "I'm so sorry this happened to her, and in the church of all places," he said in disgust. I hope Bishop Banks rots in prison," he said under his breath, shaking his head in disgust while talking to Maya. Ever since Kareem was a child, he suspected the Pastor was a fraud.

"He's going to get what he deserves for having sex with a minor and swindling his congregation," Maya said while holding Kareem's hand. "Right now, Alexis is the one who needs our support. She's a minor, so her identity is protected, but I hope to get this grant because I have her and three other young girls who need a safe place to stay.

Kareem reached over and took her hand. "A Safe Space will receive the funding. I want you to have faith that everything will be alright." Kareem said. "You are going to receive a financial blessing very soon."

"I'm claiming that!" Maya said. "Unfortunately, most of the missing and exploited Black girls aren't being kidnapped by serial killers or having their organs harvested on the black market," Maya said with a somber tone. "They are being abducted, trafficked, and sexually exploited by men and women in our community," she said, her voice filled with anger.

Kareem walked up behind Maya and began massaging her shoulders, his thumbs pressing gently into her tense muscles. She felt warmth spread through her body as he kneaded away the tension from her neck. As his hands kneaded the knots in her muscles, his mind wandered to his own life and the choices he'd made. He had a big bank account and plenty of expensive things, but he realized he needed to do more to help the community.

Maya's dedication to her community, church, and non-profit organization inspired him to do more and give back. He wanted to be a better man, not just for Maya but also for himself.

46

Paying Tithes

Four long folding tables filled with food lined the parking lot of Agape Church. The lot was packed with people in need, waiting for meals, clothing, and hygiene supplies provided by the congregation. Maya moved between the tables, filling foam containers with spaghetti, greens, yams, and rolls.

As she worked, Maya glanced at her watch. *Where is Kareem?* A look of concern appeared on Maya's face. Even though the serial killer was dead, she still worried about Kareem's safety. Plus, he was never late. He'd promised to help serve that morning.

Tahir appeared, carrying a large orange beverage cooler to her table. "You okay, sis?" he asked after setting it down.

"I'm good, Tahir," Maya replied. "Just a little worried because Kareem hasn't texted me back."

Just as Maya put her phone into her back pocket, Kareem pulled into the parking lot, driving a brand-new, pearl-blue Honda Odyssey minivan.

Kareem jumped out and jogged toward her. "Sorry, I'm late, babe. I had to pick up supplies from Costco," he said, pulling her into a hug. Even with no makeup, just a plain white T-shirt, jeans, and her hair in a single braid, she was still the most beautiful woman in the world to him.

Maya eyed the van. "Did you just buy this?"

Kareem grinned. "I sure did. Watch this." He pulled a key fob from his pocket and called Tahir to help unload. Handing him the fob, Kareem instructed him, "Press that button."

Maya watched curiously as the side door slid open and a ramp extended. Moments later, Tahir's mother, Sister Jones, exited the van in her wheelchair.

"Mama?" Tahir gasped, running to her side. Kareem smiled. "Congrats on getting your driver's license, Tahir. This is your van. No more taking the bus to church."

Tahir turned to Kareem, stunned. "For real? Bruh! Thank you!" He hugged him tightly before climbing into the driver's seat, already nodding to the music on the radio.

"Thanks, big bro!" Tahir said, hugging Kareem. Then he jumped behind the wheel of his new minivan and began bobbing his head to music on the radio. Alexis placed her son in the passenger seat and smiled.

Sister Jones reached for Kareem's hand and squeezed it. "This is a blessing," she said, her voice full of gratitude.

A few church deacons began unloading boxes from the van—socks, toothpaste, and other necessities Kareem had picked up for the community.

Maya tapped his shoulder. "Look at you, out here acting like Oprah," she teased. "You have such a good heart." She pressed a hand to his chest, then ran her fingers through the curls of his beard before standing on her toes to kiss him. "I thank God for your grandmother because she did an incredible job raising you."

Kareem thanked her and smiled. Every time Maya spoke life into him, it was like the sun breaking through storm clouds. She was more than his woman; she was his peace, best friend, and prayer partner. They had built something rare, something sacred - an intimacy that lived beyond the flesh, deeper than desire.

Pastor Rivers stepped outside and spotted the activity around the van. "Whose van is this?"

Tahir beamed. "Kareem bought it for me! Now, mama and I don't have to take the bus to church anymore."

Sister Jones explained how the Honda Odyssey's in-floor ramp made her wheelchair more manageable.

The Pastor's eyes shone with gratitude. "That is such a blessing! God bless you, Kareem."

"It's the least I can do," Kareem said humbly.

It had been over a month since Keith's funeral. During that time, Kareem had gotten back into selling real estate, working on his album, and volunteering at the church. Meanwhile, Holy Tabernacle Church was still reeling from the fallout of Bishop Banks sex scandal, and many of its former members had begun attending Agape.

After passing out the last food and supplies, Kareem turned to Maya. "Is your dad in his office? I need to talk to him."

"Don't be trying to get in good with my daddy," she joked. "Too late!" Kareem grinned.

Kareem knocked on the office door and was invited in. Pastor Rivers stood and shook his hand warmly. "Please, take a seat."

The office was small but tidy. A single window overlooked the parking lot. Bible verses lined the walls, along with a large, framed picture of the Pastor's late wife. He really loved her, Kareem said to himself.

"I wanted to talk to you about Bishop Banks," Kareem said. "His arrest is all over the news."

The Pastor sighed. "Ministers who manipulate faith need to be exposed. People have every right to be angry and disappointed." His voice was calm but firm. "Sexual scandals like this don't just hurt a church. They turn people away from God."

Leaning back in his chair, he stroked his beard. "I could've been a popular preacher if I wanted. But I don't preach prosperity. I preach charity. Luke 12:15 warns against greed." Unlike Bishop Banks, Pastor Rivers didn't want to amass a fortune; he wanted to help the masses of less fortunate.

"What saddens me is that this scandal will make people lose faith. When the shepherd is a wolf, who protects the flock?"

Kareem nodded. "I get that. I suffered from church hurt as a child. I saw the hypocrisy and greed firsthand. Part of me was even mad at God for taking my parents and my grandmother." He swallowed hard; the memory was still fresh. "But your ministry helped restore my faith."

The Pastor nodded. "When my wife got sick, I was angry at God too. Watching her suffer was the hardest thing I ever faced." His voice softened. "Why? I asked God why this had to happen?"

"One day at the hospital, my wife looked at me through her pain and said, "The fear of losing someone you love kills the joy of loving them today." Her words struck me, making me realize that life is fragile. It can be taken away in an instant." Pastor Rivers paused before continuing. "From that moment on, I cherished every second I had left with her."

Listening to Pastor Rivers helped Kareem better understand why Keith always gave so much back to the community - why he gave rappers free studio time, taught music lessons to children at the church, and spent weekends passing out free food. Keith always said that helping others was the best feeling in the world.

Pastor Rivers leaned back in his chair, stroking his beard thoughtfully. "There's a lot of amazing people helping the community here in Oakland. Take Mistah F.A.B.—not just a businessman and rapper, but someone who gives back. The *Love Life* Foundation helps at-risk youth, feeds the homeless, and promotes peace. And Steph and Ayesha Curry's *Eat.Learn.Play.* Foundation has helped hundreds of thousands here in the Bay.Area."

Pastor Rivers paused and smiled. "Muhammad Ali once said, Service to others is the rent you pay for your room here on earth."

"I agree, pastor," Kareem said. Maya's Safe Space Foundation will be a lifesaver for young girls. However, I believe we also have an opportunity to make a positive change for the entire community. With my real estate and finance background, I would like to teach classes on financial literacy, home ownership, entrepreneurship, investing, and retirement planning." The Pastor's face lit up as he nodded in agreement.

Kareem continued. "My grandmother used to tell me that the best things in life are not things. That's why I'm here today, Pastor.

Kareem pulled out an envelope. "I haven't paid tithes in over ten years. I hope this makes up for it. I've made money, but now I want to make a difference. I pray this money helps expand your ministry so that you can continue to clothe and feed people without housing. Please accept it. I only ask you not to tell anyone where this came from, including Maya."

Pastor Rivers took the envelope, eyes filled with gratitude. "The Bible says to give in secret. Your donation will remain anonymous."

Kareem smiled, shaking the Pastor's hand before walking out. Maya caught sight of them laughing together in the hallway. It felt good to see them growing closer.

***

Maya was washing dishes when her father walked in, and Le'Andria Johnson's song *Better Days* was playing from a Bluetooth speaker.

"God is good!" Pastor Rivers shouted.

Maya grinned. "All the time!"

Maya dried her hands on a dish towel and walked into the living room to see her father slumped onto the couch, his face filled with emotion.

"God is in the miracle business," he said, his voice sincere.

"What's going on, Daddy?" she asked, sitting beside him.

"The church has been struggling financially for a while now. While you were in college, I wasn't sure if I could keep it going," he said, eyes darting around the room as he spoke. "I even used some of your mom's life insurance money because I promised her I would keep the Outreach Program going."

Maya leaned in and reached for her father's hand. He exhaled, shaking his head. "But today, God showed up." He handed her a bank statement.

"A generous donor just gave over a million dollars. We will be able to clothe and feed the people for a long time!"

Maya gasped.

"That's not all. He asked me to give it to you. It's your bank account. The benefactor also donated a million dollars to A Safe Space. Your organization is going to save so many lives."

"You said he?" Maya asked with tears in her eyes. "Was it Kareem?" Maya asked.

"The donor wants to remain anonymous," her father responded.

But Maya already knew.

Kareem.

47

The Temptation of Tahir

That evening, Kareem and Tahir were in the recording studio. Since Keith's death, they had grown closer and spent hours working on each other's albums. Tahir was seated behind the mixing board while Kareem stood in the booth recording a poem called, *He Who Finds a Wife* for his upcoming Lyrics and Love album.

"I'm feeling that track, Unc! Is that poem for Maya?" Tahir asked with a sly grin.

"Of course, it's for her," Kareem replied.

"You're in love!" Tahir let out a full laugh. "Are you about to propose?" Tahir's eyes lit up.

"You'll find out."

"Well. I'm happy for both of you. Maybe I'll feel that way about a woman one day."

"What's going on with you and Alexis?" Kareem knew they were talking, but he wasn't sure if it was serious.

"I like her, but we're just friends," Tahir explained. Alexis has a son and is focused on finding a job and finishing school. She is beautiful, though. And hella thick!"

Kareem shook his head at Tahir. He wasn't sure if Tahir knew about the scandal involving Alexis and Bishop Banks, so he didn't press the issue. Instead, he changed the subject.

"How's your album coming along?" Kareem asked.

"It's almost finished," Tahir said, slapping his hands together in satisfaction. "I want to rewrite the lyrics to one track before I release it."

"Words are powerful," Kareem reminded him. "The tongue has the power of life and death. Even though it's small, it can make a huge impact on people's lives. You have a gift, Tahir. Keep using your words to empower others. This music industry doesn't always want rappers who make people think. These record labels profit off promoting ignorance and music about Black folks killing each other."

Just then, Kareem's phone buzzed. It was Maya, overjoyed about a donation her church and organization had received.

"Whoever contributed believes in what you're doing," Kareem said, smiling into the phone. "I'm so happy for you."

"I love you so much, Kareem! I need to see you now!" Maya said, unable to control her excitement.

"I love you too, babe. I just finished here with Tahir, so I can be there in ten minutes."

Tahir smirked after Kareem ended the call. "I love you, babe," he teased in a deep, mocking voice, then burst out laughing.

Kareem grinned. "Aight, I'm out, bruh. Keep working on your album."

***

After Kareem left, Tahir's phone rang. It was his friend Abdul, who was about to pull up for a session. Abdul was a local Oakland rapper and one of Tahir's childhood friends. He was also a survivor of the deadly fire that had destroyed their old apartment complex, killing Tahir's father and Abdul's aunt and leaving Tahir's mother confined to a wheelchair.

After that tragic event, Tahir and Abdul became close friends. Abdul was tall and lean, with olive skin and long, curly hair. Tahir had never been sure whether Abdul was Arab or Indian because he spoke multiple languages. Despite his nasal voice and thick accent, Abdul dreamed of becoming a rap star. Tahir initially teased him but eventually helped Abdul refine his lyrics, delivery, and stage presence.

When Abdul arrived, Tahir checked the security camera and saw a red Maserati and a black Cadillac Escalade pulled into the lot. Abdul climbed out of the Maserati, dressed head-to-toe in designer clothes with long braids cascading down his back. A moment later, a massive man stepped out of the Escalade—nearly seven feet tall, at least three hundred pounds of solid muscle.

Abdul entered the studio, followed by this imposing bodyguard. Tahir eyed him warily.

"Who is this big Deebo-looking dude? And whose Maserati is that?" Tahir asked after buzzing them inside.

"This is my bodyguard, Brute, and that's my Maserati," Abdul boasted. "Remember that beat you sold me a month ago? I used it for my track *Sin City*. In the first week, it went number one worldwide with two hundred million streams. I just signed with Eternal Flame for a one-album deal. Two-million-dollar advance."

Tahir's jaw dropped. He hadn't listened to the radio in months, having been focused on his gospel album.

"What? You signed to *Tha Flame* he asked, eyebrows raised. Eternal Flame, often called *Tha Flame,* was the hottest label around. It was based in Las Vegas and run by multi-billionaire Diablo Diggs, the wealthiest and most powerful Black man in the world.

"Check it out." Abdul pulled out a chunky gold chain with a six-pointed geometric star medallion decked in red rubies and diamonds. Tahir reached for it, but Abdul quickly pulled away.

"No one touches a Flame medallion unless you're part of the label," the bodyguard growled.

"Sorry, Tahir," Abdul said. "But I do have good news. The A&R who signed me told me she saw you perform at a gospel concert. She thinks you could get signed, too."

"Not interested," Tahir responded flatly. Abdul lit a Black & Mild, took a long drag, and exhaled a ring of smoke.

"Bruh, fuck that Christian rap shit!" Abdul snapped. "Quit tryin' to be Kirk Franklin and start countin' Benjamin Franklins!" The bodyguard snickered. Tahir tensed but refused to be intimidated by Abdul's outburst or the giant at his side.

"Don't you want to get paid, bruh?" Abdul pressed, softening his tone. "Buy your mama a house? You ain't never movin' her out the hood on gospel rap money. Think about it. If you signed with Tha Flame, you'd blow up overnight. You'd be livin' large in Las Vegas!"

"Nah, bruh. I'm not interested," Tahir said firmly, recalling Kareem's earlier advice.

"Then sell me another beat," Abdul persisted, producing a wad of cash from his pocket. "Fifty thousand for the beat. And I'll pay you another fifty if you lay down some bars. That's a hundred thousand total."

Tahir eyed the money. A hundred grand would help him move his mother into a wheelchair-accessible home and get a decent car.

"All right," he relented. "Just one beat."

Abdul grinned while Tahir settled behind the mixing board. He opened Keith's folder of hip-hop instrumentals, clicked on a basic track, and turned up the volume.

"Aw, that beat slaps!" Abdul nodded, excitement lighting up his face. Even the bodyguard started nodding, the heavy bass reverberating through the studio.

"Let's do this track together," Abdul urged. "I guarantee it'll blow up and land you a multimillion-dollar deal with Tha Flame."

Tahir's eyes burned with envy as he glared at Abdul's gleaming medallion and thought about the red Maserati parked outside. He knew he was a much better rapper than Abdul. Abdul's rapping skills were mediocre, and his lyrics lacked depth. Tahir, on the other hand, was a supreme lyricist and storyteller. Tahir entered the booth and began spitting a freestyle rap. Abdul puffed his cigar and grinned at his bodyguard, a sinister smirk stretching across his face.

48

Interior Designer

Maya and Kareem took a day off work to spend quality time together. They strolled along Lake Merritt, holding hands. Maya squeezed his hand and shared her ambitious plans for her new non-profit organization. Suddenly, she caught sight of a gondola floating on the lake and turned to Kareem with a mischievous grin. "Remember our first date?" she asked playfully. Kareem's face lit up at the memory. "How could I forget?" he replied. "I spit that love poem for you."

"Ugh, here you go with that disgusting word spit!" Maya shook her head and laughed.

"You're the first woman I ever took on a real date," Kareem confessed.

"So that's why you went all out trying to impress me. The roses, dinner, and gondola ride." Maya smiled. Before he could respond, a woman's voice interrupted their conversation.

"Kareem...Kareem," the woman yelled. They both turned around and saw the Tollers jogging up to them, wearing matching white sweatsuits. Kareem embraced Mrs. Toller and shook hands with her husband.

Mr. Toller gave Kareem a firm shake. "We love our new home, Kareem," he said with a smile. Mrs. Toller then turned to Maya, and her eyes lit up. "And who is this lovely young woman?" she asked, extending her hand for a warm handshake.

Kareem smiled and began his introduction. "Mr. and Mrs. Toller, I want to introduce you to Maya Rivers, the interior designer who decorated your new home."

Mrs. Toller's eyes widened in surprise. "Maya, it's so good to meet you. Kareem told us so many good things about you!" Maya tilted her head to the side and smiled at Kareem. "Oh really?" she asked playfully. Mrs. Toller stood with her hands on her hips and asked, "Are you two back together?"

Mr. Toller cleared his throat. "Denise, what did I tell you about getting into other people's business?"

Kareem grinned and answered, "Yes - we are back together!" Mrs. Toller clapped her hands in excitement and cheered, "Oh, I'm so happy to hear that!" She beamed at Maya. "Maya…Kareem was so heartbroken without you in his life."

Maya smiled wider and shot a mischievous glance toward Kareem. "Oh, was he?"

"Yes, girl. It reminded me of when I went to New York for a medical conference, and my husband got sick with the flu and almost died!" Mrs. Toller said, shaking her head from side to side.

"That's not true, Denise, and you know it!" Mr. Toller retorted, causing Maya and Kareem both to laugh.

Kareem took a moment to thank the Tollers. "Your words, *change is the first step toward getting a second chance,* caused me to evaluate myself. I had to transform my thinking and overcome my fear of love to receive love," Kareem admitted. "Thank you for those words!"

"Well, Kareem and Maya, I want you both to come by sometime. I'll cook dinner. Do you like Soul food?"

"We love soul food," Maya replied. "We would love to come by. You two are so adorable."

"Call us Kareem." Mr. Toller said before walking off. "You have our number, and you know the address."

"Aww. I love them!" Maya said as they walked away." Then Kareem turned to her and said, "I asked you to take the day off because a house just got listed in the Oakland Hills. Would you mind looking at it with me?" Maya's face lit up with excitement. "I would love to see it," she replied. "And who knows, maybe you'll need my interior decorating skills again," she added with a playful grin.

***

Kareem pulled into the driveway of a breathtaking two-story house in the Oakland Hills. Its cream-colored stucco walls gleamed in the sun, reflecting its modern yet elegant style. As they exited the car, Maya marveled at how the house seemed to stretch toward the clouds. They walked around its perimeter, admiring the tall windows and pristine landscaping. It looked like a mansion!

"Wow! Is this house on the market?" Maya asked in disbelief. "Yes, it is," Kareem smiled as he squeezed her hand.

"It was built a few decades ago, and it's the fourth house I ever sold. Closing this house made me the top agent in my realty company."

Kareem led Maya through the grand double doors of the luxurious two-story home, and her eyes were immediately drawn to its high ceilings and dramatic windows. The foyer opened into a spacious living room with a staircase stretching towards the sky. They made their way through an elegant dining area towards the spacious kitchen with gleaming countertops and state-of-the-art appliances.

Kareem guided Maya upstairs to give her a tour of the upper level. "It has four spacious bedrooms, three full bathrooms, a two-car garage, numerous walk-in closets, and a chef's kitchen that opens to a private deck." He showed her around the primary bedroom with an additional office room. Another spacious bedroom features walk-in closets and custom-built cabinets.

"This house is beautiful," she exclaimed as she gawked at the size of the primary bedroom's walk-in closet. "How much are you listing this property for?" Maya asked. "It must be at least ten million dollars."

Kareem grinned in response. "The fair market value for this property is about ten million, but the previous owner had to sell quickly due to his business relocating to Texas. I never thought this house would be on the market again. It's a rare gem."

"Yes, it is," Maya agreed. Kareem stepped in front of her and looked deep into her big, beautiful brown eyes. This home is a rare gem like you," he said, making Maya blush and flash her irresistible smile.

They walked back downstairs, and she marveled at the living room with its comfortable furniture and floor-to-ceiling windows. Entering the kitchen, she gazed at the modern stainless-steel appliances. *It must be nice to have this kind of money,* she thought.

Kareem opened the sliding glass door and stepped onto the large deck in the backyard. Maya followed, taking in the azure, blue pool adorned with four cabanas positioned strategically near lounge chairs at the pool's edges. In the distance, she could see the breathtaking views of the Bay Area skyline, illuminated against the sky.

"I can't believe this place!" She said, turning to Kareem and beaming with excitement. "I have so many ideas on how to decorate!"

"Good. Because I sold my condo," Kareem replied in an upbeat voice.

"What?" Maya gasped, eyes wide with surprise. "You sold your condo? Why?"

"Too many memories there," Kareem replied. "Besides, it's a bachelor pad. And it's time that I focus on starting a family and buying a home," Kareem said with a determined look.

"A home?" Maya looked at Kareem, confused.

The silence stretched between them until he asked her, "Remember that talk we had months ago about what makes a house a home?" She nodded and waited for him to continue.

Kareem reached for Maya's hand and interlocked his fingers with hers before continuing to speak. "I've learned that home is more about the person you're with than the place you reside. And you own the keys to my heart," he confessed, causing Maya's eyes to water.

"I'm glad you like this house; I purchased it a week ago for *us*. Will you help me decorate it?"

Maya looked at Kareem, tears streaming down her face. "You bought this home for us?" she whispered. Kareem held her close, feeling a surge of emotion in his chest. He wanted to give her the life she deserved with every fiber of his being.

"This is going to be our home?" Kareem said, hugging her tight. He wanted nothing more than to provide, protect, and support Maya in every way possible. And now, with this house, he could give her the dream home they had both wanted.

49

Seeking a Blessing

Kareem pulled into the Agape Assembly parking lot, his heart pounding as he rehearsed what he would say. He glanced at Pastor River's Honda Accord and took a deep breath before exiting his car. Kareem came to this church several months ago broken, desperate, and without a father figure. Pastor Rivers had become more than a mentor to Kareem; he had become the father Kareem never had.

Kareem had sold countless million-dollar homes in his career, but now he would have to summon the courage to ask the pastor one of the most critical questions of his life. He paused at the door and knocked quietly. Pastor Rivers opened the door with a warm smile and welcomed him in. Kareem sat in a chair and looked into the eyes of the man he admired.

"Pastor, when I first met Maya, I loved her but was blinded by lust. Then I heard her pray for me—something I'd only ever heard my grandmother do—and it changed me. I began to love your daughter with all my heart."

Pastor Rivers nodded, having detected the sincerity in his voice. "I've seen the way you look at Maya. It's the same way I used to look at her mother—may she rest in peace," Pastor Rivers murmured, pushing up his glasses to wipe his eyes. "I loved her with all my heart. That's the reason why I still wear my wedding ring. When I heard you recite those words from the poem in church, I began thinking that's the type of love I want a man to have for my daughter. Agape is God-given love. It's the selfless, sacrificial, unconditional love that Christ has for us."

Kareem shook his head in agreement. "Agape love is a divine love, not based on emotions or feelings but of intent and devotion. That's the type of love he had for Maya," Kareem said sincerely.

Finally, after a moment of silence, Kareem asked the question. "Pastor…May I have your blessing to marry your daughter? I know it's only been less than a year since we met, but she's the woman I want to spend my life with."

Pastor Rivers narrowed his eyes on Kareem. "I'm very protective of my daughter, Kareem. She's all that I have left in this world. So let me ask you, do you swear to love and protect my daughter for the rest of your life?"

Kareem thought about his parents. He'd never met his father or mother, but according to his grandmother, his father was deep in the drug game, leading to them being murdered. He clenched his jaw, determined never to put Maya in harm's way. "I do, pastor."

"Marriage is a covenant, a sacred union of two people coming together to share a lifelong commitment, the pastor said. "Before planning a wedding, I want to ensure you plan how the marriage will work. If Maya says yes, would you be willing to attend pre-marital counseling?" Kareem agreed.

"I give you my blessing, son," Pastor Rivers said while giving Kareem a fatherly embrace. "You have my blessing."

50

Grow Old Together

Kareem and Maya sat in the studio of 102.9 KBLX, the Bay Area's radio station for R&B and Hip Hop. Maya was excited to join Kareem as the Morning Dream Team interviewed him. The radio interview would allow her to reach at-risk girls who might want to join her organization.

"Welcome back to the Dream Team morning show," the host said. We have Kareem, an acclaimed poet and spoken word artist, and Maya Rivers, activist and founder of A Safe Space, a foundation dedicated to helping at-risk girls." He turned to them. Welcome to the show," he said.

Kareem flashed a smile, thrilled to be on air with Maya. They both leaned toward the suspended microphone and spoke in unison, "Thank you for having us."

The male host turned to Kareem. "How have you been coping after losing your best friend and producer, Keith?"

Kareem sighed, his expression somber. "It's been challenging," he admitted. He thanked the Agape Assembly Church for their prayers and support. Maya reached over, taking Kareem's hand in hers to comfort him.

"We can't forget that Keith is a hero," Maya said softly. "He put himself in harm's way and injured the serial killer, which allowed authorities to capture him, ultimately leading to his death."

"You two make a great couple," the female host observed. "How did you meet?"

Maya smiled fondly. "Keith and his late fiancée, my best friend Tasha, introduced us."

Kareem hesitated before adding, "I almost lost her because I cheated. Maya is celibate, and at first, I wasn't willing to wait until marriage. I made a mistake but apologized, and she forgave me."

The female host raised an eyebrow. "How did you apologize?"

Kareem shifted in his seat. "The best apology is changed behavior. I had to put my ego and pride aside and admit I made a huge mistake. I had to take a hard look at myself and commit to changing. Most importantly, I needed to build a healthy relationship with God before I could have a healthy relationship with Maya."

"Isn't it unrealistic to wait until marriage?" the male host asked. "How else will you know if you're sexually compatible?"

Kareem nodded. "I used to think the same way, but good sex doesn't guarantee a good relationship." He turned to Maya, meeting her eyes. "After meeting Maya—a woman with inner and outer beauty—I realized that true connection comes from touching her heart before touching her body."

He reached into his attaché case, and Maya's eyes lit up when he pulled out a copy of her book, *Single, Celibate, and Successful: Focusing on Your Purpose Instead of Waiting for a Wedding Proposal.*

"I have to brag about my woman," Kareem said. "She's brilliant, caring, loyal, and committed to uplifting the community. Before I read Maya's book, I didn't realize I was creating soul ties with the women I slept with.

"This book made me understand that I have a greater purpose than just being a player or performing erotic poetry. A quote in Maya's book says: *A man who lacks a purpose in life will become preoccupied with lust and sexual pleasure.* That hit me hard. All my adult life, I'd been a player. I was only interested in making money. I wasn't thinking about monogamy, marriage, or forming real connections. But Maya's book changed my outlook—and her love changed my life."

The radio broadcast went to a commercial break. Hearing Kareem gush over the book moved Maya. Maya grabbed his hand and held it tight. "I love you so much," she whispered, rubbing the back of his hand with her thumb during the commercial break.

When the radio went live again, the female host asked Kareem if he would put out any more erotic music.

"That era is over," Kareem said with a smile. "You won't hear me writing or recording any more erotic poetry. Only love, inspirational, and conscious music from now on."

"Tell me about this new song we're about to play. What's it called?"

"It's called *Grow Old Together.* It's from my upcoming album, *Lyrics and Love.*" The song played, and the lyrics impressed both hosts:

When we first started dating

I wasn't used to waiting

But we wanted a foundation

So, I remained patient

You changed my perspective

I became more selective

And you weren't just a woman

That I wanted to have sex with

I cherish our time together

You can't rush something

Meant to last forever

Can we grow old together?

You're the one I want to hold forever

You're more than a friend to me

So I'm proposing to you now

While on bended knee

"Wow! That's such a beautiful song," the female radio host said.

"Maya inspired all of the songs on my *Lyrics and Love* album," Kareem declared, his eyes full of love and admiration. "She's the woman I want to grow old and grey with."

Suddenly, Pastor Rivers entered the studio, accompanied by Tahir, Alexis, and several church members. Maya stood up, stunned. Everyone gasped as they noticed Kareem on bended knee in front of her. The radio host announced over the airwaves that a marriage proposal was happening live in the studio.

Kareem took both of Maya's hands and began to passionately profess his love for her, pouring out his heart in his proposal:

I've loved you

from the very first moment we met

I know that we haven't known each other for very long,

But I've known all along

that you're the one that I want to spend the rest of my life with

Kareem opened a black velvet box containing the ring. Maya gasped at the size of the diamond. She couldn't believe what was happening, her hands flying to her mouth as tears filled her eyes.

Kareem knelt on one knee and took her hands in his. "Maya, I want to spend the rest of my life with you. I love you. Will you marry me?"

Too overwhelmed to speak, Maya nodded and threw her arms around him. "Yes, baby, yes!" she finally gasped, tears streaming down her face. Kareem stood and kissed her softly before slipping the ring onto her finger. He pulled her close and whispered, "I thank God for bringing you into my life. You're my soulmate."

Maya felt an immense wave of joy as they embraced and kissed passionately. Suddenly, she heard a familiar voice from behind. Spinning around, she saw her best friend, Tasha, who had flown back from Alabama for the special occasion.

"Congratulations, best friend!" Tasha yelled excitedly.

Maya ran over and embraced her tightly. "You know I wouldn't miss this for the world," Tasha said. "Keith is smiling down on both of you right now."

Everyone in the studio was emotional. Kareem embraced the pastor in a firm hug. "You're family now," Pastor Rivers whispered to Kareem.

51

A Woman Scorned

Leah seethed with rage as she threw a wineglass at her TV. For the past few months, she'd been overwhelmed with anxiety from watching the news reports about her father's arrest for sexual assault, fraud, theft, and embezzlement. Every channel, from CNN to the local news, had been running stories about her father's arrest nonstop.

Not only was Bishop Banks facing charges of sexual assault, but he was also accused of misusing church funds, falsifying financial records, and filing fraudulent tax returns. The IRS had frozen all his assets, while FBI agents seized items from his house. The board of directors at the church also informed Leah that their church's tax-exempt status was now in jeopardy.

Leah was broke! For the first time in her life, she couldn't shop and was forced to watch her privileged lifestyle slip away—no more Gucci, Prada, Chanel, or Dior. And as if that wasn't enough, she had just listened to Kareem propose to Maya over the radio.

Leah screamed with fury as she threw an expensive vase to the ground, causing shards of glass crystal to fly everywhere. Tears streamed down her face as she shouted, "You're supposed to be my husband, Kareem! My husband! How could you marry that bitch?!!!" She clenched her fists and ground her teeth as an uncontrollable rage surged through her veins.

All those years, she'd slept with Kareem's grandmother's Bible in her bed, waiting for him to return to church. Fate had reunited her with Kareem, and now Maya Rivers had stolen him from her!

Leah grabbed her phone and typed out an angry message to Kareem:

1:30 p.m. We need to talk, Kareem!

1:32 p.m. Call me back, Kareem!

1:32 p.m. CALL ME BACK RIGHT NOW!!!! 😺 😺

1:33 p.m. I can't believe you're marrying that bitch! I hate you!!!!

Leah texted and called Kareem, but he blocked her. She created a fake profile to view his private Instagram page, but he denied her the request to follow within minutes. How else could she track him? - *Maya!*

Maya hadn't blocked the Gospel Network's Instagram page that Leah managed. Leah's eyes narrowed as she browsed Maya's profile for information. As Leah scrolled through Maya's social media posts, she found photos of Kareem's new home and Maya hanging out with Alexis. A sudden realization hit her:

Alexis!!!! That's the girl who must've accused my father. That explains her presence outside of his office and at the Gospel Fest!

Alexis was the girl who had accused her father. Maya must've conspired with Alexis to imprison her father! Maya also stole Kareem from her!

Leah began to grind her teeth in anger, a malicious grin appearing on her lips. As she looked at Maya's photos, Leah swore an oath of vengeance. Maya will pay! *I'll kill her,* Leah thought. A twisted smile appeared on her face. Soon, Maya would discover that hell hath no fury like Leah Banks scorned! Leah would get revenge because whatever Leah Banks wanted, Leah Banks got!

52

Housewarming Gift

After their engagement, Maya and Kareem were inseparable. She moved into their new home and began decorating the living room and bedrooms. Both decided to remain celibate until their honeymoon. Celibacy strengthened their emotional and spiritual bond. It also removed distractions and helped them become more disciplined in their business dealings. Kareem was selling real estate rapidly again, and Maya's nonprofit provided a safe space for at-risk girls.

Kareem had grown to love Maya in ways that he never thought possible. For Maya, the proposal at the radio station was all the proof that she needed that she was the only woman Kareem loved, but the dream house he bought for them confirmed it even more. She couldn't wait for their wedding day.

One day, Maya went to check on the *Safe Space* home, and when Kareem's phone rang, the familiar tune of his friend Tshaka's ringtone filled the room. Tshaka had just returned from his trip to Africa and had received news about Keith's death. Kareem texted his new address to Tshaka and ran outside to meet him when his sleek black Bentley pulled into the driveway.

When Tshaka stepped out of his car, Kareem was immediately struck by his solemn expression. They embraced in a brotherly hug before going inside the house. Once they were seated in the living room, Kareem told Tshaka about the serial killer targeting him, the details about the murders Vincent had committed, and how Keith had given his life protecting Tasha. Tshaka bowed his head as he spoke, his eyes brimming with tears.

When Kareem finished, a long, heavy silence followed. Finally, Tshaka spoke. "There's an African proverb that says, *Good men must die, but death cannot kill their names*. Keith was a good man. He was our brother. His name will live on; I'll make sure of that." He paused, letting out a long sigh.

"I'm only in town for a few days," Tshaka said. "I'm leaving for Brazil on Tuesday. It turns out that I have distant relatives in Cuba. He paused, as if considering what words to say next.

Kareem looked Tshaka in the eyes, his curiosity evident. "Why do you travel so much? You disappear for months at a time."

Tshaka's gaze hardened. "There are forces that want to see me dead," he spat in rage. "Anyone who has fought for the freedom and liberation of our people has been executed." He continued. "David Walker, Marcus Garvey, Malcolm X, Tshaka Nkrumah, Steve Biko, Fred Hampton, Amilcar Cabral were all exiled or murdered. I'm a Pan-Africanist. I want to unite African people worldwide. I won't give up until it's done." His voice reverberated through the room with fire and determination.

"I believe that forces are trying to kill you," Kareem said as he recalled the night at Tshaka's gym. Six men entered that evening when Tshaka, Keith, and Kareem were working out. At the time, Tshaka's gym was open to the public. All six men began working out, and Kareem sensed they were in trouble. One of them approached Tshaka and asked for a photograph with him, which Tshaka refused. The next thing you know, all four men began to attack, and Keith and Kareem jumped in.

Tshaka was an unstoppable force that night, taking down four of his attackers with swift precision while Kareem and Keith handled the other two. Tshaka's fists flew like lightning as he threw punches at a speed that Kareem had never seen before. He moved like a real-life superhero. After the fight ended, the three of them formed an unbreakable bond. Tshaka knew he could trust Kareem and Keith with his life, and they'd been close as brothers ever since.

"I'll never forget that night. I remember the police found semi-automatic weapons in their gym bags," Kareem recalled. Tshaka took a deep breath and exhaled before continuing to speak. "After they were arrested, I contacted Oakland Police only to find out they had no documented record of the incident or their arrest." Kareem shook his head in disbelief. "What?! Are you serious?"

"I'm serious," Tshaka said with a serious look. "But enough of that! I have a housewarming gift that I want to give you before I leave. Tshaka reached for a large box that he'd brought. "This is no ordinary gift," Tshaka said sternly. I intended to give it to Keith as a wedding gift. But now I want to give it to you. Open it up."

Kareem carefully unwrapped the box and gasped when he saw what lay inside. "It's a sword," Kareem said. The sword's hilt is pure gold, and the blade is engraved with African Adinkra symbols.

"Not just any sword. "This is *Akrafena,*" Tshaka said reverently, and it originates from the Ashanti people of Ghana. This sword was forged by the sacred Blacksmiths of West Africa thousands of years ago. It symbolizes courage, responsibility, and bravery and will protect you from evil."

"If only Keith were here to see you give me this sword!" Kareem started laughing. "He would've said, *Rebuke that sword and seek protection from the Lord.*" Kareem joked, causing Tshaka to burst out laughing. "One thing I loved about our friendship is that we always joked, but never argued about religion," Tshaka said, laughing. "Keith was a Christian, and I'm spiritual, but we never allowed our beliefs to divide us," he continued. "The day we learn to stop allowing religion to divide us is the day we unite."

The two friends continued to talk for another hour before Tshaka got up to leave. "So much has changed in such a short time," Tshaka said while embracing Kareem in a brotherly hug. "I'm glad to see you and Maya are getting married. That's beautiful. Call me whenever you need me, fam. I'll be there!"

So much had changed, Kareem thought to himself. If someone had told him that he would lose his best friend, accept God back into his life, purchase a new home, and get engaged to Maya, all within months, he would've looked at them like they were crazy.

When Maya returned home that evening, Kareem showed her the sword Tshaka had gifted them. Maya stared at the sword with concern. "Ummm, where is this sword supposed to go?" Maya asked in a disapproving voice. "Put it wherever you like, babe," Kareem said. Maya reached for the sword and placed it inside the broom closet. "That's where I like it," she smirked. Kareem shook his head in laughter.

Later that evening, Kareem and Maya snuggled on the sofa while H.E.R.'s music played in the background. Maya lay underneath a large throw, sipping hot chocolate while Kareem was on his iPad. "What are you writing, babe? Maya asked, moving beside him and resting her head on his shoulder. Kareem smiled as he felt her voluptuous body next to his. "A love poem for you," he smiled.

"Can I hear it?" Maya pleaded. Kareem chuckled. "Now, C'mon, babe. You know what you have to say if you want to hear the poem,"

Anytime Maya wanted to hear a poem that Kareem had written for her, she had to say *Spit it* first. It was an ongoing joke they played with each other since they first met. Maya nudged Kareem in his rib. "You know I don't like that term, she whined. "Ok, babe, spit it!" Kareem told her part of the unfinished poem:

Before I met you

> *I was lost*
> *Floating aimlesslessly*
> *in an ocean of lust*
> *God led me to you*
> *Your smile was a lighthouse*
> *Your beautiful face was a beacon*
> *And your hug has become my safe harbor*

"I'm blessed to have you in my life," Kareem said, gently rubbing the back of her hand with his thumb as they cuddled together.

Maya played in Kareem's beard. She gazed at him briefly before laying her head on his chest. She marveled at how much Kareem had changed since becoming saved. He talked less about sex, poetry, and music and more about investing, starting a family, and building generational wealth.

Suddenly, a loud doorbell rang through the house, interrupting their cuddle session. Kareem reached for his phone and checked the live view on their doorbell app to see who was waiting outside. His eyes focused on an older woman with white hair pulled back into a neat bun. She stood at their doorstep, her hands trembling. As Kareem swung open the door, he caught sight of her puffy red eyes and knew something was wrong.

"Hello! I'm your neighbor from down the street," she said, her voice filled with sadness. "Are you ok?" Kareem asked, sounding concerned. The neighbor explained that her beloved dog, Marcy, had gone missing the previous day. She showed them a photo of the small, white dog on her cell phone - a *small Coton de Tulear* that resembled a fluffy cotton ball. "I don't know how she got out of the house," she said with a heavy heart, "but I found her body yesterday."

"Oh no," Maya said. "My deepest condolences. Where did you find the body?"

"Right there," she pointed to the front of their home. "On your front lawn."

Maya gasped. "What? I'm so sorry."

"Do you think it could have been a mountain lion?" Kareem asked, remembering that someone had shared footage of a mountain lion roaming their backyard on the neighborhood watch app. "Or a raccoon?" He also recalled seeing raccoons in the backyard a few nights ago — his neighbor had warned him when he moved into the house that a raccoon had once attacked and almost killed his cat.

"I… don't know," she muttered through her tears. "If you have any pets, please keep them from outside. I'll miss my Marcy."

Kareem wished they could have met under better circumstances. He and Maya gave their condolences before closing the door. Kareem made a mental note to call a pest control service.

53

A Wake-Up Call

Detective Murphy's phone vibrated on the nightstand. Startled, he rubbed his sleep-filled eyes and squinted at the phone screen - it was 1:58 a.m. He saw an unknown number from Atlanta, GA. With a deep breath, he answered the call and was met with the frantic voice of FBI Agent Nelson on the other end.

"Bad news," Agent Nelson screamed over the phone. "The DNA results came back. The body wasn't Vincent's. It belonged to a transient named Reginald Harris from Berkeley, California. His teeth matched those of the body in the SUV. Toxicology revealed high levels of gamma-hydroxybutyric acid in his blood."

"Damn it!" Detective Murphy sensed something didn't feel right the night of the crash. The van careening off the cliff was a diversion to throw us off his trail," Murphy realized. *Vincent is still alive!*

Vincent had planned this all along. The body inside the van was part of his elaborate plan to escape. Vincent knew it would take weeks for forensics to identify the remains. By the time they realized that the body inside the vehicle belonged to Reginald Harris, Vincent Thomas would be long gone. Questions raced through Murphy's head. *Why had it taken so long for the FBI to get the DNA analysis?* Murphy remembered that Vincent was an FBI trainee. *Would they cover for him?* No...that wouldn't happen. *Or would it?*

Detective Murphy hung up and called his friend, Pastor Rivers. He needed Kareem's new address and wanted to let him know his life was in danger.

54

Blackout

Kareem looked at the time on his computer. It was 1:20 a.m. He'd been up late formatting the cover of his poetry book, *Lyrics and Love,* which he dedicated to Maya. He planned to give copies to their wedding guests. He was working in an office that had once been a spare room, but he'd transformed it into his private workspace. With her eye for design and color, Maya painted the walls in warm tones to create a cozy atmosphere.

Kareem shifted in his chair and sighed. He'd been feeling restless lately. He couldn't quite place his hand on it, but something didn't feel right.

Suddenly, the power to the computer went off. *Another blackout,* Kareem thought to himself. The local electric company, PG&E, had been having rolling blackouts throughout the Bay Area due to high winds and increased fire danger. He checked the alarm app on his phone and saw that his home security system was still activated, drawing its power from the battery backup. *No need to wake Maya up,* he thought. She'd already been traumatized by the neighbor's dog being killed near the house's entrance.

He thought about going to bed, but something told him to go downstairs and check the circuit breaker. He turned his cellphone's flashlight on to guide his path down the stairs. His eyes adjusted to the darkness, but his heart pounded in the eerie darkness as he walked to the breaker room.

Moonlight filtered through the horizontal slats of the kitchen blinds. Kareem walked towards the refrigerator and smelled a foul stench in the air. *Did I forget to empty the garbage?* After checking the trash and sink, he determined the smell was coming from a closet in the hallway.

His heart thumping, Kareem focused his iPhone flashlight on the hallway closet. He opened it and noticed the crawl space covering was open. It smelled rotten, like decomposing animals below. Fear coursed through him as he realized someone had broken in through the crawl space and cut the power.

Kareem frantically rushed towards the laundry room and found the circuit breaker panel open. The intruder had opened the panel and tripped the main breaker. With trembling fingers, he pressed it - but nothing happened. Then, a movement in the living room startled him.

His eyes scanned the living room and focused on a light emitting from a phone. He followed the light to the living room table. It didn't look like Maya's cell. He picked it up and dropped his phone once he saw the images. The pictures on the phone were of Lisa's mutilated body.

Kareem stood still, his muscles tense and his heart pounding. A chill ran down his spine as he froze in place — he was not alone. A silhouette of someone lurking in the shadows near the living room window caught his attention. The figure clutched a large knife, and the blade glimmered in the moonlight.

Vincent! Vincent's in the house! But how? He's dead!

The intruder lunged forward, plunging his hunting knife deep into Kareem's shoulder with a force that made him scream in pain. He'd never been stabbed before, and the wound caused an indescribably hot pain that felt like wildfire spreading through his shoulder.

Kareem gasped in agony and tried to back away, but the intruder advanced swiftly toward Kareem's chest, ready to deliver the death blow. The intruder was quick, but Kareem was quicker. With a surge of strength, he grabbed the intruder's wrist and delivered a powerful kick that sent the intruder crashing to the ground.

Kareem stumbled back, clutching his wounded shoulder as he watched his attacker struggle to get up. Blood rushed from the wound in his shoulder, forming a steady stream down his arm and onto his stomach.

As an overwhelming surge of adrenaline fueled his body, Kareem launched himself at the intruder again. With a fierce kick, he knocked off the man's night-vision goggles, exposing his face in the harsh light. But what Kareem saw left him stunned and shaking with rage:

Vincent!

Vincent's eyes were fixated on Kareem in a chilling stare. His face was still disfigured from the damage that Keith had inflicted. Kareem was frozen in disbelief. *How is he still alive?*

"After I kill you, I'm going to bleed your bitch!" Vincent threatened in a raspy and menacing voice.

The thought of Vincent harming Maya angered Kareem. He'd already lost his best friend to this psychopath. He wasn't going to lose the woman he loved.

Vincent lunged forward with a knife aimed at Kareem's heart, but Kareem expertly dodged the attack. Kareem punched him in the face, causing him to fall to the floor. Kareem then attacked Vincent with a flurry of jabs on his body. Each blow landed with bone-crushing force, but Vincent's body armor dulled the impact.

He considered running to the kitchen and grabbing a knife, but that would expose the bedroom to Maya. He remembered the sword that Tshaka had given him was in the closet. He would expose the stairwell if he ran to get it, allowing Vincent a path to Maya. Kareem couldn't risk it.

Vincent plunged the hunting knife toward Kareem's neck; his face twisted into a demented grimace. But Kareem was stronger than Vincent anticipated. Even with his shoulder bleeding, Kareem continued to pummel Vincent's face, causing the knife to fall out of Vincent's hands.

It was dark, and Kareem couldn't see where the knife landed, but he knew he had to kill Vincent. This man had murdered his best friend and would kill Maya if he wasn't stopped. His arm and chest were bleeding, and excruciating pain radiated from his shoulder. Kareem's strength was fading. He knew he had to act fast; if Vincent recovered, he would have no chance of saving Maya.

Vincent mustered the strength to shove Kareem off him. But Kareem wasn't done yet, fueled by adrenaline and years of intense training with Tshaka in the gym. Kareem remembered the spinning Capoeira kick move called *Armada*, which he'd learned from Tshaka. An image of Tshaka flashed in his mind, reminding Kareem of how enslaved Africans in Brazil created Capoeira to defend themselves from their oppressors. Even with their hands chained, Black Brazilians found ways to protect themselves using their legs.

Despite his injured arm and shoulder, Kareem was determined to use the move to his advantage. Kareem lunged at Vincent, extending his arms for balance as he spun on his left foot and struck Vincent in his head with maximum force. The power of his kick knocked Vincent back, sending him sprawling into the wall. Kareem drove his knee into Vincent's skull, fragments of bone cracking beneath the pressure. Ignoring the gash in his shoulder that was throbbing with pain, Kareem continued his relentless assault.

"Maya! Run! Get out of here now!" Kareem screamed, "Vincent is in the house!" He remembered the promise he had made to her father to protect Maya. He was bleeding profusely but couldn't allow Vincent to harm her. *God, give me strength, he* said to himself as he drove an elbow into Vincent's face, who lay unconscious.

The urgency in Kareem's voice woke Maya from her sleep. It was dark, and she was nervous. She grabbed her phone and tiptoed towards the stairs. Her pulse raced as her fingers fumbled along the wall until she found an electrical switch. She flipped it, but no lights came on.

"Kareem?" Maya screamed from the top of the stairs. "Kareem? Are you ok?" Maya yelled again louder.

"Vincent is in the house!" Kareem yelled.

Instinctively, Maya pulled out her phone and called 911. The operator dispatched an officer as Maya raced downstairs. Maya gasped in horror when she saw Kareem's body on the floor in a pool of blood next to Vincent.

Suddenly, she remembered the African sword that Tshaka had given them as a gift. She had placed it in the closet near the foyer. Maya yanked open the closet and grabbed the sword. Without hesitation, she charged forward and thrust the blade into Vincent's chest, feeling a surge of energy with each swing that pierced his Kevlar vest.

"That's for Keith, mothafucka!" She screamed while plunging the sword deeper into his chest. "And this is for all the Black women you've murdered!" She yelled, swinging the sword more aggressively into his body each time. After numerous blows, the sword was dripping with blood. Vincent was dead.

Maya threw down the sword and hugged Kareem. He was conscious but lying in a pool of blood. Tears fell on her face as she knelt next to him.

"I-I called 911," she stammered as tears cascaded down her face. Kareem laughed faintly, and Maya felt her chest heave with sobs.

"You're bleeding! Why are you laughing?" Maya screamed hysterically. Kareem held his hand up to her face and said, "Because I never thought I would hear you cuss." He laughed again, coughing up blood.

Maya's tears rolled down her soft cheeks as Kareem's breathing grew shallow. His hand trembled as he touched her face gently, whispering, "Don't cry, love. I never liked to see you cry." Kareem felt himself losing consciousness. He was dying. But Maya, the woman he loved, was safe, and that's all that mattered.

The police burst through the door, their guns blazing, with Detective Murphy right behind them. They immediately stopped when they saw Vincent lying on the floor, a pool of crimson blood staining the tiles around him. Detective Murphy rushed over to Kareem, slumped in Maya's arms, her tears falling freely onto his motionless body.

55

Hope

Maya sat in the hospital waiting room of Highland Hospital, one of the country's top trauma centers. Kareem had been in surgery for over an hour, and Maya prayed that he would pull through. Although her parents had raised her to be a *warrior*, not a *worrier*, she was beyond emotional and worried about his condition.

Pastor Rivers arrived and rushed over to hug his daughter. Maya wiped away her tears as she recalled the incident, reliving the horror of seeing Vincent in her house. She had so many unanswered questions. "How did this happen?" she asked between sobs. *Vincent was supposed to be dead!*

Pastor Rivers led Maya back toward the seating area. He sat beside his daughter and began praying. He held her hand, determined to be the rock she needed. They sat in silence for a few minutes until the doctor emerged, still wearing his scrubs and hair cover.

"How is he, doctor?" Maya asked.

"He just got out of surgery," the doctor said, the lines in his forehead creased in concern. "He suffered a deep stab wound to his subclavian artery and numerous wounds to his shoulders. We managed to stop the bleeding, but his vital signs are still fluctuating. I can't guarantee that he will make it. We have to keep him here for a few days to ensure he stabilizes."

"Can I go see my fiancée?" Maya pleaded; her voice desperate. "I need to be by his side."

"He's lost a lot of blood," the doctor said gravely. "He's on a ventilator in an induced coma while we wait to see if he will recover. I'll have a nurse see you to his room."

56

Detective Murphy stood outside Kareem and Maya's home, watching as the police secured a perimeter around the property. After flipping the circuit breaker that Vincent had shut off, the house came back on. The crawl space hatch beneath the porch stood wide open, confirming how Vincent had likely sneaked inside. Murphy's gut told him Vincent hadn't worked alone. *Someone had to help him plan this. But who?*

Stepping over pools of blood, Detective Murphy approached the sofa. The CSI team was already photographing every inch, methodically searching for evidence. Murphy carefully lifted a cushion, and the metallic glint of a cell phone caught his eye. Changing into fresh gloves, he retrieved the device and stared at the screen.

It was an older Android, unlocked and unprotected. He tapped the screen—and the sight made his stomach clench. There, in the phone's gallery, were photos of a bound Black woman, her body mutilated and smeared with blood. Murphy forced himself to exhale slowly, willing his composure to remain intact. He closed the photo app and read the text messages:

Are you inside the house yet?

15 minutes later, somebody sent another text:

Did you kill her?

His eyes narrowed in on the third text:

**Did you slit her fucking throat yet?!!!! What's
taking so long???!!!**

A chill ran down Murphy's spine. Vincent wasn't acting alone.
He had an accomplice. Someone was texting him, waiting for
confirmation of a murder.

Detective Murphy crossed the room to where his partner,
Detective Andy Cho, the department's mobile forensics expert, was
examining a laptop. "We need to trace this number," Murphy said,
showing Cho the incriminating messages and call logs. Cho switched
from latex to nitrile gloves and pulled up his specialized software. Within
moments, he announced it was a Google Voice number.

"I'll submit an emergency disclosure request to Google," Cho
said, tapping rapidly on his device. "I'll also request a geofence warrant
for location data. Hopefully, we'll have account details and an IP address
in a few hours."

Detective Murphy grew anxious as he waited for the caller's
information. When Detective Cho revealed the name of Vincent's co-
conspirator, his jaw dropped in shock.

"I can't believe this," he muttered, dialing Pastor Rivers with
shaking fingers.

"Pastor, it's Detective Murphy. Are you still at the hospital with
Maya? We just identified Vincent's accomplice."

The pastor's voice trembled on the other end. "I left about an
hour ago to pick up some clothes for her. She won't leave Kareem's side
until he wakes."

Murphy spoke urgently, words rushing out. "We have Vincent's phone. The text messages provide Kareem's new address, as well as details on when he and Maya come and go. He paused, bracing himself. "The phone number belongs to Leah Banks - Bishop Banks daughter."

"Wait! What?" Pastor Rivers gasped in shock.

A stunned silence filled the line, and then Pastor Rivers sucked in a ragged breath. "I'm heading back to the hospital now. Maya is still in the ICU with Kareem.

Murphy's pulse thundered in his ears. If Leah is involved, Maya and Kareem could be in grave danger. I'll send officers to lock down the ICU."

57

Visiting Hours

Leah followed the ambulance to Highland Hospital, her heart racing. When Vincent didn't answer the phone or leave Kareem's house within an hour, as they had planned, she sensed something had gone wrong. Seeing Maya run outside with the paramedics confirmed it: Vincent had failed in his attempt to kill her.

"Fuck! Fuck! Fuck!" Leah hissed under her breath.

Leah recalled the day Vincent had cornered her after witnessing the heated confrontation at Vegan Mob. He'd offered to murder Maya for a price, flaunting his credentials as a professional hitman. Leah had doubted him - until he showed her gruesome photos and videos of his past jobs in foreign countries. The cold truth set in when she saw the handgun tucked in his waistband. Desperate for revenge against Maya, Leah withdrew $10,000 in cash from the bank and handed it over to Vincent.

When Vincent's plan to kidnap Tasha and kill Maya failed, he called Leah and told her to follow him on the highway. After staging the fiery car crash, she hid Vincent in her trunk and drove him to Six Rivers National Forest, where he lived off the grid for months, nursing his injuries. Throughout his recovery, Leah provided updates on Kareem and Maya, fueling Vincent's desire for vengeance.

But now that Vincent was dead, Leah was determined to make sure Maya got what she deserved. Maya had stolen Kareem from her and helped send her father to prison. Leah's life was ruined all because of Maya. Leah vowed that Maya would pay - with her life!

Leah burst through the Emergency Room doors and glanced around frantically. The room was empty except for a security guard and an older woman slumped back in the waiting chair, fast asleep. The security guard looked up from his cell phone and asked if she needed help, eyeing her suspiciously.

Leah used her best acting skills, forcing tears to stream down her cheeks as she fabricated her story.

"My brother was rushed in a few hours ago," she said, visibly shaken. "His name is Kareem Simmons."

The guard radioed for information. Kareem Simmons has just come out of surgery. He's in the ICU," he relayed, eyeing Leah with caution.

"I need to see him," Leah sobbed hysterically, awakening the woman in the chair and releasing more fake tears to appear convincing. The security guard handed Leah a pen to sign in, quickly making a temporary visitor badge, and then directed her to the ICU area.

The ICU was an open one without visiting hours. Leah, her face partially obscured by large, dark sunglasses, moved with a sense of urgency toward the nurse's station.

"My brother, Kareem Simmons…he was just admitted. "Please, I need to see him," she pleaded, her eyes welling up with fake tears.

The head nurse directed Leah to the ICU room where Kareem was staying. She had no idea that Leah had a loaded gun in her small purse.

***

Maya sat at Kareem's bedside; her eyes red from crying. The rhythmic beeping of the ventilator and the slow rise and fall of Kareem's chest were the only signs that he was still alive. Multiple stab wounds had left him clinging to life. Maya took his hand in hers and held it tight, praying for a miracle.

Maya hated hospitals, and sitting in the ICU with tubes hooked to Kareem reminded her of her mother's battle with cancer. She couldn't bear the thought of losing him, of living her life without him by her side.

She remembered the day they'd met at the studio—his gentle eyes and warm, disarming smile. She thought of all their plans and the future they were building together. Now, it all seemed uncertain. The doctor warned her that Kareem's chances of full recovery were slim, but Maya refused to give up hope.

She drank two cups of coffee throughout the night and read numerous scriptures from Kareem's grandmother's Bible. It was the only thing she could grab before leaving the house. She'd been rereading scriptures on healing that Kareem's grandmother had highlighted in her Bible. Suddenly, the door to the ICU room banged open. Maya spun around, expecting a nurse to check on Kareem's vital signs.

Instead, Leah Banks stood there, her eyes burning with raw hatred as she glared at Maya.

"Leah? What are you doing here?" Maya asked, her eyes wide with shock.

Without a word, Leah pulled a gun from her purse and aimed it directly at Maya. "I'm here to finish the job," Leah snarled, her voice trembling with rage. "I'm going to kill you, bitch!"

Maya stared down the barrel of the gun. She forced herself to stand, carefully placing the Bible on Kareem's chest. "Why are you doing this?" she whispered.

"You don't get to ask questions, bitch!" Leah stepped forward, pointing the gun straight at Maya's chest. "You stole Kareem from me and helped put my father in jail! All of this is your fault! If you had just left us alone, none of this would be happening!"

"Your father is a -"

"Shut up bitch!" Leah cocked the weapon. "You're going to die!"

Maya's gut instinct told her to push the button and call the emergency nurse, but she didn't want to risk anyone else getting shot. Maya had turned her cell phone off at the request of the head nurse. Leah's face was hard and unreadable, and she kept the gun pointed at Maya. The two women stared at each other in silence; the only sound in the room was the beeping of the EKG machine hooked up to Kareem.

Leah's lips curled into a sinister smile. "Vincent taught me one thing," she hissed. "The best way to torture someone is by killing who they love first. If I can't have Kareem, then no one can."

With lightning speed, Leah pointed the gun at Kareem's wounded body lying on the hospital bed. Before Maya could process what was happening, Leah pulled the trigger, and a flash of fire exploded from the gun barrel.

"No!" Maya flung herself at Leah, channeling every ounce of adrenaline into her attack. The gun skidded across the floor. Enraged, Maya pummeled Leah's face with wild punches. Blinded by tears, she hit Leah over and over with a flurry of punches until her knuckles were raw, and Leah lay bloody and unconscious.

The hospital room erupted into chaos as police officers charged in, weapons drawn. Gasping for breath, Maya staggered away from Leah's motionless body. A frantic nurse screamed that Kareem had been shot.

Maya's heart sank. It was too late.

58

The funeral was held at *Agape Assembly*. Maya walked in, her head bowed, her long black dress trailing behind her. A silky black scarf draped her shoulders, and her diamond engagement ring, her most cherished gift, sparkled on her finger. She passed the mourners to the front pew, where she knelt and prayed, her eyes filled with tears. The man who had guided, inspired, and loved her was gone.

The music started, and a chorus of mourners joined in as they sang the gospel song *Take Me To The King*, one last time for the man they all loved. Friends and family of the deceased spoke, their voices trembling with emotion.

Finally, a figure approached the pulpit. His face was solemn, and he glanced briefly at Maya before beginning his sermon. He was the only man who could comfort her during this time of grief. . He asked God to give him the right words to ease her grief.

***

Kareem stood at the pulpit, his heart heavy with grief. It had been weeks since Pastor Rivers sudden death. The circumstances surrounding Pastor Rivers passing were still shrouded in mystery, with a criminal investigation now underway.

One year had passed since Leah attempted to kill Kareem. Miraculously, his grandmother's Bible had stopped the bullet from Leah's gun from killing him. Even from the grave, his grandmother, his guardian angel, was still protecting. During his recovery, Kareem and Maya wed in a small ceremony. Her father, Pastor Rivers, walked her down the aisle, carrying a picture of his deceased wife during their wedding. And now, here Kareem was, eulogizing the man who had become the father he never had.

Kareem cleared his throat, his voice shaking as he spoke to the congregation. The church was filled with people who had come to pay their respects and honor the man who had meant so much to so many.

Kareem cleared his throat, his knuckles grasping the edge of the pulpit. "I thank God for Pastor Rivers," he began. "He came into my life when tragedy struck. I'm so blessed to be standing here a year later, married to his beautiful daughter, Maya. Thank you, Pastor Rivers, for being the father that I never had. I know you're at peace, hugging your beautiful wife in heaven. Thank you for teaching me the true meaning of Agape love."

Kareem paused and lifted his gaze to the heavens, imagining Pastor Rivers looking down from above. He felt deeply grateful for the man who had changed his life and brought him closer to God.

Kareem's eyes brimmed with tears as he focused on Maya. He'd promised her father that he would love and protect her, which he intended to do. They were married now, and Maya was pregnant. Kareem had grown to love her in a way he never imagined possible. Their love was *Agape* - selfless and sacrificial.

After the funeral, Maya hugged Tasha tightly and felt her best friend's warmth spread through her body. Tasha had flown back from Alabama to be with her during this difficult time. She felt a hand on her shoulder and saw Alexis standing beside her. Alexis had joined *Agape Assembly* and became a Sunday school teacher and outreach coordinator for *A Safe Space,* the nonprofit that Maya had founded. Maya smiled softly, grateful for the love and support that both her friends had shown her.

Kareem looked around the church and noticed one person absent from the funeral: Tahir. Tahir had taken Keith's beats, relocated to Las Vegas, and signed a deal with Eternal Flame Entertainment. Kareem clenched his teeth in anger. He felt betrayed by Tahir. He had a bad feeling that things would get worse in the future, but for now, he had to stay strong for Maya and their unborn child.

Kareem and Maya exited the church, with the chauffeur opening the limousine door. The ride to Rolling Hills Cemetery in Richmond was sad, with the car's silence only broken by Maya's occasional sobs. At the cemetery, Pastor Rivers was buried beside his wife. Kareem had beautiful headstones erected to commemorate their lives together.

After the ceremony at the cemetery, the sun had begun to set, and the light glinted off Maya's dark sunglasses as she tightly clutched her father's obituary. Kareem had included photos of both of Maya's parents in the obituary. He wrapped a supportive arm around Maya's shoulders, allowing her to lean against him for strength as they walked back to the limousine.

Slumping into the back seat of the limousine, Maya let out a heavy sigh. Kareem looked at her, his heart aching for her. "I love you," he said softly.

She shook her head, fresh tears rolling down her cheeks. "I miss my daddy," she whispered, her grip tightening on Kareem's hand. He pulled her close, his strong arm wrapping around her. "I'm sure he's in heaven right now, hugging your mother," he murmured. "And he's watching over us both."

Determined not to let her stress endanger the baby, Kareem stroked her hair and recalled a scripture that had once consoled him: "He will wipe every tear from their eyes. There will be no more death or mourning or crying or pain."

Kareem leaned in. "Maya Simmons," he said softly. "Can I share something with you?"

"Maya Simmons, can I tell you something?" Kareem asked.

She looked up, eyes still glassy. "Yes."

"I thank God for your parents! They did an incredible job raising you!"

Maya smiled, trying hard to fight back the tears. She remembered how she often told Kareem the same thing about his grandmother. Then Kareem pulled out his phone.

"I wrote a love poem for you last night. I haven't written in a while, so I'm rusty. Would you like to hear it?" Kareem asked.

Maya nodded and then smiled, letting her tears flow freely.

"Spit it, baby!" she said. "Spit it!"

The sleek black limousine pulled away from the cemetery, and Kareem gently stroked her fingers as he recited the love poem he had written for her, hoping to ease her pain.

Deep down, Kareem knew that there was foul play involved in Pastor Rivers death. His gut told him that Tahir, who now lived in Las Vegas, was also in grave danger. But for now, he had to focus on protecting his pregnant wife and their unborn child. As he laid a hand on her pregnant belly, a fierce determination burned within him to protect his family from any future danger, no matter what the cost.